Tiffany Aching's land is a lot like our own.

It has rolling fields, grassy hills, grazing sheep and shepherdesses.
But there are small differences:
tiny blue men with big tempers,
monsters in rivers,
headless horsemen in the streets,
elves and goblins and never-ending winters.
There is magic in this land –
the Chalk, they call it.

And if we move out just a little, we can see
more lands, more creatures, more magic.

Move even further out, and you can see this world
is in fact a flat disc, carried on the backs of four
elephants astride a giant turtle floating through space.
It's known as Discworld®, and you could write pages and pages
about its adventures (indeed, a rather brilliant man, Sir Terry
Pratchett, has written over ten thousand pages about it).

But while the world of the Disc is wonderful and varied,
this is Tiffany's story. Because this tiny bit of the Disc,
the Chalk, *needs* Tiffany.

There are people to save, battles to win, magic to learn.
Through five incredible stories, follow Tiffany Aching
as she joins witches and fairies to protect a world that,
it turns out, is rather different from our own . . .

Also by TERRY PRATCHETT

for younger readers

A full list of Terry Pratchett's books
can be found on **www.terrypratchett.co.uk**

About the Author

Terry Pratchett was the acclaimed creator of the global bestselling Discworld® series, the first of which, *The Colour of Magic*, was published in 1983. In all, he was the author of over fifty bestselling books. His novels have been widely adapted for stage and screen, and he was the winner of multiple prizes, including the Carnegie Medal, as well as being awarded a knighthood for services to literature. He died in March 2015.

www.terrypratchett.co.uk

About the Illustrator

When she's not trying to take over the world or fighting sock-stealing monsters, **Laura Ellen Anderson** is a professional children's book author and illustrator who lives in north London. The creator of *Evil Emperor Penguin* for the *Phoenix* comic, she is also the illustrator of Sibéal Pounder's Witch Wars series and CBeebies presenter Cerrie Burnell's picture books and Harper fiction series. Laura's first author/illustrator picture book, *I Don't Want Curly Hair*, was published by Bloomsbury in 2017. She has also created new cover illustrations for Enid Blyton's Famous Five series.

www.lauraellenanderson.co.uk

@Lillustrator

TERRY PRATCHETT

The Wee
Free Men

A TIFFANY ACHING NOVEL

CORGI BOOKS

CORGI BOOKS

UK | USA | Canada | Ireland | Australia
India | New Zealand | South Africa

Corgi Books is part of the Penguin Random House group of companies
whose addresses can be found at global.penguinrandomhouse.com.

www.penguin.co.uk
www.puffin.co.uk
www.ladybird.co.uk

First published in Great Britain by Doubleday 2003
Published by Corgi Books 2004
This edition published 2017

006

Typeset in Minion 12/14.5pt by Falcon Oast Graphic Art Ltd
Printed in Great Britain by Clays Ltd, Elcograf S.p.A.

A CIP catalogue record for this book is available from the British Library

ISBN: 978–0–552–57630–7

All correspondence to:
Corgi Books
Penguin Random House Children's
80 Strand, London WC2R 0RL

CHAPTER 1

A Clang Well Done

Some things start before other things.

It was a summer shower but didn't appear to know it, and it was pouring rain as fast as a winter storm.

Miss Perspicacia Tick sat in what little shelter a raggedy hedge could give her and explored the universe. She didn't notice the rain. Witches dried out quickly.

The exploring of the universe was being done with a couple of twigs tied together with string, a stone with a hole in it, an egg, one of Miss Tick's stockings which also had a hole in it, a pin, a piece of paper and a tiny stub of pencil. Unlike wizards, witches learn to make do with a little.

The items had been tied and twisted together to make a . . . device. It moved oddly when she prodded it. One of the sticks seemed to pass right through the

1

egg, for example, and came out the other side without leaving a mark.

'Yes,' she said quietly, as rain poured off the rim of her hat. 'There it is. A definite ripple in the walls of the world. Very worrying. There's probably another world making contact. That's never good. I ought to go there. But . . . according to my left elbow, there's a witch there already . . .'

'She'll sort it out, then,' said a small and, for now, mysterious voice from somewhere near her feet.

'No, it can't be right. That's chalk country over that way,' said Miss Tick. 'You can't grow a good witch on chalk. The stuff's barely harder than clay. You need good hard rock to grow a witch, believe me.' Miss Tick shook her head, sending raindrops flying. 'But my elbows are generally very reliable.'*

'Why talk about it? Let's go and see,' said the voice. 'We're not doing very well around here, are we?'

That was true. The lowlands weren't good to witches. Miss Tick was making pennies by doing bits of medicine and misfortune-telling,† and slept in barns most nights. She'd twice been thrown in ponds.

'I can't barge in,' she said. 'Not on another witch's territory. That never, ever works. But . . .' she paused, 'witches don't just turn up out of nowhere. Let's have a look . . .'

---

* People say things like 'listen to your heart', but witches learn to listen to other things too. It's amazing what your kidneys can tell you.

† Ordinary fortune-tellers tell you what you *want* to happen; witches tell you what's going to happen whether you want it to or not. Strangely enough, witches tend to be more accurate but less popular.

She pulled a cracked saucer out of her pocket, and tipped into it the rainwater that had collected on her hat. Then she took a bottle of ink out of another pocket and poured in just enough to turn the water black.

She cupped it in her hands to keep the raindrops out, and listened to her eyes.

Tiffany Aching was lying on her stomach by the river, tickling trout. She liked to hear them laugh. It came up in bubbles.

A little way away, where the river bank became a sort of pebble beach, her brother Wentworth was messing around with a stick, and almost certainly making himself sticky.

Anything could make Wentworth sticky. Washed and dried and left in the middle of a clean floor for five minutes, Wentworth would be sticky. It didn't seem to come from anywhere. He just got sticky. But he was an easy child to mind, provided you stopped him eating frogs.

There was a small part of Tiffany's brain that wasn't too certain about the name Tiffany. She was nine years old and felt that Tiffany was going to be a hard name to live up to. Besides, she'd decided only last week that she wanted to be a witch when she grew up, and she was certain Tiffany just wouldn't work. People would laugh.

Another and larger part of Tiffany's brain was thinking of the word 'susurrus'. It was a word that not many people have thought about, ever. As her fingers rubbed the trout under its chin she rolled the word round and round in her head.

Susurrus . . . according to her grandmother's dictionary, it meant 'a low soft sound, as of whispering or muttering'. Tiffany liked the taste of the word. It made her think of mysterious people in long cloaks whispering important secrets behind a door: *susurrususssurrusss* . . .

She'd read the dictionary all the way through. No one told her you weren't supposed to.

As she thought this, she realized that the happy trout had swum away. But something else was in the water, only a few inches from her face.

It was a round basket, no bigger than half a coconut shell, coated with something to block up the holes and make it float. A little man, only six inches high, was standing up in it. He had a mass of untidy red hair, into which a few feathers, beads and bits of cloth had been woven. He had a red beard, which was pretty much as bad as the hair. The rest of him that wasn't covered with blue tattoos was covered with a tiny kilt. And he was waving a fist at her, and shouting:

'Crivens! Gang awa' oot o' here, ye daft wee hinny! 'Ware the green *heid*!'

And with that he pulled at a piece of string that was hanging over the side of his boat and a second red-headed man surfaced, gulping air.

'Nae time for fishin'!' said the first man, hauling him aboard. 'The green heid's coming!'

'Crivens!' said the swimmer, water pouring off him. 'Let's offski!'

And with that he grabbed one very small oar and, with rapid back and forth movements, made the basket speed away.

'Excuse me!' Tiffany shouted. 'Are you fairies?'

But there was no answer. The little round boat had disappeared in the reeds.

Probably not, Tiffany decided.

Then, to her dark delight, there was a susurrus. There was no wind, but the leaves on the alder bushes by the river bank began to shake and rustle. So did the reeds. They didn't bend, they just blurred. *Everything* blurred, as if something had picked up the world and was shaking it. The air fizzed. People whispered behind closed doors . . .

The water began to bubble, just under the bank. It wasn't very deep here – it would only have reached Tiffany's knees if she'd paddled – but it was suddenly darker and greener and, somehow, much deeper . . .

She took a couple of steps backwards just before long skinny arms fountained out of the water and clawed madly at the bank where she had been. For a moment she saw a thin face with long sharp teeth, *huge* round eyes and dripping green hair like waterweed, and then the thing plunged back into the depths.

By the time the water closed over it Tiffany was already running along the bank to the little beach where Wentworth was making frog pies. She snatched up the child just as a stream of bubbles came around the curve in the bank. Once again the water boiled, the green-haired creature shot up, and the long arms clawed at the mud. Then it screamed, and dropped back into the water.

'I wanna go-a *toy-lut*!' screamed Wentworth.

Tiffany ignored him. She was watching the river with a thoughtful expression.

I'm not scared at all, she thought. How strange. I ought to be scared, but I'm just angry. I mean, I can *feel* the scared, like a red-hot ball, but the angry isn't letting it out . . .

'Wenny wanna wanna *wanna* go-a *toy-lut*!' Wentworth shrieked.

'Go on, then,' said Tiffany absent-mindedly. The ripples were still sloshing against the bank.

There was no point in telling anyone about this. Everyone would just say 'What an imagination the child has' if they were feeling in a good mood, or 'Don't tell stories!' if they weren't.

She was still very angry. How dare a monster turn up in the river? Especially one so . . . so . . . ridiculous! Who did it think she was?

This is Tiffany, walking back home. Start with the boots. They are big and heavy boots, much repaired by her father and they'd belonged to various sisters before her; she wore several pairs of socks to keep them on. They are *big*. Tiffany sometimes feels she is nothing more than a way of moving boots around.

Then there is the dress. It has been owned by many sisters before her and has been taken up, taken out, taken down and taken in by her mother so many times that it really ought to have been taken away. But

Tiffany rather likes it. It comes down to her ankles and, whatever colour it had been to start with, is now a milky blue which is, incidentally, exactly the same colour as the butterflies skittering beside the path.

Then there is Tiffany's face. Light pink, with brown eyes, and brown hair. Nothing special. Her head might strike anyone watching – in a saucer of black water, for example – as being just slightly too big for the rest of her, but perhaps she'd grow into it.

And then go further up, and further, until the track becomes a ribbon and Tiffany and her brother two little dots, and there is her country . . .

They call it the Chalk. Green downlands roll under the hot midsummer sun. From up here, the flocks of sheep, moving slowly, drift over the short turf like clouds on a green sky. Here and there sheepdogs speed over the turf like comets.

And then, as the eyes pull back, it is a long green mound, lying like a great whale on the world . . .

. . . surrounded by the inky rainwater in the saucer.

Miss Tick looked up.

'That little creature in the boat was a Nac Mac Feegle!' she said. 'The most feared of all the fairy races! Even trolls run away from the Wee Free Men! And one of them warned her!'

'She's the witch, then, is she?' said the voice.

'At that age? Impossible!' said Miss Tick. 'There's been no one to teach her! There're no witches on the Chalk! It's too *soft*. And yet . . . she wasn't scared . . .'

The rain had stopped. Miss Tick looked up at the

Chalk, rising above the low, wrung-out clouds. It was about five miles away.

'This child needs watching,' she said. 'But chalk's too soft to grow a witch on . . .'

Only the mountains were higher than the Chalk. They stood sharp and purple and grey, streaming long trails of snow from their tops even in summer. 'Brides o' the sky', Granny Aching had called them once, and it was so rare that she ever said anything at all, let alone anything that wasn't to do with sheep, that Tiffany had remembered it. Besides, it was exactly right. That's what the mountains looked like in the winter, when they were all in white and the snow streams blew like veils.

Granny used old words, and came out with odd, old sayings. She didn't call the downland the Chalk, she called it 'the wold'. Up on the wold the wind blows cold, Tiffany had thought, and the word had stuck that way.

She arrived at the farm.

People tended to leave Tiffany alone. There was nothing particularly cruel or unpleasant about this, but the farm was big and everyone had their jobs to do, and she did hers very well and so she became, in a way, invisible. She was the dairymaid, and good at it. She made better butter than her mother did, and people commented about how good she was with cheese. It was a talent. Sometimes, when the wandering teachers came to the village, she went and got a bit of education. But mostly she worked in the dairy, which was dark and cool. She enjoyed it. It meant she was doing something for the farm.

It was actually *called* the Home Farm. Her father rented it from the Baron, who owned the land, but there had been Achings farming it for hundreds of years and so, her father said (quietly, sometimes, after he'd had a beer in the evenings), as far as the *land* knew, it was owned by the Achings. Tiffany's mother used to tell him not to speak like that, although the Baron was always very respectful to Mr Aching since Granny had died two years ago, calling him the finest shepherd in these hills, and was generally held by the people in the village to be not too bad these days. It paid to be respectful, said Tiffany's mother, and the poor man had sorrows of his own.

But sometimes her father insisted that there had been Achings (or Akins, or Archens, or Akens, or Akenns – spelling had been optional) mentioned in old documents about the area for hundreds and hundreds of years. They had these hills in their bones, he said, and they'd always been shepherds.

Tiffany felt quite proud of this, in an odd way, because it might also be nice to be proud of the fact that your ancestors moved around a bit too, or occasionally tried new things. But you've got to be proud of *something*. And for as long as she could remember she'd heard her father, an otherwise quiet, slow man, make the Joke, the one that must have been handed down from Aching to Aching for hundreds of years.

He'd say, 'Another day of work and I'm still Aching',

or 'I get up Aching and I go to bed Aching', or even 'I'm Aching all over'. They weren't particularly funny after about the third time, but she'd miss it if he didn't say at least one of them every week. They didn't have to be funny, they were *father* jokes. Anyway, however they were spelled, all her ancestors had been Aching to stay, not Aching to leave.

There was no one around in the kitchen. Her mother had probably gone up to the shearing pens with a bite of lunch for the men, who were shearing this week. Her sisters Hannah and Fastidia were up there too, rolling fleeces and paying attention to some of the younger men. They were always quite keen to work during shearing.

Near the big black stove was the shelf that was still called Granny Aching's Library by her mother, who liked the idea of having a library. Everyone else called it Granny's Shelf.

It was a small shelf, since the books were wedged between a jar of crystallized ginger and the china shepherdess that Tiffany had won at a fair when she was six.

There were only five books if you didn't include the big farm diary, which in Tiffany's view didn't count as a real book because you had to write it yourself. There was the dictionary. There was the Almanack, which got changed every year. And next to that was *Diseases of the Sheep*, which was fat with the bookmarks that her grandmother had put there.

Granny Aching had been an expert on sheep, even though she called them 'just bags of bones, eyeballs and teeth, lookin' for new ways to die'. Other shepherds would walk miles to get her to come and cure their beasts of ailments. *They* said she had the Touch, although she just said that the best medicine for sheep or man was a dose of turpentine, a good cussin' and a kick. Bits of paper with Granny's own recipes for sheep cures stuck out all over the book. Mostly they involved turpentine, but some included cussin'.

Next to the book on sheep was a thin little volume called *Flowers of the Chalk*. The turf of the downs was full of tiny, intricate flowers, like cowslips and harebells, and even smaller ones that somehow survived the grazing. On the Chalk, flowers had to be tough and cunning to survive the sheep and the winter blizzards.

Someone had coloured in the pictures of the flowers, a long time ago. On the flyleaf of the book was written in neat handwriting 'Sarah Grizzel', which had been Granny's name before she was married. She probably thought that Aching was at least better than Grizzel.

And finally there was *The Goode Childe's Booke of Faerie Tales*, so old that it belonged to an age when there were far more 'e's around.

Tiffany stood on a chair and took it down. She turned the pages until she found the one she was looking for, and stared at it for a while. Then she put the book back, replaced the chair, and opened the crockery cupboard.

She found a soup plate, went over to a drawer, took

out the tape measure her mother used for dressmaking, and measured the plate.

'Hmm,' she said. 'Eight inches. Why didn't they just *say*?'

She unhooked the largest frying pan, the one that could cook breakfast for half a dozen people all at once, and took some sweets from the jar on the dresser and put them in an old paper bag. Then, to Wentworth's sullen bewilderment, she took him by a sticky hand and headed back down towards the stream.

Things still looked very normal down there, but she was not going to let *that* fool her. All the trout had fled and the birds weren't singing.

She found a place on the river bank with the right-sized bush. Then she hammered a piece of wood into the ground as hard as she could, close to the edge of the water, and tied the bag of sweets to it.

'Sweeties, Wentworth,' she shouted.

She gripped the frying pan and stepped smartly behind the bush.

Wentworth trotted over to the sweets and tried to pick up the bag. It wouldn't move.

'I wanna go-a *toy-lut*!' he yelled, because it was a threat that usually worked. His fat fingers scrabbled at the knots.

Tiffany watched the water carefully. Was it getting darker? Was it getting greener? Was that just waterweed down there? Were those bubbles just a trout, laughing?

No.

She ran out of her hiding place with the frying pan swinging like a bat. The screaming monster, leaping out of the water, met the frying pan coming the other way with a clang.

It was a good clang, with the *oiyoiyoioioioioioi-nnnnngggggg* that is the mark of a clang well done.

The creature hung there for a moment, a few teeth and bits of green weed splashing into the water, then slid down slowly and sank with some massive bubbles.

The water cleared and was once again the same old river, shallow and icy cold and floored with pebbles.

'Wanna wanna *sweeties*!' screamed Wentworth, who never noticed anything else in the presence of sweets.

Tiffany undid the string and gave them to him. He ate them far too quickly, as he always did with sweets. She waited until he was sick, and then went back home in a thoughtful state of mind.

In the reeds, quite low down, small voices whispered:

'Crivens, Wee Bobby, did yer no' see that?'

'Aye. We'd better offski an' tell the Big Man we've found the hag.'

Miss Tick was running up the dusty road. Witches don't like to be seen running. It looks unprofessional. It's also not done to be seen carrying things, and she had her tent on her back.

She was also trailing clouds of steam. Witches dry out from the inside.

13

'It had all those teeth!' said the mystery voice, this time from her hat.

'I know!' snapped Miss Tick.

'And she just hauled off and hit it!'

'Yes. I *know*.'

'Just like that!'

'Yes. Very impressive,' said Miss Tick. She was getting out of breath. Besides, they were already on the lower slopes of the downs now, and she wasn't good on chalk. A wandering witch likes firm ground under her, not a rock so soft you could cut it with a knife.

'Impressive?' said the voice. 'She used her *brother* as *bait*!'

'Amazing, wasn't it?' said Miss Tick. 'Such quick thinking . . . oh, no . . .' She stopped running, and leaned against a field wall as a wave of dizziness hit her.

'What's happening? What's happening?' said the voice from the hat. 'I nearly fell off!'

'It's this wretched chalk! I can feel it already! I can do magic on honest soil, and rock is always fine, and I'm not too bad on clay, even . . . but chalk's neither one thing nor the other! I'm very *sensitive* to geology, you know.'

'What are you trying to tell me?' said the voice.

'Chalk . . . is a hungry soil. I don't really have much power on chalk.'

The owner of the voice, who was hidden, said: 'Are you going to fall over?'

'No, no! It's just the magic that doesn't work . . .'

Miss Tick did not look like a witch. Most witches don't, at least the ones who wander from place to place. Looking like a witch can be dangerous when you walk among the uneducated. And for that reason she didn't wear any occult jewellery, or have a glowing magical knife or a silver goblet with a pattern of skulls all round it, or carry a broomstick with sparks coming out of it, all of which are tiny hints that there may be a witch around. Her pockets never carried anything more magical than a few twigs, maybe a piece of string, a coin or two and, of course, a lucky charm.

Everyone in the country carried lucky charms, and Miss Tick had worked out that if you didn't have one people would suspect that you *were* a witch. You had to be a bit cunning to be a witch.

Miss Tick *did* have a pointy hat, but it was a stealth hat and only pointed when she wanted it to.

The only thing in her bag that might have made anyone suspicious was a very small, grubby booklet entitled 'An Introduction to Escapology', by The Great Williamson. If one of the risks of your job is being thrown into a pond with your hands tied together, then the ability to swim thirty yards under water, fully clothed, plus the ability to lurk under the weeds breathing air through a hollow reed counts as nothing if you aren't also *amazingly* good with knots.

'You can't do magic here?' said the voice in the hat.

'No, I can't,' said Miss Tick.

She looked up at the sounds of jingling. A strange procession was coming up the white road. It was mostly made up of donkeys pulling small carts with brightly painted covers on them. People walked alongside the carts, dusty to the waist. They were mostly men, they wore bright robes – or robes, at least, that had been bright before being trailed through mud and dust for years – and every one of them wore a strange black square hat.

Miss Tick smiled.

They looked like tinkers, but there wasn't one amongst them, she knew, who could mend a kettle. What they did was sell invisible things. And after they'd sold what they had, they still had it. They sold what everyone needed but often didn't want. They sold the key to the universe to people who didn't even know it was locked.

'I can't *do*,' said Miss Tick, straightening up. 'But I *can* teach!'

Tiffany worked for the rest of the morning in the dairy. There was cheese that needed doing.

There was bread and jam for lunch. Her mother said: 'The teachers are coming to town today. You can go, if you've done your chores.'

Tiffany agreed that, yes, there were one or two things she'd quite like to know more about.

'Then you can have half a dozen carrots and an egg. I dare say they could do with an egg, poor things,' said her mother.

Tiffany took them with her after lunch, and went to get an egg's worth of education.

Most boys in the village grew up to do the same

jobs as their fathers or, at least, some other job somewhere in the village where someone's father would teach them as they went along. The girls were expected to grow up to be somebody's wife. They were also expected to be able to read and write, those being considered soft indoor jobs that were too fiddly for the boys.

However, everyone also felt that there were a few other things that even the boys ought to know, to stop them wasting time wondering about details like 'What's on the other side of the mountains?' and 'How come rain falls out of the sky?'

Every family in the village bought a copy of the Almanack every year, and a sort of education came from that. It was big and thick and printed somewhere far off, and it had lots of details about things like phases of the moon and the right time to plant beans. It also contained a few prophecies about the coming year, and mentioned faraway places with names like Klatch and Hersheba. Tiffany had seen a picture of Klatch in the Almanack. It showed a camel standing in a desert. She'd only found out what both those things were because her mother had told her. And that was Klatch, a camel in a desert. She'd wondered if there wasn't a bit more to it, but it seemed that 'Klatch = camel, desert' was all anyone knew.

And that was the trouble. If you didn't find some way of stopping it, people would go *on* asking questions.

The teachers were useful there. Bands of them

wandered through the mountains, along with the tinkers, portable blacksmiths, miracle medicine men, cloth pedlars, fortune-tellers and all the other travellers who sold things people didn't need every day but occasionally found useful.

They went from village to village delivering short lessons on many subjects. They kept apart from the other travellers, and were quite mysterious in their ragged robes and strange square hats. They used long words, like 'corrugated iron'. They lived rough lives, surviving on what food they could earn from giving lessons to anyone who would listen. When no one would listen, they lived on baked hedgehog. They went to sleep under the stars, which the maths teachers would count, the astronomy teachers would measure and the literature teachers would name. The geography teachers got lost in the woods and fell into bear traps.

People were usually quite pleased to see them. They taught children enough to shut them up, which was the main thing after all. But they always had to be driven out of the villages by nightfall in case they stole chickens.

Today the brightly coloured little booths and tents were pitched in a field just outside the village. Behind them small square areas had been fenced off with high canvas walls and were patrolled by apprentice teachers looking for anyone trying to overhear Education without paying.

The first tent Tiffany saw had a sign which said:

JOGRAFFY!
JOGRAFFY!
JOGRAFFY!

For today only: all major land masses and oceans
PLUS everything you need to kno about glassiers!
One penny or All Major Vejtables Acsepted!

Tiffany had read enough to know that, while he might be a whiz at major land masses, this particular teacher could have done with some help from the man running the stall next door:

The Wonders of Punctuation and Spelling

1 - Absolute Certainty about the Comma
2 - I before E Completely Sorted Out
3 - The Mystery of the Semi-Colon Revealed
4 - See the Ampersand (Small extra charge)
5 - Fun with Brackets

Will accept vegetables, eggs, and clean used clothing

The next stall along was decorated with scenes out of history, generally of kings cutting one another's heads off and similar interesting highlights. The teacher in front was dressed in ragged red robes, with rabbitskin trimmings, and wore an old top hat with flags stuck in it. He had a small megaphone, which he aimed at Tiffany.

'The Death of Kings Through the Ages?' he said. 'Very educational, lots of blood!'

'Not really,' said Tiffany.

'Oh, you've *got* to know where you've come from, miss,' said the teacher. 'Otherwise how will you know where you're going?'

'I come from a long line of Aching people,' said Tiffany. 'And I think I'm moving on.'

She found what she was looking for at a booth hung with pictures of animals including, she was pleased to see, a camel.

The sign said: **Useful Creatures. Today: Our Friend the Hedgehog.**

She wondered how useful the thing in the river had been, but this looked like the only place to find out. A few children were waiting on the benches inside the booth for the lesson to begin, but the teacher was still standing out in front, in the hope of filling up the empty spaces.

'Hello, little girl,' he said, which was only his first big mistake. 'I'm sure *you* want to know all about hedgehogs, eh?'

'I did this one last summer,' said Tiffany.

The man looked closer, and his grin faded. 'Oh, yes,'

he said. 'I remember. You asked all those . . . little questions.'

'I would like a question answered today,' said Tiffany.

'Provided it's not the one about how you get baby hedgehogs,' said the man.

'No,' said Tiffany patiently. 'It's about zoology.'

'Zoology, eh? That's a big word, isn't it.'

'No, actually it isn't,' said Tiffany. 'Patronizing is a big word. Zoology is really quite short.'

The teacher's eyes narrowed further. Children like Tiffany were bad news. 'I can see you're a clever one,' he said. 'But I don't know any teachers of zoology in these parts. Vetin'ry, yes, but not zoology. Any particular animal?'

'Jenny Green-Teeth. A water-dwelling monster with big teeth and claws and eyes like soup plates,' said Tiffany.

'What size of soup plates? Do you mean big soup plates, a whole full portion bowl with maybe some biscuits, possibly even a bread roll, or do you mean the little cup you might get if, for example, you just ordered soup and a salad?'

'The size of soup plates that are eight inches across,' said Tiffany, who'd never ordered soup and a salad anywhere in her life. 'I checked.'

'Hmm, that is a puzzler,' said the teacher. 'Don't think I know that one. It's certainly not useful, I know that. It sounds made-up to me.'

'Yes, that's what *I* thought,' said Tiffany. 'But I'd still like to know more about it.'

'Well, you could try her. She's new.'

The teacher jerked his thumb towards a little tent at the end of the row. It was black and quite shabby. There weren't any posters, and absolutely no exclamation marks.

'What does she teach?' she asked.

'Couldn't say,' said the teacher. 'She *says* it's thinking, but I don't know how you teach *that*. That'll be one carrot, thank you.'

When she went closer Tiffany saw a small notice pinned to the outside of the tent. It said, in letters which whispered rather than shouted:

'I CAN TEACH YOU A LESSON
YOU WON'T FORGET IN A HURRY'

CHAPTER 2

Miss Tick

Tiffany read the sign and smiled.

'Aha,' she said. There was nothing to knock on, so she added 'Knock, knock' in a louder voice.

A woman's voice from within said: 'Who's there?'

'Tiffany,' said Tiffany.

'Tiffany who?' said the voice.

'Tiffany who isn't trying to make a joke.'

'Ah. That sounds promising. Come in.'

She pushed aside the flap. It was dark inside the tent, as well as stuffy and hot. A skinny figure sat behind a small table. She had a very sharp, thin nose and was wearing a large black straw hat with paper flowers on it. It was completely unsuitable for a face like that.

'Are you a witch?' said Tiffany. 'I don't mind if you are.'

'What a strange question to spring on someone,' said the woman, looking slightly shocked. 'Your baron bans witches in this country, you know that, and the first thing you say to me is "Are you a witch?" Why would I be a witch?'

'Well, you're wearing all black,' said Tiffany.

'Anyone can wear black,' said the woman. 'That doesn't mean a thing.'

'And you're wearing a straw hat with flowers in it,' Tiffany went on.

'Aha!' said the woman. 'That proves it, then. Witches wear tall pointy hats. Everyone knows that, foolish child.'

'Yes, but witches are also very clever,' said Tiffany calmly. There was something about the twinkle in the woman's eyes that told her to carry on. 'They sneak about. Probably they often don't look like witches. And a witch coming here would know about the Baron and so she'd wear the kind of hat that everyone knows witches don't wear.'

The woman stared at her. 'That was an incredible feat of reasoning,' she said at last. 'You'd make a good witch-finder. You know they used to set fire to witches? Whatever kind of hat I've got on, you'd say it proves I'm a witch, yes?'

'Well, the frog sitting on your hat is a bit of a clue too,' said Tiffany.

'I'm a toad, actually,' said the creature, which had been peering at Tiffany from between the paper flowers.

'You're very yellow for a toad.'

'I've been a bit ill,' said the toad.

'And you talk,' said Tiffany.

'You only have my word for it,' said the toad, disappearing into the paper flowers. 'You can't prove anything.'

'You don't have matches on you, do you?' said the woman to Tiffany.

'No.'

'Fine, fine. Just checking.'

Again, there was a pause while the woman gave Tiffany a long stare, as if making up her mind about something.

'My name,' she said at last, 'is Miss Tick. And I *am* a witch. It's a good name for a witch, of course.'

'You mean blood-sucking parasite?' said Tiffany, wrinkling her forehead.

'I'm sorry?' said Miss Tick coldly.

'Ticks,' said Tiffany. 'Sheep get them. But if you use turpentine—'

'I *meant* that it *sounds* like "mystic",' said Miss Tick.

'Oh, you mean a pune*, or play on words,' said Tiffany. 'In that case it would be even better if you were Miss *Teak*, a hard foreign wood, because that would sound like "mystique", or you could be Miss Take, which would—'

'I can see we're going to get along like a house on fire,' said Miss Tick. 'There may be no survivors.'

'You really *are* a witch?'

---

* Tiffany had read lots of words in the dictionary that she'd never heard spoken, so she had to guess at how they were pronounced.

'Oh, pur-lease,' said Miss Tick. 'Yes, yes, I am a witch. I have a talking animal, a tendency to correct other people's pronunciation – it's *pun*, by the way, not "pune" – and a fascination for poking my nose into other people's affairs and, yes, a *pointy hat*.'

'Can I operate the spring now?' said the toad.

'Yes,' said Miss Tick, her eyes still on Tiffany. 'You can operate the spring.'

'I like operating the spring,' said the toad, crawling around to the back of the hat.

There was a click, and a slow *thwap-thwap* noise, and the centre of the hat rose slowly and jerkily up out of the paper flowers, which fell away.

'Er . . .' said Tiffany.

'You have a question?' said Miss Tick.

With a last *thwop*, the top of the hat made a perfect point.

'How do you know I won't run away right now and tell the Baron?' said Tiffany.

'Because you haven't the slightest desire to do so,' said Miss Tick. 'You're absolutely fascinated. You want to *be* a witch, am I right? You probably want to fly on a broomstick, yes?'

'Oh, yes!' She'd often dreamed of flying. Miss Tick's next words brought her down to earth.

'Really? You like having to wear really, really thick pants? Believe me, if I've got to fly I wear two pairs of woollen ones and a canvas pair on the outside which, I may tell you, are not very feminine no matter how much lace you sew on. It can get *cold* up there. People forget that. And then there's the bristles. Don't ask me

26

about the bristles. I will not talk about the bristles.'

'But can't you use a keeping-warm spell?' said Tiffany.

'I could. But a witch doesn't do that sort of thing. Once you use magic to keep yourself warm, then you'll start using it for other things.'

'But isn't that what a witch is supposed to—' Tiffany began.

'Once you learn about magic, I mean really *learn* about magic, learn everything you can learn about magic, then you've got the most important lesson still to learn,' said Miss Tick.

'What's that?'

'Not to use it. Witches don't use magic unless they really have to. It's hard work and difficult to control. We do other things. A witch pays attention to everything that's going on. A witch uses her head. A witch is sure of herself. A witch always has a piece of string—'

'I always *do* have a piece of string!' said Tiffany. 'It's always handy!'

'Good. Although there's more to witchcraft than string. A witch delights in small details. A witch sees through things and round things. A witch sees further than most. A witch sees things from the other side. A witch knows where she is, and *when* she is. A witch would see Jenny Green-Teeth,' she added. 'What happened?'

'How did you know I saw Jenny Green-Teeth?'

'I'm a witch. Guess,' said Miss Tick.

Tiffany looked around the tent. There wasn't much

to see, even now that her eyes were getting accustomed to the gloom. The sounds of the outside world filtered through the heavy material.

'I think—'

'Yes?' said the witch.

'I think you heard me telling the teacher.'

'Correct. I just used my ears,' said Miss Tick, saying nothing at all about saucers of ink. 'Tell me about this monster with eyes the size of the kind of soup plates that are eight inches across. Where do soup plates come into it?'

'The monster is mentioned in a book of stories I've got,' explained Tiffany. 'It said Jenny Green-Teeth has eyes the size of soup plates. There's a picture, but it's not a good one. So I measured a soup plate, so I could be exact.'

Miss Tick put her chin on her hand and gave Tiffany an odd sort of smile.

'That was all right, wasn't it?' said Tiffany.

'What? Oh, yes. Yes. Um . . . yes. Very . . . exact. Go on.'

Tiffany told her about the fight with Jenny, although she didn't mention Wentworth in case Miss Tick got funny about it. Miss Tick listened carefully.

'Why the frying pan?' she said. 'You could've found a stick.'

'A frying pan just seemed a better idea,' said Tiffany.

'Hah! It *was*. Jenny would've eaten you up if you'd used a stick. A frying pan is made of iron. Creatures of that kidney can't stand iron.'

'But it's a monster out of a storybook!' said Tiffany.

'What's it doing turning up in our little river?'

Miss Tick stared at Tiffany for a while, and then said: 'Why do you want to be a witch, Tiffany?'

It had started with The Goode Childe's Booke of Faerie Tales. *Actually, it had probably started with a lot of things, but the stories most of all.*

Her mother had read them to her when she was little, and then she'd read them to herself. And all the stories had, somewhere, the witch. The *wicked old witch*.

And Tiffany had thought: Where's the *evidence*?

The stories never said *why* she was wicked. It was enough to be an old woman, enough to be all alone, enough to look strange because you had no teeth. It was enough to be *called* a witch.

If it came to that, the book never gave you the *evidence* of anything. It talked about 'a handsome prince' . . . was he really, or was it just because he was a prince that people called him handsome? As for 'a girl who was as beautiful as the day was long' . . . well, which day? In midwinter it hardly ever got light! The stories didn't want you to think, they just wanted you to believe what you were told . . .

And you were told that the old witch lived all by herself in a strange cottage made of gingerbread or which ran around on giant hen's feet, and talked to animals, and could do magic.

Tiffany only ever knew one old woman who lived all alone in a strange cottage . . .

Well, no. That wasn't quite true. But she had only ever known one old woman who lived in a strange house *that moved about*, and that was Granny Aching. And she could do magic, sheep magic, and she talked to animals and there was nothing wicked about her. That *proved* you couldn't believe the stories.

And there had been the *other* old woman, the one who *everyone* said was a witch. And what had happened to her had made Tiffany very . . . thoughtful.

Anyway, she preferred the witches to the smug handsome princes and especially to the stupid smirking princesses, who didn't have the sense of a beetle. They had lovely golden hair too, and Tiffany didn't. Her hair was brown, plain brown. Her mother called it chestnut, or sometimes auburn, but Tiffany knew it was brown, brown, brown, just like her eyes. Brown as earth. And did the book have any adventures for people who had brown eyes and brown hair? No, no, no . . . it was the blond people with blue eyes and the redheads with green eyes who got the stories. If you had brown hair you were probably just a servant or a woodcutter or something. Or a dairymaid. Well, that was not going to happen, even if she *was* good at cheese. She couldn't be the prince, and she'd never be a princess, and she didn't want to be a woodcutter, so she'd be the witch and *know* things, just like Granny Aching—

'Who was Granny Aching?' said a voice.

Who was Granny Aching? People would start asking that now. And the answer was: what Granny Aching was, was there. She was always there. It seemed that the lives of all the Achings revolved around Granny Aching. Down in the village decisions were made, things were done, life went on in the knowledge that in her old wheeled shepherding hut on the hills Granny Aching was there, watching.

And she was the silence of the hills. Perhaps that's why she liked Tiffany, in her awkward, hesitant way. Her older sisters chattered, and Granny didn't like noise. Tiffany didn't make noise when she was up at the hut. She just loved being there. She'd watch the buzzards, and listen to the noise of the silence.

It did have a noise, up there. Sounds, voices, animal noises floating up onto the downs, somehow made the silence deep and complex. And Granny Aching wrapped this silence around herself and made room inside it for Tiffany. It was always too busy on the farm. There were a lot of people with a lot to do. There wasn't enough time for silence. There wasn't time for listening. But Granny Aching was silent and listened all the time.

'What?' said Tiffany, blinking.

'You just said "Granny Aching listened to me all the time",' said Miss Tick.

Tiffany swallowed. 'I think my grandmother was slightly a witch,' she said, with a touch of pride.

'Really? How do you know?'

'Well, witches can curse people, right?' said Tiffany.

'So it is said,' said Miss Tick diplomatically.

'Well, my father said Granny Aching cussed the sky blue,' said Tiffany.

TERRY PRATCHETT

Miss Tick coughed. 'Well, cussing, now, cussing isn't like genuine *cursing*. Cussing's more like dang and botheration and darned and drat, you know? Cursing is more on the lines of "I hope your nose explodes and your ears go flying away."'

'I think Granny's cussing was a bit more than that,' said Tiffany, in a very definite voice. 'And she talked to her dogs.'

'And what kind of things did she say to them?' said Miss Tick.

'Oh, things like *come by* and *away to me* and *that'll do*,' said Tiffany. 'They always did what she told them.'

'But those are just sheepdog commands,' said Miss Tick dismissively. 'That's not exactly witchcraft.'

'Well, that still makes them familiars, doesn't it?' Tiffany retorted, feeling annoyed. 'Witches have animals they can talk to, called familiars. Like your toad there.'

'I'm not familiar,' said a voice from among the paper flowers. 'I'm just slightly presumptuous.'

'And she knew about all kinds of herbs,' Tiffany persisted. Granny Aching was going to be a witch even if Tiffany had to argue all day. 'She could cure anything. My father said she could make a shepherd's pie stand up and baa.' Tiffany lowered her voice. 'She could *bring lambs back to life . . .'*

You hardly ever saw Granny Aching indoors in the spring and summer. She spent most of the year sleeping in the old wheeled hut, which could be dragged across the downs after the flocks. But the first time Tiffany

32

could remember seeing the old woman in the farm-house, she was kneeling in front of the fire, putting a dead lamb in the big black oven.

Tiffany had screamed and screamed. And Granny had gently picked her up, a little awkwardly, and sat her on her lap and shushed her and called her 'my little jiggit', while on the floor her sheepdogs, Thunder and Lightning, watched her in doggish amazement. Granny wasn't particularly at home around children, because they didn't baa.

When Tiffany had stopped crying out of sheer lack of breath, Granny had put her down on the rug and opened the oven, and Tiffany had watched the lamb come alive again.

When Tiffany got a little older, she found out that 'jiggit' meant twenty in the Yan Tan Tethera, the ancient counting language of the shepherds. The older people still used it when they were counting things they thought of as special. She was Granny Aching's twentieth grandchild.

And when she was older she also understood all about the warming oven, which never got more than, well, warm. Her mother would let the bread dough rise in it, and Ratbag the cat would sleep in it, sometimes on the dough. It was just the place to revive a weak lamb that had been born on a snowy night and was near death from the cold. That was how it worked. No magic at all. But that time it had been magic. And it didn't stop being magic just because you found out how it was done.

*

'Good, but still not *exactly* witchcraft,' said Miss Tick, breaking the spell again. 'Anyway, you don't have to have a witch ancestor to be a witch. It helps, of course, because of heredity.'

'You mean like having talents?' said Tiffany, wrinkling her brow.

'Partly, I suppose,' said Miss Tick. 'But I was thinking of pointy hats, for example. If you have a grandmother who can pass on her pointy hat to you, that saves a great deal of expense. They are incredibly hard to come by, especially ones strong enough to withstand falling farmhouses. Did Mrs Aching have anything like that?'

'I don't think so,' said Tiffany. 'She hardly ever wore a hat except in the very cold weather. She wore an old grain sack as a sort of hood. Um . . . does that count?'

For the first time, Miss Tick looked a little less flinty. 'Possibly, possibly,' she said. 'Do you have any brothers and sisters, Tiffany?'

'I have six sisters,' said Tiffany. 'I'm the youngest. Most of them don't live with us now.'

'And then you weren't the baby any more because you had a dear little brother,' said Miss Tick. 'The only boy too. That must have been a nice surprise.'

Suddenly, Tiffany found Miss Tick's faint smile slightly annoying.

'How do you know about my brother?' she said.

The smile faded. Miss Tick thought: This child is *sharp*. 'Just a guess,' she said. No one likes admitting to spying.

'Are you using persykology on me?' said Tiffany hotly.

'I think you mean psychology,' said Miss Tick.

'Whatever,' said Tiffany. 'You think I don't like him because my parents make a fuss of him and spoil him, yes?'

'Well, it did cross my mind,' said Miss Tick, and gave up worrying about the spying. She was a witch, and that was all there was to it. 'I think it was the bit when you used him as bait for a slathering monster that gave me a hint,' she added.

'He's just a nuisance!' said Tiffany. 'He takes up my time and I'm always having to look after him and he always wants sweets. Anyway,' she continued, 'I had to think fast.'

'Quite so,' said Miss Tick.

'Granny Aching would have done something about monsters in our river,' said Tiffany, ignoring that. 'Even if they are out of books.' And she'd have done something about what happened to old Mrs Snapperly, she added to herself. She'd have spoken up, and people would have listened . . . They always listened when Granny spoke up. *Speak up for those who don't have voices*, she always said.

'Good,' said Miss Tick. 'So she should. Witches deal with things. You said the river was very shallow where Jenny leaped up? And the world looked blurred and shaky? Was there a susurrus?'

Tiffany beamed. 'Yes, there certainly was!'

'Ah. Something bad is happening.'

Tiffany looked worried.

'Can I stop it?'

'And now I'm slightly impressed,' said Miss Tick. 'You said, "Can I stop it?", not "Can anyone stop it?" or "Can we stop it?" That's good. You accept responsibility. That's a good start. And you keep a cool head. But, no, you can't stop it.'

'I walloped Jenny Green-Teeth!'

'Lucky hit,' said Miss Tick. 'There may be worse than her on the way, believe me. I believe an incursion of major proportions is going to start here and, clever though you are, my girl, you have as much chance as one of your lambs on a snowy night. You keep clear. I'll try to fetch help.'

'What, from the Baron?'

'Good gracious, no. He'd be no use at all.'

'But he protects us,' said Tiffany. 'That's what my mother says.'

'Does he?' said Miss Tick. 'Who from? I mean, from whom?'

'Well, from, you know . . . attack, I suppose. From other barons, my father says.'

'Has he got a big army?'

'Well, er, he's got Sergeant Roberts, and Kevin and Neville and Trevor,' said Tiffany. 'We all know them. They mostly guard the castle.'

'Any of them got magical powers?' said Miss Tick.

'I saw Neville do card tricks once,' said Tiffany.

'A wow at parties, but probably not much use even against something like Jenny,' said Miss Tick. 'Are there no oth— Are there no witches here at all?'

Tiffany hesitated.

'There was old Mrs Snapperly,' she said. Oh, yes. She'd lived all alone in a strange cottage all right . . .

'Good name,' said Miss Tick. 'Can't say I've heard it before, though. Where is she?'

'She died in the snow last winter,' said Tiffany slowly.

'And now tell me what you're not telling me,' said Miss Tick, sharp as a knife.

'Er . . . she was begging, people think, but no one opened their doors to her and, er . . . it was a cold night, and . . . she died.'

'And she was a witch, was she?'

'Everyone *said* she was a witch,' said Tiffany. She really did not want to talk about this. No one in the villages around here wanted to talk about it. No one went near the ruins of the cottage in the woods, either.

'You don't think so?'

'Um . . .' Tiffany squirmed. 'You see . . . the Baron had a son called Roland. He was only twelve, I think. And he went riding in the woods by himself last summer and his dogs came back without him.'

'Mrs Snapperly lived in those woods?' said Miss Tick.

'Yes.'

'And people think she killed him?' said Miss Tick. She sighed. 'They probably think she cooked him in the oven, or something.'

'They never actually *said*,' said Tiffany. 'But I think it was something like that, yes.'

'And did his horse turn up?' said Miss Tick.

'No,' said Tiffany. 'And that was strange, because if

it'd turned up anywhere along the hills the people would have noticed it . . .'

Miss Tick folded her hands, sniffed, and smiled a smile with no humour in it at all.

'Easily explained,' she said. 'Mrs Snapperly must have had a really *big* oven, eh?'

'No, it was really quite small,' said Tiffany. 'Only ten inches deep.'

'I bet Mrs Snapperly had no teeth and talked to herself, right?' said Miss Tick.

'Yes. And she had a cat. And a squint,' said Tiffany. And it all came out in a rush: 'And so after he vanished they went to her cottage and they looked in the oven and they dug up her garden and they threw stones at her old cat until it died and they turned her out of her cottage and piled up all her old books in the middle of the room and set fire to them and burned the place to the ground and everyone said she was an old witch.'

'They burned the books,' said Miss Tick, in a flat voice.

'Because they said they had old writing in them,' said Tiffany. 'And pictures of stars.'

'And when you went to look, did they?' said Miss Tick.

Tiffany suddenly felt cold. 'How did you know?' she said.

'I'm good at listening. Well, did they?'

Tiffany sighed. 'Yes, I went to the cottage next day and some of the pages, you know, had kind of floated up in the heat. And I found a part of one, and it had all old lettering and gold and blue edging. And I buried her cat.'

'You buried the cat?'

'Yes! Someone had to!' said Tiffany hotly.

'And you measured the oven,' said Miss Tick. 'I know you did, because you just told me what size it was.' And you measure soup plates, Miss Tick added to herself. What *have* I found here?

'Well, yes. I did. I mean . . . it was tiny! And if she could magic away a boy and a whole horse, why didn't she magic away the men who came for her? It didn't make any sense—!'

Miss Tick waved her into silence. 'And then what happened?'

'Then the Baron said no one was to have anything to do with her,' said Tiffany. 'He said *any* witches found in the country would be tied up and thrown in the pond. Er, you could be in danger,' she added uncertainly.

'I can untie knots with my teeth and I have a Gold Swimming Certificate from the Quirm College for Young Ladies,' said Miss Tick. 'All that practice at jumping into the swimming pool with my clothes on was time well spent.' She leaned forward. 'Let me guess what happened to Mrs Snapperly,' she said. 'She lived from the summer until the snow, right? She stole food from barns and probably women gave her food at the back door if the men weren't around? I expect the bigger boys threw things at her if they saw her.'

'How do you *know* all this?' said Tiffany.

'It doesn't take a huge leap of imagination, believe

me,' said Miss Tick. 'And she wasn't a witch, was she?'

'I think she was just a sick old lady who was no use to anyone and smelled a bit and looked odd because she had no teeth,' said Tiffany. 'She just looked like a witch in a story. Anyone with half a mind could see that.'

Miss Tick sighed. 'Yes. But sometimes it's so hard to find half a mind when you need one.'

'Can't you teach me what I need to know to be a witch?' said Tiffany.

'Tell me why you *still* want to be a witch, bearing in mind what happened to Mrs Snapperly?'

'So that sort of thing doesn't happen again,' said Tiffany.

She even buried the old witch's cat, thought Miss Tick. What kind of child is this?

'Good answer. You might make a decent witch one day,' she said. 'But I don't teach people to *be* witches. I teach people *about* witches. Witches learn in a special school. I just show them the way, if they're any good. All witches have special interests, and I like children.'

'Why?'

'Because they're much easier to fit in the oven,' said Miss Tick.

But Tiffany wasn't frightened, just annoyed.

'That was a nasty thing to say,' she said.

'Well, witches don't have to be *nice*,' said Miss Tick, pulling a large black bag from under the table. 'I'm glad to see you pay attention.'

'There really is a school for witches?' said Tiffany.

'In a manner of speaking, yes,' said Miss Tick.

'Where?'

'Very close.'

'It is magical?'

'Very magical.'

'A wonderful place?'

'There's nowhere quite like it.'

'Can I go there by magic? Does, like, a unicorn turn up to carry me there or something?'

'Why should it? A unicorn is nothing more than a big horse that comes to a point, anyway. Nothing to get so excited about,' said Miss Tick. 'And that will be one egg, please.'

'Exactly where can I find the school?' said Tiffany, handing over the egg.

'Aha. A root vegetable question, I think,' said Miss Tick. 'Two carrots, please.'

Tiffany handed them over.

'Thank you. Ready? To find the school for witches, go to a high place near here, climb to the top, open your eyes . . .' Miss Tick hesitated.

'Yes?'

'. . . and then open your eyes again.'

'But—' Tiffany began.

'Got any more eggs?'

'No, but—'

'No more education, then. But I have a question to ask you.'

'Got any eggs?' said Tiffany instantly.

'Hah! Did you see anything *else* by the river, Tiffany?'

Silence suddenly filled the tent. The sound of bad

spelling and erratic geography filtered through from outside as Tiffany and Miss Tick stared into one another's eyes.

'No,' lied Tiffany.

'Are you sure?' said Miss Tick.

'Yes.'

They continued the staring match. But Tiffany could outstare a cat.

'I *see*,' said Miss Tick, looking away. 'Very well. In that case, please tell me . . . when you stopped outside my tent just now you said "Aha" in what I considered to be a smug tone of voice. Were you thinking, This is a strange little black tent with a mysterious little sign on the door, so going inside could be the start of an adventure, *or* were you thinking, This could be the tent of some wicked witch like they thought Mrs Snapperly was, who'll put some horrible spell on me as soon as I go in? It's all right, you can stop staring now. Your eyes are watering.'

'I thought both those things,' said Tiffany, blinking.

'But you came in anyway. Why?'

'To find out.'

'Good answer. Witches are naturally nosy,' said Miss Tick, standing up. 'Well, I must go. I hope we shall meet again. I will give you some free advice, though.'

'Will it cost me anything?'

'What? I just said it was free!' said Miss Tick.

'Yes, but my father said that free advice often turns out to be expensive,' said Tiffany.

Miss Tick sniffed. 'You could say this advice is

priceless,' she said. 'Are you listening?'

'Yes,' said Tiffany.

'Good. Now . . . if you trust in yourself . . .'

'Yes?'

'. . . and believe in your dreams . . .'

'Yes?'

'. . . and follow your star . . .' Miss Tick went on.

'Yes?'

'. . . you'll still get beaten by people who spent *their* time working hard and learning things and weren't so lazy. Goodbye.'

The tent seemed to grow darker. It was time to leave. Tiffany found herself back in the square where the other teachers were taking down their stalls.

She didn't look round. She knew enough not to look round. Either the tent would still be there, which would be a disappointment, or it would have mysteriously disappeared, and that would be worrying.

She headed home, and wondered if she should have mentioned the little red-haired men. She hadn't, for a whole lot of reasons. She wasn't sure, now, that she'd really seen them; she had a feeling that they wouldn't have wanted her to; and it was nice to have something Miss Tick didn't know. Yes. That was the best part. Miss Tick was a bit too clever, in Tiffany's opinion.

On the way home she climbed to the top of Arken Hill, which was just outside the village. It wasn't very big, not even as high as the downs above the farm and certainly nothing like as high as the mountains.

The hill was more . . . homely. There was a flat

place at the top where nothing ever grew, and Tiffany knew there was a story that a hero had once fought a dragon up there and its blood had burned the ground where it fell. There was another story that said there was a heap of treasure under the hill, *defended* by the dragon, and *another* story that said a king was buried there in armour of solid gold. There were lots of stories about the hill; it was surprising it hadn't sunk under the weight of them.

Tiffany stood on the bare soil and looked at the view.

She could see the village and the river and Home Farm, and the Baron's castle and, beyond the fields she knew, she could see grey woods and heathlands.

She closed her eyes and opened them again. And blinked, and opened them *again*.

There was no magic door, no hidden building revealed, no strange signs.

For a moment, though, the air buzzed, and smelled of snow.

When she got home she looked up 'incursion' in the dictionary. It meant 'invasion'.

An incursion of major proportions, Miss Tick had said.

And, now, little unseen eyes watched Tiffany from the top of the shelf . . .

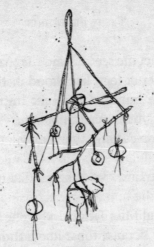

CHAPTER 3

Hunt The Hag

Miss Tick removed her hat, reached inside and pulled a piece of string. With little clicks and flapping noises the hat took up the shape of a rather elderly straw hat. She picked up the paper flowers from the ground and stuck them on, carefully.

Then she said: 'Phew!'

'You can't just let the kid go like that,' said the toad, who was sitting on the table.

'Like what?'

'She's clearly got First Sight *and* Second Thoughts. That's a powerful combination.'

'She's a little know-it-all,' said Miss Tick.

'Right. Just like you. She's impressed you, right? I know she did because you were quite nasty to her, and you always do that to people who impress you.'

'Do you want to be turned into a frog?'

45

'Well, now, let me see . . .' said the toad sarcastically. 'Better skin, better legs, likelihood of being kissed by a princess one hundred per cent improved . . . why, yes. Whenever you're ready, madam.'

'There're worse things than being a toad,' said Miss Tick darkly.

'Try it some time,' said the toad. 'Anyway, I rather liked her.'

'So did I,' said Miss Tick briskly. 'She hears about an old lady dying because these idiots thought she was a witch, and *she* decides to become a witch so that they don't try that again. A monster roars up out of her river and she bashes it with a frying pan! Have you ever heard the saying "The land finds its witch"? It's happened here, I'll bet. But a *chalk* witch? Witches like granite and basalt, hard rock all the way down! Do you know what chalk *is*?'

'You're going to tell me,' said the toad.

'It's the shells of billions and billions of tiny, helpless little sea creatures that died millions of years ago,' said Miss Tick. 'It's . . . tiny, tiny bones. Soft. Soggy. Damp. Even limestone is better than that. But . . . she's grown up on chalk and *she* is hard, and sharp too. She's a born witch. On *chalk*! Which is *impossible*!'

'She bashed Jenny!' said the toad. 'The girl has got talent!'

'Maybe, but she needs more than that. Jenny isn't clever,' said Miss Tick. 'She's only a Grade One Prohibitory Monster. And she was probably bewildered to find herself in a stream, when her natural home is in stagnant water. There'll be much, much worse than her.'

'What do you mean, "a Grade One Prohibitory Monster"?' asked the toad. 'I've never heard her called that.'

'I *am* a teacher as well as a witch,' said Miss Tick, adjusting her hat carefully. 'Therefore I make lists. I make assessments. I write things down in a neat, firm hand with pens of two colours. Jenny is one of a number of creatures invented by adults to scare children away from dangerous places.' She sighed. 'If only people would *think* before they make up monsters.'

'You ought to stay and help her,' said the toad.

'I've got practically no power here,' said Miss Tick. 'I told you. It's the chalk. And remember the red-headed men. A Nac Mac Feegle *spoke* to her! *Warned* her! I've never seen one in my life! If she's got *them* on her side, who knows what she can do?'

She picked up the toad. 'D'you know what'll be turning up?' she continued. 'All the things they locked away in those old stories. All those reasons why you shouldn't stray off the path, or open the forbidden door, or say the wrong word, or spill the salt. All the stories that gave children nightmares. All the monsters from under the biggest bed in the world. Somewhere, all stories are real and all dreams come true. And they'll come true here if they're not stopped. If it wasn't for the Nac Mac Feegle I'd be really worried. As it is, I'm going to try and get some help. That's going to take me at least two days without a broomstick!'

'It's unfair to leave her alone with them,' said the toad.

'She won't be alone,' said Miss Tick. 'She'll have you.'

'Oh,' said the toad.

Tiffany shared a bedroom with Fastidia and Hannah. She woke up when she heard them come to bed, and lay in the dark until she heard their breathing settle down and they started to dream of young sheep shearers with their shirts off.

Outside, summer lightning flashed around the hills, and there was a rumble of thunder . . .

Thunder and Lightning. She knew them as dogs before she knew them as the sound and light of a storm. Granny always had her sheepdogs with her, indoors and out. One moment they would be black and white streaks across the distant turf and then they were suddenly there, panting, eyes never leaving Granny's face. Half the dogs on the hills were Lightning's puppies, trained by Granny Aching.

Tiffany had gone with the family to the big Sheepdog Trials. Every shepherd on the Chalk went to them, and the very best entered the arena to show how well they could work their dogs. The dogs would round up sheep, separate them, drive them into the pens – or sometimes run off, or snap at one another, because even the best dog can have a bad day. But Granny never entered with Thunder and Lightning. She'd lean on the fence with the dogs lying in front of her, watching the show intently and puffing her foul pipe. And Tiffany's father had said that, after each shepherd had worked his dogs, the judges would look nervously across at Granny Aching to see what she thought. In fact, all the shepherds watched her. Granny never, ever entered the arena because she was the Trials. If Granny thought you were a good shepherd – if she nodded at you when you walked out of the arena, if she puffed at her pipe and said 'That'll do' – you walked like a giant for a day, you owned the Chalk . . .

When she was small and up on the wold with Granny, Thunder and Lightning would baby-sit Tiffany, lying attentively a few feet away as she played. And she'd been so proud when Granny had let her use them to round up a flock. She'd run about excitedly in all directions shouting 'Come by!' and 'There!' and 'Walk up!' and, glory be, the dogs had worked perfectly.

She knew now that they'd have worked perfectly whatever she'd shouted. Granny was just sitting there, smoking her pipe, and by now the dogs could read her mind. They only ever took orders from Granny Aching . . .

The storm died down after a while and there was the gentle sound of rain.

At some point Ratbag the cat pushed open the door and jumped onto the bed. He was big to start with, but Ratbag *flowed*. He was so fat that, on any reasonably flat surface, he gradually spread out in a great puddle of fur. He hated Tiffany, but would never let personal feelings get in the way of a warm place to sleep.

She must have slept, because she woke up when she heard the voices.

They seemed very close but, somehow, very small.

'Crivens! It's a' verra well sayin' "find the hag", but what should we be lookin' for, can ye tell me that? All these bigjobs look just the same tae me!'

'Not-totally-wee Geordie doon at the fishin' said she was a big, big girl!'

'A great help that is, I dinnae think! They're all big, big girls!'

'Ye paira dafties! Everyone knows a hag wears a pointy bonnet!'

'So they canna be a hag if they're sleepin', then?'

'Hello?' whispered Tiffany.

There was silence, embroidered with the breathing of her sisters. But in a way Tiffany couldn't quite describe, it was the silence of people trying hard not to make any noise.

She leaned down and looked under the bed. There was nothing there but the guzunder.

The little man in the river had talked just like that.

She lay back in the moonlight, listening until her ears ached.

Then she wondered what the school for witches would be like and why she hadn't seen it yet.

She knew every inch of the country for two miles around. She liked the river best, with the backwaters where striped pike sunbathed just above the weeds and the banks where kingfishers nested. There was a heronry a mile or so upriver and she liked to creep up on the birds when they came down here to fish in the reeds, because there's nothing funnier than a heron trying to get airborne in a hurry . . .

She drifted off to sleep again, thinking about the land around the farm. She knew all of it. There were no secret places that she didn't know about.

But maybe there were magical doors. That's what she'd make, if she had a magical school. There should be secret doorways everywhere, even hundreds of miles away. Look at a special rock by, say, moonlight, and there would be yet another door.

But the school, now, the school. There would be lessons in broomstick riding and how to sharpen your hat to a point, and magical meals, and lots of new friends.

'Is the bairn asleep?'

'Aye, I canna' hear her movin'.'

Tiffany opened her eyes in the darkness. The voices under the bed had a slightly echoey edge. Thank goodness the guzunder was nice and clean.

'Right, let's get oot o' this wee pot, then.'

The voices moved off across the room. Tiffany's ears tried to swivel to follow them.

'Hey, see here, it's a hoose! See, with wee chairies and things!'

They've found the doll's house, Tiffany thought.

It was quite a large one, made by Mr Block the farm carpenter when Tiffany's oldest sister, who already had two babies of her own now, was a little girl. It wasn't the most fragile of items. Mr Block did not go in for delicate work. But over the years the girls had decorated it with bits of material and some rough and ready furniture.

By the sound of it the owners of the voices thought it was a palace.

'Hey, hey, hey, we're in the cushy stuff noo! There's a beid in this room. Wi' pillows!'

'Keep it doon, we don't want any o' them to wake up!'

'Crivens, I'm as quiet as a wee moose! Aargh! There's sojers!'

'Whut d'ye mean, sojers?'

'There's redcoats in the room!'

They've found the toy soldiers, thought Tiffany, trying not to breathe loudly.

Strictly speaking, they had no place in the doll's house, but Wentworth wasn't old enough for them and so they'd got used as innocent bystanders back in those days when Tiffany had made tea parties for her dolls. Well, what passed for dolls. Such toys as there were in the farmhouse had to be tough to survive intact through the generations and didn't always manage it. Last time Tiffany had tried to arrange a party, the guests had been a rag doll with no head, two wooden soldiers and three-quarters of a small teddy bear.

Thuds and bangs came from the direction of the doll's house.

'I got one! Hey, pal, can yer mammie sew? Stitch this! Aargh! He's got a heid on him like a tree!'

'Crivens! There's a body here wi' no heid at a'!'

'*Aye, nae wonder, 'cos here's a bear! Feel ma boot, ye washoon!*'

It seemed to Tiffany that although the owners of the three voices were fighting things that couldn't possibly fight back, including a teddy bear with only one leg, the fight still wasn't going all one way.

'*I got 'im! I got 'im! I got 'im! Yer gonna get a gummer, yer wee hard disease!*'

'*Someone bit ma leg! Someone bit ma leg!*'

'*Come here! Ach, yer fightin' yersels, ye eejits! Ah'm fed up wi' the paira yees!*'

Tiffany felt Ratbag stir. He might be fat and lazy, but he was lightning fast when it came to leaping on small creatures. She couldn't let him get the . . . whatever they were, however bad they sounded.

She coughed loudly.

'*See?*' said a voice from the doll's house. '*Yer woked them up! Ah'm offski!*'

Silence fell again and this time, Tiffany decided after a while, it was the silence of no one there rather than the silence of people being incredibly quiet. Ratbag went back to sleep, twitching occasionally as he disembowelled something in his fat cat dreams.

Tiffany waited a little while and then got out of bed and crept towards the bedroom door, avoiding the two squeaky floorboards. She went downstairs in the dark, found a chair by moonlight, fished the book of Faerie Tales off Granny's shelf, then lifted the latch on the back door and stepped out into the warm midsummer night.

There was a lot of mist around, but a few stars were

visible overhead and there was a gibbous moon in the sky. Tiffany knew it was gibbous because she'd read in the Almanack that 'gibbous' meant what the moon looked like when it was just a bit fatter than half full, and so she made a point of paying attention to it around those times just so that she could say to herself: 'Ah, I see the moon's very gibbous tonight . . .'

It's possible that this tells you more about Tiffany than she would want you to know.

Against the rising moon the downs were a black wall that filled half the sky. For a moment she looked for the light of Granny Aching's lantern . . .

Granny never lost a lamb. That was one of Tiffany's first memories: of being held by her mother at the window one frosty night in early spring, with a million brilliant stars glinting over the mountains and, on the darkness of the downs, the one yellow star in the constellation of Granny Aching, zigzagging through the night. She wouldn't go to bed while a lamb was lost, however bad the weather . . .

There was only one place where it was possible for someone in a large family to be private, and that was in the privy. It was a three-holer, and it was where everyone went if they wanted to be alone for a while.

There was a candle in there, and last year's Almanack hanging on a string. The printers knew their readership, and printed the Almanack on soft thin paper.

Tiffany lit the candle, made herself comfortable,

and looked at the book of Faerie Tales. The moon gibbous'd at her through the crescent-shaped hole cut in the door.

She'd never really liked the book. It seemed to her that it tried to tell her what to do and what to think. Don't stray from the path, don't open that door, but hate the wicked witch because she is *wicked*. Oh, and believe that shoe size is a good way of choosing a wife.

A lot of the stories were highly suspicious, in her opinion. There was the one that ended when the two good children pushed the wicked witch into her own oven. Tiffany had worried about that after all that trouble with Mrs Snapperly. Stories like this stopped people thinking properly, she was sure. She'd read that one and thought, Excuse me? *No one* has an oven big enough to get a whole person in, and what made the children think they could just walk around eating people's houses in any case? And why does some boy too stupid to know a cow is worth a lot more than five beans have the *right* to murder a giant and steal all his gold? Not to mention commit an act of ecological vandalism? And some girl who can't tell the difference between a wolf and her grandmother must either have been as dense as teak or come from an extremely ugly family. The stories *weren't real*. But Mrs Snapperly had died because of stories.

She flicked past page after page, looking for the right pictures. Because, although the stories made her angry, the pictures, ah, the pictures were the most beautiful things she'd ever seen.

She turned a page and there it was.

Most of the pictures of fairies were not very impressive. Frankly, they looked like a small girls' ballet class that'd just had to run through a bramble patch. But this one . . . was different. The colours were strange, and there were no shadows. Giant grasses and daisies grew everywhere, so the fairies must have been quite small, but they *looked* big. They looked like rather strange humans. They certainly didn't look much like fairies. Hardly any of them had wings. They were odd shapes, in fact. In fact, some of them looked like monsters. The girls in the tutus wouldn't have stood much chance.

And the odd thing was that, alone of all the pictures in the book, *this* one looked as if it had been done by an artist who had painted what was in front of him. The other pictures, the ballet girls and the romper-suit babies, had a made-up, syrupy look. This one didn't. This one said that the artist had been there . . .

. . . at least in his head, Tiffany thought.

She concentrated on the bottom left-hand corner, and there it was. She'd seen it before, but you had to know where to look. It was definitely a little red-haired man, naked except for a kilt and a skinny waistcoat, scowling out of the picture. He looked very angry. And . . . Tiffany moved the candle to see more clearly . . . he was *definitely* making a gesture with his hand.

Even if you didn't know it was a rude one, it was easy to guess.

She heard voices. She pushed the door open with

her foot to hear them better, because a witch always listens to other people's conversations.

The sound was coming from the other side of the hedge, where there was a field that should have been full of nothing but sheep, waiting to go to market. Sheep are not known for their conversation. She snuck out carefully in the misty dawn and found a small gap that had been made by rabbits, which just gave her a good enough view.

There was a ram grazing near the hedge and the conversation was coming from it or, rather, somewhere in the long grass underneath it. There seemed to be at least four speakers, who sounded bad-tempered.

'*Crivens! We wanna coo beastie, no' a ship beastie!*'

'*Ach, one's as goo' as t'other! C'mon, lads, a' grab a holt o' a leg!*'

'*Aye, all the coos are inna shed, we tak' what we can!*'

'*Keep it doon, keep it doon, will ya!*'

'*Ach, who's listnin'? OK, lads – yan . . . tan . . . teth'ra!*'

The sheep rose a little in the air, and bleated in alarm as it started to go across the field backwards. Tiffany thought she saw a hint of red hair in the grass around its legs, but that vanished as the ram was carried away into the mist.

She pushed her way through the hedge, ignoring the twigs that scratched at her. Granny Aching wouldn't have let anyone get away with stealing a sheep, even if they were invisible.

But the mist was thick and, now, Tiffany heard noises from the henhouse.

The disappearing-backwards sheep could wait. Now the *hens* needed her. A fox had got in twice in the last two weeks and the hens that hadn't been taken were barely laying.

Tiffany ran through the garden, catching her nightdress on pea sticks and gooseberry bushes, and flung open the henhouse door.

There were no flying feathers, and nothing like the panic a fox would cause. But the chickens were clucking excitedly and Prunes, the cockerel, was strutting nervously up and down. One of the hens looked a bit embarrassed. Tiffany lifted it up quickly.

There were two tiny blue, red-haired men underneath. They were each holding an egg, clasped in their arms. They looked up with very guilty expressions.

'Ach, no!' said one. 'It's the bairn! *She's* the hag . . .'

'You're stealing our eggs,' said Tiffany. 'How dare you! And I'm *not* a hag!'

The little men looked at one another, and then at the eggs.

'Whut eiggs?' said one.

'The eggs you are holding,' said Tiffany meaningfully.

'Whut? Oh, these? These are *eiggs*, are they?' said the one who'd spoken first, looking at the eggs as if he'd never seen them before. 'There's a thing. And there was us thinking they was, er, stones.'

'Stones,' said the other one nervously.

'We crawled under yon chookie for a wee bitty warmth,' said the first one. 'And there was all these things, we thought they was stones, which was why the puir fowl was clucking all the time . . .'

'Clucking,' said the second one, nodding vigorously.

'. . . so we took pity on the puir thing and—'

'*Put* . . . the . . . eggs . . . *back*,' said Tiffany slowly.

The one who hadn't been doing much talking nudged the other one. 'Best do as she says,' it said. 'It's a' gang agley. Ye canna cross an Aching an' this one's a hag. She dinged Jenny an' no one ha' ever done *that* afore.'

'Aye, I didnae think o' that . . .'

Both of the tiny men put the eggs back very carefully. One of them even breathed on the shell of his and made a show of polishing it with the ragged hem of his kilt.

'No harm done, mistress,' he said. He looked at the other man. And then they vanished. But there was a suspicion of a red blur in the air and some straw by the henhouse door flew up in the air.

'And I'm a miss!' shouted Tiffany. She lowered the hen back onto the eggs, and went to the door. 'And I'm *not* a hag! Are you fairies of some sort? And what about our ship – I mean, sheep?' she added.

There was no answer but a clanking of buckets near the house, which meant that other people were getting up.

She rescued the Faerie Tales, blew out the candle and made her way into the house. Her mother was lighting the fire and asked what she was doing up, and she said that she'd heard a commotion in the henhouse and had gone out to see if it was the fox again. That wasn't a lie. In fact, it was completely true, even if it wasn't exactly accurate.

Tiffany was on the whole quite a truthful person, but it seemed to her that there were times when things didn't divide easily into 'true' and 'false', but instead could be 'things that people needed to know at the moment' and 'things that they didn't need to know at the moment'.

Besides, she wasn't sure what *she* knew at the moment.

There was porridge for breakfast. She ate it hurriedly, meaning to get back out into the paddock and see about that sheep. There might be tracks in the grass, or something . . .

She looked up, not knowing why.

Ratbag had been asleep in front of the oven. Now he was sitting up, alert. Tiffany felt a prickling on the back of her neck, and tried to see what the cat was looking at.

On the dresser was a row of blue and white jars which weren't very useful for anything. They'd been left to her mother by an elderly aunt, and she was proud of them because they looked nice but were completely useless. There was little room on the farm for useless things that looked nice, so they were treasured.

Ratbag was watching the lid of one of them. It was rising very slowly, and under it was a hint of red hair and two beady, staring eyes.

It lowered again when Tiffany gave it a long stare. A

moment later she heard a faint rattle and, when she looked up, the pot was wobbling back and forth and there was a little cloud of dust rising along the top of the dresser. Ratbag was looking around in bewilderment.

They certainly were *very* fast.

She ran out into the paddock and looked around. The mist was off the grass now, and skylarks were rising on the downs.

'If that sheep doesn't come back *this minute*,' she shouted at the sky, 'there will be a *reckoning*!'

The sound bounced off the hills. And then she heard, very faint but close by, the sound of small voices:

'*Whut did the hag say?*' said the first voice.

'*She said there'd be a reck'ning!*'

'*Oh, waily, waily, waily! We're in trouble noo!*'

Tiffany looked around, face red with anger.

'We have a *duty*,' she said, to the air and the grass.

It was something Granny Aching had said once, when Tiffany had been crying about a lamb. She had an old-fashioned way of speaking, and had said: 'We are as gods to the beasts o' the field, my jiggit. We order the time o' their birth and the time o' their death. Between times, we ha' a duty.'

'We have a duty,' Tiffany repeated, more softly. She glared around the field. 'I know you can hear me, whoever you are. If that sheep doesn't come back, there will be . . . trouble . . .'

The larks sang over the sheepfolds, making the silence deeper.

Tiffany had to do the chores before she had any more time to herself. That meant feeding the chickens and collecting the eggs, and feeling slightly proud of the fact that there were two more than there might otherwise have been. It meant fetching six buckets of water from the well and filling the log basket by the stove, but she put those jobs off because she didn't like doing them much. She did quite like churning butter, though. It gave her time to think.

When I'm a witch with a pointy hat and a broomstick, she thought as she pumped the handle, I'll wave my hand and the butter will come just like *that*. And any little red-headed devils that even *think* about taking our beasts will be—

There was a slopping sound behind her, where she'd lined up the six buckets to take to the well.

One of them was now full of water, which was still sloshing backwards and forwards.

She went back to the churning as if nothing had happened but stopped after a while and went over to the flour bin. She took a small handful of flour and dusted it over the doorstep, and then went back to the churning.

A few minutes later there was another watery sound behind her. When she turned round there was, yes, another full bucket. And in the flour on the stone doorstep were just two lines of little footprints, one leading out of the dairy and one coming back.

It was all Tiffany could do to lift one of the heavy wooden buckets when it was full.

So, she thought, they are immensely strong as well

as being incredibly fast. I'm really being very calm about this.

She looked up at the big wooden beams that ran across the room, and a little dust fell down, as if something had quickly moved out of the way.

I think I ought to put a stop to this right now, she thought. On the other hand, there's no harm in waiting until all the buckets are filled up.

'And then I'll have to fill the log box in the scullery,' she said aloud. Well, it was worth a try.

She went back to the churning, and didn't bother to turn her head when she heard four more sloshes behind her. Nor did she look round when she heard little *whooshwhoosh* noises and the clatter of logs in the box. She only turned to see when the noise stopped.

The log box was full up to the ceiling, and all the buckets were full. The patch of flour was a mass of footprints.

She stopped churning. She had a feeling that eyes were watching her, a *lot* of eyes.

'Er . . . thank you,' she said. No, that wasn't right. She sounded nervous. She let go of the butter paddle and stood up, trying to look as fierce as possible.

'And what about our sheep?' she said. 'I won't believe you're really sorry until I see the sheep come back!'

There was a bleating from the paddock. She ran out to the bottom of the garden and looked through the hedge.

The sheep *was* coming back, backwards and at high

speed. It jerked to a halt a little way from the hedge and dropped down as the little men let it go. One of the red-headed men appeared for a moment on its head. He huffed on a horn, polished it with his kilt, and vanished in a blur.

Tiffany walked back to the dairy looking thoughtful.

Oh, and when she got back the butter had been churned. Not just churned, in fact, but patted into a dozen fat golden oblongs on the marble she used when she did it. There was even a sprig of parsley on each one.

Are they brownies? she wondered. According to the Faerie Tales, brownies hung around the house doing chores in exchange for a saucer of milk. But in the picture they'd been cheery little creatures with long pointy hoods. The red-haired men didn't look as if they'd ever drunk milk in their lives, but perhaps it was worth a try.

'Well,' she said aloud, still aware of the hidden watchers. 'That'll do. Thank you. I'm glad you're sorry for what you did.'

She took one of the cat's saucers from the pile by the sink, washed it carefully, filled it with milk from today's churn, then put it down on the floor and stood back. 'Are you brownies?' she said.

The air blurred. Milk splashed across the floor and the saucer spun round and round.

'I'll take that as a no, then,' said Tiffany. 'So what are you?'

There were unlimited supplies of no answer at all.

She lay down and looked under the sink, and then peered behind the cheese shelves. She stared up into the dark, spidery shadows of the room. It felt empty.

And she thought: I think I need a whole egg's worth of education, in a hurry . . .

Tiffany had walked along the steep track from the farm down into the village hundreds of times. It was less than half a mile long, and over the centuries the carts had worn it down so that it was more like a gully in the chalk and ran like a milky stream in wet weather.

She was halfway down when the susurrus started. The hedges rustled without a wind. The skylarks stopped singing and, while she hadn't really noticed their song, their silence was a shock. Nothing's louder than the end of a song that's always been there.

When she looked up at the sky it was like looking through a diamond. It sparkled, and the air went cold so quickly that it was like stepping into an icy bath.

Then there was snow under foot, snow on the hedges. And the sound of hooves.

They were in the field beside her. A horse was galloping through the snow, behind the hedge that was now, suddenly, just a wall of white.

The hoofbeats stopped. There was a moment of silence and then a horse landed in the lane, skidding on the snow. It pulled itself upright, and the rider turned it to face Tiffany.

The rider himself couldn't face Tiffany. He had no face. He had no head to hang it on.

She ran. Her boots slipped on the snow as she moved, but suddenly her mind was cold as the ice.

She had two legs, slipping on ice. A horse had twice as many legs to slip. She'd seen horses try to tackle this hill in icy weather. She had a chance.

She heard a breathy, whistling noise behind her, and a whinny from the horse. She risked a glance. The horse was coming after her, but slowly, half walking and half sliding. Steam poured off it.

About halfway down the slope the lane passed under an arch of trees, looking like crashed clouds now under their weight of snow. And beyond them, Tiffany knew, the lane flattened out. The headless man would catch her on the flat. She didn't know what would happen after that, but she was sure it would be unpleasantly short.

Flakes of snow dropped on her as she passed under the trees, and she decided to make a run for it. She might reach the village. She was good at running.

But if she got there, then what? She'd never reach a door in time. And people would shout, and run about. The dark horseman didn't look like someone who'd take much notice of that. No, she had to *deal* with it.

If only she'd brought the frying pan.

'Here, wee hag! Stannit ye still, right noo!'

She stared up.

A tiny blue man had poked his head up out of the snow on top of the hedge.

'There's a headless horseman after me!' she shouted.

'He'll no' make it, hinny. Stand ye still! Look him in the eye!'

'He hasn't got any eyes!'

'Crivens! Are ye a hag or no'? Look him in the eyes he hasnae got!'

The blue man disappeared into the snow.

Tiffany turned round. The horseman was trotting under the trees now, the horse more certain as the ground levelled. He had a sword in his hand, and he *was* looking at her, with the eyes he didn't have. There was the breathy noise again, not good to hear.

The little men are watching me, she thought. I can't run. Granny Aching wouldn't have run from a thing with no head.

She folded her arms and glared.

The horseman stopped, as if puzzled, and then urged the horse forward.

A blue and red shape, larger than the other little men, dropped out of the trees. He landed on the horse's forehead, between its eyes, and grabbed an ear in both hands.

Tiffany heard the man shout: 'Here's a face full o' dandruff for ye, yer bogle, courtesy of Big Yan!' and then the man hit the horse between the eyes *with his head*.

To her amazement the horse staggered sideways.

'Aw right?' shouted the tiny fighter. 'Big toughie, is ye? Once more wi' *feelin'*!'

This time the horse danced uneasily the other way, and then its back legs slid from under it and it collapsed in the snow.

Little blue men erupted from the hedge. The horseman, trying to get to his feet, disappeared under a blue and red storm of screaming creatures—

And vanished. The snow vanished. The horse vanished.

The blue men, for a moment, were in a pile on the hot, dusty road. One of them said, 'Aw, crivens! I kicked meself in me own heid!' And then they, too, vanished, but for a moment Tiffany saw blue and red blurs disappearing into the hedge.

Then the skylarks were back. The hedges were green and full of flowers. Not a twig was broken, not a flower disturbed. The sky was blue, with no flashes of diamond.

Tiffany looked down. On the toes of her boots, snow was melting. She was, strangely, glad about that. It meant that what had just happened was magical, not madness. Because, if she closed her eyes, she could still hear the wheezy breathing of the headless man.

What she needed right now was people, and ordinary things happening. But more than anything else, she wanted answers.

Actually, what she wanted more than anything else was not to hear the wheezy breathing when she shut her eyes . . .

The tents had gone. Except for a few pieces of broken chalk, apple cores, some stamped-down grass and, alas, a few chicken feathers, there was nothing at all to show that the teachers had ever been there.

A small voice said, 'Psst!'

She looked down. A toad crept out from under a dock leaf.

'Miss Tick said you'd be back,' it said. 'I expect there're some things you need to know, right?'

'*Everything*,' said Tiffany. 'We're swamped with tiny men! I can't understand half of what they say! They keep calling me a hag!'

'Ah, yes,' said the toad. 'You've got Nac Mac Feegles!'

'It snowed, and then it hadn't! I was chased by a horseman with no *head*! And one of the . . . what did you say they were?'

'Nac Mac Feegles,' said the toad. 'Also known as pictsies. *They* call themselves the Wee Free Men.'

'Well, one of them head-butted the horse! It fell over! It was a huge horse too!'

'Ah, that sounds like a Feegle,' said the toad.

'I gave them some milk and they tipped it over!'

'You gave the Nac Mac Feegles *milk*?'

'Well, you said they're pixies!'

'Not pixies, *pictsies*. They certainly don't drink milk!'

'Are they from the same place as Jenny?' Tiffany demanded.

'No. They're rebels,' said the toad.

'Rebels? Against who?'

'Everyone. Anything,' said the toad. 'Now pick me up.'

'Why?'

'Because there's a woman at the well over there

giving you a funny look. Put me in your apron pocket, for goodness' sake.'

Tiffany snatched up the toad, and smiled at the woman. 'I'm making a collection of pressed toads,' she said.

'That's nice, dear,' said the woman, and hurried away.

'That wasn't very funny,' said the toad from her apron.

'People don't listen anyway,' said Tiffany.

She sat down under a tree and took the toad out of her pocket.

'The Feegles tried to steal some of our eggs and one of our sheep,' she said. 'But I got them back.'

'You got something back from the Nac Mac Feegle?' said the toad. 'Were they ill?'

'No. They were a bit . . . well, sweet, actually. They even did the chores for me.'

'The *Feegles* did *chores*?' said the toad. 'They *never* do chores! They're not helpful at all!'

'And then there was the headless horseman!' said Tiffany. 'He had no *head*!'

'Well, that is the major job qualification,' said the toad.

'What's going on, toad?' said Tiffany. 'Is it the Feegles who are invading?'

The toad looked a bit shifty. 'Miss Tick doesn't really want you to handle this,' it said. 'She'll be back soon with help . . .'

'Is she going to be in time?' Tiffany demanded.

'I don't know. Probably. But you shouldn't—'

'I want to know what is happening!'

'She's gone to get some other witches,' said the toad. 'Uh . . . she doesn't think you should—'

'You'd better tell me what you know, toad,' said Tiffany. 'Miss Tick isn't here. I am.'

'Another world is colliding with this one,' said the toad. 'There. Happy now? That's what Miss Tick thinks. But it's happening faster than she expected. All the monsters are coming back.'

'Why?'

'There's no one to stop them.'

There was silence for a moment.

'There's me,' said Tiffany.

CHAPTER 4

The Wee Free Men

Nothing happened on the way back to the farm. The sky stayed blue, none of the sheep in the home paddocks appeared to be travelling backwards very fast, and an air of hot emptiness lay over everything.

Ratbag was on the path leading up to the back door, and he had something trapped in his paws. As soon as he saw Tiffany he picked it up and exited around the corner of the house at high speed, legs spinning in the high-speed slink of a guilty cat. Tiffany was too good a shot with a clod of earth.

But at least there wasn't something red and blue in his mouth.

'Look at him,' she said. 'Great cowardly blob! I really wish I could stop him catching baby birds, it's so sad!'

'You haven't got a hat you can wear, have you?' said the toad, from her apron pocket. 'I hate not being able to see.'

They went into the dairy, which Tiffany normally had to herself for most of the day.

In the bushes by the door there was a muffled conversation. It went like this:

'*Whut did the wee hag say?*'

'*She said she wants yon cat to stop scraffin' the puir wee burdies.*'

'*Is that a'? Crivens! Nae problemo!*'

Tiffany put the toad on the table as carefully as possible.

'What do you eat?' she said. It was polite to offer guests food, she knew.

'I've got used to slugs and worms and stuff,' said the toad. 'It wasn't easy. Don't worry if you don't have any. I expect you weren't expecting a toad to drop in.'

'How about some milk?'

'You're very kind.'

Tiffany fetched some, and poured it into a saucer. She watched while the toad crawled in.

'Were you a handsome prince?' she asked.

'Yeah, right, maybe,' said the toad, dribbling milk.

'So why did Miss Tick put a spell on you?'

'Her? Huh, she couldn't do that,' said the toad. 'It's serious magic, turning someone into a toad but leaving them thinking they're human. No, it was a fairy godmother. Never cross a woman with a star on a stick, young lady. They've got a mean streak.'

'Why did she do it?'

The toad looked embarrassed. 'I don't know,' it said. 'It's all a bit . . . foggy. I just *know* I've been a person. At least, I think I know. It gives me the willies. Sometimes I wake up in the night and I think, was I ever *really* human? Or was I just a toad that got on her nerves and she made me *think* I was human once? That'd be a real torture, right? Supposing there's nothing for me to turn back into?' The toad turned worried yellow eyes on her. 'After all, it can't be very hard to mess with a toad's head, yeah? It must be much simpler than turning, oh, a one-hundred-and-sixty-pound human into eight ounces of toad, yes? After all, where's the rest of the mass going to go, I ask myself? Is it just sort of, you know, left over? Very worrying. I mean, I've got one or two memories of being a human, of course, but what's a memory? Just a thought in your brain. You can't be sure it's *real*. Honestly, on nights when I've eaten a bad slug I wake up screaming, except all that comes out is a croak. Thank you for the milk, it was very nice.'

Tiffany stared in silence at the toad.

'You know,' she said, 'magic is a lot more complicated than I thought.'

'*Flappitty-flappitty flap! Cheep, cheep! Ach, poor wee me, cheepitty-cheep!*'

Tiffany ran over to the window.

There was a Feegle on the path. It had made itself some crude wings out of a piece of rag, and a kind of beaky cap out of straw, and was wobbling around in a circle like a wounded bird.

'Ach, cheepitty-cheep! Fluttery-flutter! I certainly hope dere's no' a pussycat aroound! Ach, dearie me!' it yelled.

And down the path Ratbag, arch-enemy of all baby birds, slunk closer, dribbling. As Tiffany opened her mouth to yell, he leaped and landed with all four feet on the little man.

Or at least where the little man had been, because he had somersaulted in mid-air and was now right in front of Ratbag's face and had grabbed a cat ear with each hand.

'Ach, see you, pussycat, scunner that y'are!' he yelled. 'Here's a giftie from the t' wee burdies, yah schemie!'

He butted the cat hard on the nose. Ratbag spun in the air and landed on his back with his eyes crossed. He squinted in cold terror as the little man leaned down at him and shouted, 'CHEEP!'

Then he levitated in the way that cats do and became a ginger streak, rocketing down the path, through the open door and shooting past Tiffany to hide under the sink.

The Feegle looked up, grinning, and saw Tiffany.

'Please don't go—' she began quickly, but he went, in a blur.

Tiffany's mother was hurrying down the path. Tiffany picked up the toad and put it back in her apron pocket just in time.

'Where's Wentworth? Is he here?' her mother asked urgently. 'Did he come back? Answer me!'

'Didn't he go up to the shearing with you, Mum?'

said Tiffany, suddenly nervous. She could feel the panic pouring off her mother like smoke.

'We can't find him!' There was a wild look in her mother's eyes. 'I only turned my back for a minute! Are you *sure* you haven't seen him?'

'But he couldn't come all the way back here—'

'Go and look in the house! Go on!'

Mrs Aching hurried away. Hastily, Tiffany put the toad on the floor and chivvied him under the sink. She heard him croak and Ratbag, mad with fear and bewilderment, came out from under the sink in a whirl of legs and rocketed out of the door.

She stood up. Her first, shameful thought was: He *wanted* to go up to watch the shearing. How could he get lost? He went with Mum and Hannah and Fastidia!

And how closely would Fastidia and Hannah watch him with all those young men up there?

She tried to pretend she hadn't thought that, but she was treacherously good at spotting when she was lying. That's the trouble with a brain: it thinks more than you sometimes want it to.

But he's never interested in moving far away from people! It's half a mile up to the shearing pens! And he doesn't move that fast. After a few feet he flops down and demands sweets!

But it would be a bit more peaceful around here if he did get lost . . .

There it went again, a nasty, shameful thought which she tried to drown out by getting busy. But first she took some sweets out of the jar, as bait, and rustled the bag as she ran from room to room.

She heard boots in the yard as some of the men came down from the shearing sheds, but got on with looking under beds and in cupboards, even ones so high that a toddler couldn't possibly reach them, and then looked *again* under beds that she'd already looked under, because it was that kind of search. It was the kind of search where you go and look in the attic, even though the door is always locked.

After a few minutes there were two or three voices outside, calling for Wentworth, and she heard her father say, 'Try down by the river!'

. . . and that meant he was frantic too, because Wentworth would never walk that far without a bribe. He was not a child who was happy away from sweets.

It's your fault.

The thought felt like a piece of ice in her mind.

It's *your* fault because you didn't love him very much. He turned up and you weren't the youngest any more, and you had to have him trailing around after you, and you kept wishing, didn't you?, that he'd go away.

'That's not true!' Tiffany whispered to herself. 'I . . . quite liked him . . .'

Not very much, admittedly. Not all the time. He didn't know how to play properly, and he never did what he was told. *You* thought it would be better if he *did* get lost.

Anyway, she added in her head, you can't love people all the time when they have a permanently runny nose. And *anyway* . . . I wonder . . .

'I wish I could find my brother,' she said aloud.

This seemed to have no effect. But the house was full of people, opening and shutting doors and calling out and getting in one another's way, and the . . . Feegles were shy, despite many of them having faces like a hatful of knuckles.

Don't *wish*, Miss Tick had said. *Do* things.

She went downstairs. Even some of the women who'd been packing fleeces up at the shearing had come down. They were clustered around her mother, who was sitting at the table, crying. No one noticed Tiffany. That often happened.

She slipped into the dairy, closed the door carefully behind her, and leaned down to peer under the sink.

The door burst open again and her father ran in. He stopped. Tiffany looked up guiltily.

'He can't be under there, girl!' her father said.

'Well, er . . .' said Tiffany.

'Did you look upstairs?'

'Even the attic, Dad—'

'Well—' her father looked panicky and impatient at the same time – 'go and . . . do something!'

'Yes, Dad.'

When the door had shut Tiffany peered under the sink again.

'Are you there, toad?'

'Very poor pickings under here,' the toad answered, crawling out. 'You keep it very clean. Not even a spider.'

'This is *urgent*!' snapped Tiffany. 'My little brother

has gone missing. In broad daylight! Up on the downs, where you can see for miles!'

'Oh, *croap*,' said the toad.

'Pardon?' said Tiffany.

'Er, that was, er, swearing in Toad,' said the toad. 'Sorry, but—'

'Has what's going on got something to do with magic?' said Tiffany. 'It has, hasn't it . . . ?'

'I hope it hasn't,' said the toad, 'but I think it has.'

'Have those little men stolen Wentworth?'

'Who, the Feegles? *They* don't steal children!'

There was something in the way the toad said it. *They* don't steal . . .

'Do you know who *has* taken my brother, then?' Tiffany demanded.

'No. But . . . *they* might,' said the toad. 'Look, Miss Tick told me that you were not to—'

'My brother has been *stolen*,' said Tiffany sharply. 'Are you going to tell me not to do anything about it?'

'No, but—'

'Good! Where are the Feegles now?'

'Lying low, I expect. The place is full of people searching, after all, but—'

'How can I bring them back? I *need* them!'

'Um, Miss Tick said—'

'*How can I bring them back?*'

'Er . . . you want to bring them back, then?' said the toad, looking mournful.

'Yes!'

'It's just that's something not many people have ever wanted to do,' said the toad. 'They're not like brownies. If you get Nac Mac Feegles in the house, it's usually best to move away.' He sighed. 'Tell me, is your father a drinking man?'

'He has a beer sometimes,' said Tiffany. 'What's that got to do with anything?'

'Only beer?'

'Well, I'm not supposed to know about what my father calls the Special Sheep Liniment,' said Tiffany. 'Granny Aching used to make it in the old cowshed.'

'Strong stuff, is it?'

'It dissolves spoons,' said Tiffany. 'It's for special occasions. Father says it's not for women because it puts hairs on your chest.'

'Then if you want to be *sure* of finding the Nac Mac Feegles, go and fetch some,' said the toad. 'It will work, believe me.'

Five minutes later Tiffany was ready. Few things are hidden from a quiet child with good eyesight, and she knew where the bottles were stored and she had one now. The cork was hammered in over a piece of rag, but it was old and she was able to lever it out with the tip of a knife. The fumes made her eyes water.

She went to pour some of the golden-brown liquid into a saucer—

'No! We'll be trampled to death if you do that,' said the toad. 'Just leave the cork off.'

Fumes rose from the top of the bottle, wavering like the air over rocks on a hot day.

She felt it – a sensation, in the dim, cool room, of riveted attention.

She sat down on a milking stool and said, 'All right, you can come out now.'

There were *hundreds*. They rose up from behind buckets. They lowered themselves on string from the ceiling beams. They sidled sheepishly from behind the cheese racks. They crept out from under the sink. They came out of places where you'd think a man with hair like an orange gone nova couldn't possibly hide.

They were all about six inches tall and mostly coloured blue, although it was hard to know if that was the actual colour of their skins or just the dye from their tattoos, which covered every inch that wasn't covered with red hair. They wore short kilts, and some wore other bits of clothing too, like skinny waistcoats. A few of them wore rabbit or rat skulls on their heads, as a sort of helmet. And every single one of them carried, slung across his back, a sword nearly as big as he was.

However, what Tiffany noticed more than anything else was that they were scared of her. Mostly they were looking at their own feet, which was no errand for the faint-hearted because their feet were large, dirty and half tied up with animal skins to make very bad shoes. None of them wanted to look her in the eye.

'You were the people who filled the water buckets?' she said.

There was a lot of foot shuffling and coughing and a chorus of 'Ayes'.

'And the wood box?'

There were more 'Ayes'.

Tiffany glared at them.

'And what about the sheep?'

This time they all looked down.

'Why did you steal the sheep?'

There was a lot of muttering and nudging and then one of the tiny men removed his rabbit skull helmet and twiddled it nervously in his hands.

'We wuz hungerin', mistress,' he muttered. 'But when we kenned it was thine, we did put the beastie back in the fold.'

They looked so crestfallen that Tiffany took pity on them.

'I expect you wouldn't have stolen it if you weren't so hungry, then,' she said.

There were several hundred astonished looks.

'Oh, we would, mistress,' said the helmet- twiddler.

'You would?'

Tiffany sounded so surprised that the twiddler looked around at his colleagues for support. They all nodded.

'Yes, mistress. We have tae. We are a famously stealin' folk. Aren't we, lads? Whut's it we're famous for?'

'Stealin'!' shouted the blue men.

'And what else, lads?'

'Fightin'!'

'And what else?'

'Drinkin'!'

'And what else?'

There was a certain amount of thought about this, but they all reached the same conclusion.

'Drinkin' *and* fightin'!'

'And there was summat else,' muttered the twiddler. 'Ach, yes. Tell the hag, lads!'

'Stealin' an' drinkin' an' fightin'!' shouted the blue men cheerfully.

'Tell the wee hag who we are, lads,' said the helmet-twiddler.

There was the scrape of many small swords being drawn and thrust into the air.

'Nac Mac Feegle! The Wee Free Men! Nae king! Nae quin! Nae laird! Nae master! *We willna' be fooled again!*'

Tiffany stared at them. They were all watching her to see what she was going to do next, and the longer she said nothing, the more worried they became. They lowered their swords, looking embarrassed.

'But we wouldna' dare deny a powerful hag, except mebbe for strong drink,' said the twiddler, his helmet spinning desperately in his hands and his eyes on the bottle of Special Sheep Liniment. 'Will ye no' help us?'

'Help you?' said Tiffany. 'I want *you* to help *me*! Someone has taken my brother in broad daylight.'

'Oh waily, waily waily!' said the helmet-twiddler. 'She's come, then. She's come a-fetchin'. We're too late! It's the Quin!'

'There was only one of them!' said Tiffany.

'They mean the Queen,' said the toad. 'The Queen of the—'

'Hush yer gob!' shouted the helmet-twiddler, but his voice was lost in the wails and groans of the Nac Mac Feegles. They were pulling at their hair and stamping on the ground and shouting 'Alackaday!' and 'Waily waily waily!' and the toad was arguing with the helmet-twiddler and everyone was getting louder to make themselves heard—

Tiffany stood up. 'Everybody shut up right now!' she said.

Silence fell, except for a few sniffs and faint 'wailys' from the back.

'We wuz only dreeing our weird, mistress,' said the helmet-twiddler, almost crouching in fear.

'But not in here!' snapped Tiffany, shaking with anger. 'This is a *dairy*! I have to keep it clean!'

'Er . . . dreeing your weird means "facing your fate",' said the toad.

''Cuz if the Quin is here then it means our kelda is weakenin' fast,' said the helmet-twiddler. 'An' we'll ha' naeone tae look after us.'

To look after us, thought Tiffany. Hundreds of tough little men who could each win the Worst Broken Nose Contest need someone to look after them?

She took a deep breath.

'My mother's in the house crying,' she said, 'and . . .' I don't know how to comfort her, she added to herself. I'm no *good* at this sort of thing, I never know what I should be saying. Out loud she said: 'And she wants him back. Er. A lot.' She added, hating to say it: 'He's her favourite.'

She pointed to the helmet-twiddler, who backed away.

'First of all,' she said, 'I can't keep thinking of you as

84

the helmet-twiddler, so what is your name?'

A gasp went up from the Nac Mac Feegles, and Tiffany heard one of them murmur, 'Aye, she's the hag, sure enough. That's a hag's question!'

The helmet-twiddler looked around at them as if seeking help.

'We dinnae give oor names,' he muttered. But another Feegle, somewhere safe at the back, said, 'Wheest! You cannae refuse a hag!'

The little man looked up, very worried.

'I'm the Big Man o' the clan, mistress,' he said. 'An' my name it is . . .' He swallowed. 'Rob Anybody Feegle, mistress. But I beg ye not to use it agin me!'

The toad was ready for this.

'They think names have magic in them,' he murmured. 'They don't tell them to people in case they are written down.'

'Aye, an' put upon comp-li-cated documents,' said a Feegle.

'An' summonses and such things,' said another.

'Or "Wanted" posters!' said another.

'Aye, an' bills an' affidavits,' said another.

'Writs of distrainment, even!' The Feegles looked around in panic at the very thought of written-down things.

'They think written words are even more powerful,' whispered the toad. 'They think all writing is magic. Words worry them. See their swords? They glow blue in the presence of lawyers.'

'All *right*,' said Tiffany. 'We're getting somewhere. I promise not to write his name down. Now tell me about this Queen who's taken Wentworth. Queen of what?'

'Canna say it aloud, mistress,' said Rob Anybody. 'She hears her name wherever it's said, and she comes callin'.'

'Actually, that's true,' said the toad. 'You do not want to meet her, ever.'

'She's bad?'

'Worse. Just call her the Queen.'

'Aye, the Quin,' said Rob Anybody. He looked at Tiffany with bright, worried eyes. 'Ye dinnae ken o' the Quin? An' you the wean o' Granny Aching, who had these hills in her bones? Ye dinnae ken the ways? She did not show ye the ways? Ye're no' a hag? How can this be? Ye slammered Jenny Green-Teeth and stared the Heidless Horseman in the eyes he hasnae got, and you dinnae ken?'

Tiffany gave him a brittle smile, and then whispered to the toad, 'Who's Ken? And what about his dinner? And what's a wean of Granny Aching?'

'As far as I can make out,' said the toad, 'they're amazed that you don't know about the Queen and . . . er, the magical ways, what with you being a child of Granny Aching and standing up to the monsters. "Ken" means "know".'

'And his dinner?'

'Forget about his dinner for now,' said the toad. 'They thought Granny Aching told you her magic. Hold me up to your ear, will you?' Tiffany did so, and the toad whispered, 'Best not to disappoint them, eh?'

She swallowed. 'But she never told me about any

magic—' she began. And stopped. It was true. Granny Aching hadn't told her about any magic. But she showed people magic every day.

. . . There was the time when the Baron's champion hound was caught killing sheep. It was a hunting dog, after all, but it had got out onto the downs and, because sheep run, it had chased . . .

The Baron knew the penalty for sheep-worrying. There were laws on the Chalk, so old that no one remembered who made them, and everyone knew this one: sheep-killing dogs were killed.

But this dog was worth five hundred gold dollars, and so – the story went – the Baron sent his servant up onto the downs to Granny's hut on wheels. She was sitting on the step, smoking her pipe and watching the flocks.

The man rode up on his horse and didn't bother to dismount. That was not a good thing to do if you wanted Granny Aching to be your friend. Iron-shod hooves cut the turf. She didn't like that.

He said: 'The Baron commands that you find a way to save his dog, Mistress Aching. In return, he will give you a hundred silver dollars.'

Granny had smiled at the horizon, puffed at her pipe for a while, and replied: 'A man who takes arms against his lord, that man is hanged. A starving man who steals his lord's sheep, that man is hanged. A dog that kills sheep, that dog is put to death. Those laws are on these hills and these hills are in my bones. What is a baron, that the law be brake for him?'

She went back to staring at the sheep.

'The Baron owns this country,' said the servant. 'It is his law.'

The look Granny Aching gave him turned the man's hair white. That was the story, anyway. But all stories about Granny Aching had a bit of fairy tale about them.

'If it is, as ye say, his law, then let him break it and see how things may then be,' she said.

A few hours later the Baron sent his bailiff, who was far more important but had known Granny Aching for longer. He said: 'Mrs Aching, the Baron requests that you use your influence to save his dog. He will happily give you fifty gold dollars to help ease this difficult situation. I am sure you can see how this will benefit everyone concerned.'

Granny smoked her pipe and stared at the new lambs and said: 'Ye speak for your master, your master speaks for his dog. Who speaks for the hills? Where is the Baron, that the law be brake for him?'

They said that when the Baron was told this he went very quiet. But although he was pompous, and often un-reasonable, and far too haughty, he was not stupid. In the evening he walked up to the hut and sat down on the turf nearby. After a while, Granny Aching said: 'Can I help you, my lord?'

'Granny Aching, I plead for the life of my dog,' said the Baron.

'Bring ye siller? Bring ye gilt?' said Granny Aching.

'No silver. No gold,' said the Baron.

'Good. A law that is brake by siller or gilt is no worthwhile law. And so, my lord?'

'I plead, Granny Aching.'

'Ye try to break the law with a word?'

'That's right, Granny Aching.'

Granny Aching, the story went, stared at the sunset for a while and then said: 'Then be down at the little old stone barn at dawn tomorrow and we'll see if an old dog can learn new tricks. There will be a reckoning. Good night to ye.'

Most of the village was hanging around the old stone barn the next morning. Granny arrived with one of the smaller farm wagons. It held a ewe with her new-born lamb. She put them in the barn.

Some of the men turned up with the dog. It was nervy and snappy, having spent the night chained up in a shed, and kept trying to bite the men who were holding it by two leather straps. It was hairy. It had fangs.

The Baron rode up with the bailiff. Granny Aching nodded at them and opened the barn door.

'You're putting the dog into the barn with a sheep, Mrs Aching?' said the bailiff. 'Do you want it to choke to death on lamb?'

This didn't get much of a laugh. No one really liked the bailiff.

'We shall see,' said Granny. The men dragged the dog to the doorway, threw it inside the barn and slammed the door quickly. People rushed to the little windows.

There was the bleating of the lamb, a growl from the dog, and then a baa from the lamb's mother. But this wasn't the normal baa of a sheep. It had an edge to it.

Something hit the door and it bounced on its hinges. Inside, the dog yelped.

Granny Aching picked up Tiffany and held her up to a window.

The shaken dog was trying to get to its feet, but it didn't manage it before the ewe charged it again, seventy pounds of enraged sheep slamming into it like a battering ram.

Granny lowered Tiffany again and lit her pipe. She puffed it peacefully as the building behind her shook and the dog yelped and whimpered.

After a couple of minutes she nodded at the men. They opened the door.

The dog came out limping on three legs, but it hadn't managed to get more than a few feet before the ewe shot out behind it and butted it so hard that it rolled over.

It lay still. Perhaps it had learned what would happen if it tried to get up again.

Granny Aching had nodded to the men, who grabbed the sheep and dragged it back into the barn.

The Baron had been watching with his mouth open.

'He killed a wild boar last year!' he said. 'What did you do to him?'

'He'll mend,' said Granny Aching, carefully ignoring the question. ''Tis mostly his pride that's hurt. But he won't look at a sheep again, you have my thumb on that.' And she licked her right thumb and held it out.

After a moment's hesitation, the Baron licked his thumb, reached down and pressed it against hers. Everyone knew what it meant. On the Chalk, a thumb bargain was unbreakable.

'For you, at a word, the law was brake,' said Granny Aching. 'Will ye mind that, ye who sit in judgement? Will yer remember this day? Ye'll have cause to.'

The Baron nodded to her.

'That'll do,' said Granny Aching, and their thumbs parted.

Next day the Baron technically did give Granny Aching gold, but it was only the gold-coloured foil on an ounce of Jolly Sailor, the cheap and horrible pipe tobacco that was the only one Granny Aching would ever smoke. She was always in a bad mood if the pedlars were late and she'd run out. You couldn't bribe Granny Aching for all the gold in the world, but you could definitely attract her attention with an ounce of Jolly Sailor.

Things were a lot easier after that. The bailiff was a little less unpleasant when rents were late, the Baron was a little more polite to people, and Tiffany's father said one night after two beers that the Baron had been shown what happens when sheep rise up, and things might be different one day, and her mother hissed at him not to talk like that because you never knew who was listening.

And, one day, Tiffany heard him telling her mother, quietly: ''Twas an old shepherds' trick, that's all. An old ewe will fight like a lion for her lamb, we all know that.'

That was how it worked. No magic at all. But that time it had been magic. And it didn't stop being magic just because you found out how it was done . . .

The Nac Mac Feegles were watching Tiffany carefully, with occasional longing glances at the bottle of Special Sheep Liniment.

I haven't even found the witches' school, she thought. I don't know a single spell. I don't even have a pointy hat. My talents are an instinct for making cheese and not running around panicking when things go wrong. Oh, and I've got a toad.

And I don't understand half of what these little men are saying. But they know who's taken my brother.

Somehow I don't think the Baron would have a clue how to deal with this. I don't, either, but I think I can be clueless in more sensible ways.

'I . . . remember a lot of things about Granny Aching,' she said. 'What do you want me to do?'

'The kelda sent us,' said Rob Anybody. 'She sensed the Quin comin'. She kenned there wuz going to be trouble. She tole us, it's gonna be bad, find the new hag who's kin to Granny Aching, she'll ken what to do.'

Tiffany looked at the hundreds of expectant faces. Some of the Feegles had feathers in their hair, and necklaces of mole teeth. You couldn't tell someone with half his face dyed dark blue and a sword as big as he was that you weren't really a witch. You couldn't disappoint someone like that.

'And will you help me get my brother back?' she said. The Feegles' expressions didn't change. She tried again. 'Can you help me steal my brother back from the Quin?'

Hundreds of small yet ugly faces brightened up considerably.

'Ach, *noo* yer talkin' *oour* language,' said Rob Anybody.

'Not . . . quite,' said Tiffany. 'Can you all just wait a

moment? I'll just pack some things,' she said, trying to sound as if she knew what she was doing. She put the cork back on the bottle of Special Sheep Liniment. The Nac Mac Feegles sighed.

She darted back into the kitchen, found a sack, took some bandages and ointments out of the medicine box, added the bottle of Special Sheep Liniment because her father said it always did *him* good and, as an afterthought, added the book *Diseases of the Sheep* and picked up the frying pan. Both might come in useful.

The little men were nowhere to be seen when she went back into the dairy.

She knew she ought to tell her parents what was happening. But it wouldn't work. It would be 'telling stories'. Anyway, with any luck she could get Wentworth back before she was even missed. But, just in case . . .

She kept a diary in the dairy. Cheese needed to be kept track of, and she always wrote down details of the amount of butter she'd made and how much milk she'd been using.

She turned to a fresh page, picked up her pencil and, with her tongue sticking out of the corner of her mouth, began to write.

The Nac Mac Feegles gradually reappeared. They didn't obviously step out from behind things, and they certainly didn't pop magically into existence. They appeared in the same way that faces appear in clouds and fires; they seemed to turn up if you just looked hard enough and wanted to see them.

They watched the moving pencil in awe, and she could hear them murmuring.

'Look at that writin' stick noo, will ye, bobbin' along. That's hag business.'

'Ach, she has the kennin' o' the writin', sure enough.'

'But you'll no' write doon oour names, eh, mistress?'

'Aye, a body can be put in the pris'n if they have written evidence.'

Tiffany stopped writing and read the note:

> Dear Mum and Dad,
> I have gone to look for Wentworth. I am
> ~~perfectly~~ probably quite safe, because I am
> with some ~~friends~~ ~~acquaintances~~ people who
> knew Granny, ps the cheeses on rack three
> will need turning tomorrow if I'm not back.
> Love, Tiffany

Tiffany looked up at Rob Anybody, who had shinned up the table leg and was watching the pencil intently, in case it wrote something dangerous.

'You could have just come and asked me right at the start,' she said.

'We dinnae ken it was thee we were lookin' for, mistress. Lots of bigjob women walkin' aroond this farm. We didnae ken it was thee until you caught Daft Wullie.'

It might not be, thought Tiffany.

'Yes, but stealing the sheep and the eggs, there was no need for that,' she said sternly.

'But they wasnae nailed doon, mistress,' said Rob Anybody, as if that was an excuse.

'You can't nail down an egg!' snapped Tiffany.

'Ach, well, you'd have the kennin' of wise stuff like that, mistress,' said Rob Anybody. 'I see you's done wi' the writin', so we'd best be goin'. Ye hae a besom?'

'Broomstick,' murmured the toad.

'Er, no,' said Tiffany. 'The important thing about magic,' she added, haughtily, 'is to know when not to use it.'

'Fair enough,' said Rob Anybody, sliding back down the table leg. 'Come here, Daft Wullie.' One of the Feegles that looked very much like that morning's egg-thief came and stood by Rob Anybody, and they both bent over slightly. 'If you'd care to step on us, mistress,' said Rob Anybody.

Before Tiffany could open her mouth, the toad said out of the corner of its mouth, and being a toad that means quite a lot of corner, 'One Feegle can lift a grown man. You couldn't squash one if you tried.'

'I don't *want* to try!'

Tiffany very cautiously raised a big boot. Daft Wullie ran underneath it, and she felt the boot being pushed upwards. She might as well have trodden on a brick.

'Now t'other wee bootie,' said Rob Anybody.

'I'll fall over!'

'Nae, we're *good* at this . . .'

And then Tiffany was standing up on two pictsies. She felt them moving backwards and forwards underneath her, keeping her balanced. She felt quite secure, though. It was just like wearing really *thick* soles.

'Let's gae,' said Rob Anybody, down below. 'An' don't worry about yon pussycat scraffin' the wee burdies. Some of the lads is stayin' behind to mind things!'

Ratbag crept along a branch. He wasn't a cat who was good at changing the ways he thought. But he was good at finding nests. He'd heard the cheeping from the other end of the garden and even from the bottom of the tree he'd been able to see three little yellow beaks in the nest. Now he advanced, dribbling. Nearly there . . .

Three Nac Mac Feegles pulled off their straw beaks and grinned happily at him.

'Hello, Mister Pussycat,' said one of them. 'Ye dinnae learn, do ye? CHEEP!'

CHAPTER 5

The Green Sea

Tiffany flew a few inches above the ground, standing still. Wind rushed around her as the Feegles sped out of the farmyard's top gate and onto the turf of the downs ...

This is the girl, flying. At the moment there's a toad on her head, holding onto her hair.

Pull back, and here is the long green whaleback of the downs. Now she's a pale blue dot against the endless grass, mowed by the sheep to the length of a carpet. But the green sea isn't unbroken. Here and there, humans have been.

Last year Tiffany had spent three carrots and an apple on half an hour of geology, although she'd been refunded a carrot after explaining to the teacher that 'Geology' shouldn't be spelled on his sign as 'G olly G'. He said that the chalk had been formed under water millions of years before from tiny seashells.

That made sense to Tiffany. Sometimes you found little fossils in the chalk. But the teacher didn't know much about the flint. You found flints, harder than steel, in chalk, the softest of rocks. Sometimes the shepherds chipped the flints, one flint against another, into knives. Not even the best steel knives could take an edge as sharp as flint.

And men in what was called on the Chalk 'the olden days' had dug pits for it. They were still there, deep holes in the rolling green, filled with thickets of thorn and brambles.

Huge, knobbly flints still turned up in the village gardens too. Sometimes they were larger than a man's head. They often looked like heads too. They were so melted and twisted and curved that you could look at a flint and see almost anything – a face, a strange animal, a sea monster. Sometimes the more interesting ones would be put on garden walls, for show.

The old people called those 'calkins', which meant 'chalk children'. They'd always seemed . . . odd to Tiffany, as if the stone was striving to become alive. Some flints looked like bits of meat, or bones, or something off a butcher's slab. In the dark, under the sea, it looked as though the chalk had been trying to make the shapes of living creatures.

There weren't just the chalk pits. Men had been everywhere on the Chalk. There were stone circles, half fallen down, and burial mounds like green pimples where, it was said, chieftains of the olden days

THE WEE FREE MEN

had been buried with their treasure. No one fancied digging into them to find out.

There were odd carvings in the chalk too, which the shepherds sometimes weeded when they were out on the downs with the flocks and there was not a lot to do. The chalk was only a few inches under the turf. Hoofprints could last a season, but the carvings had lasted for thousands of years. They were pictures of horses and giants, but the strange thing was that you couldn't see them properly from anywhere on the ground. They looked as if they'd been made for viewers in the sky.

And then there were the weird places, like Old Man's Forge, which was just four big flat rocks placed so they made a kind of half-buried hut in the side of a mound. It was only a few feet deep. It didn't look anything special, but if you shouted your name into it, it was several seconds before the echo came back.

There were signs of people everywhere. The Chalk had been *important*.

Tiffany left the shearing sheds way behind. No one was watching. Sheared sheep took no notice at all of a girl moving without her feet touching the ground.

The lowlands dropped away behind her and now she was properly on the downs. Only the occasional baa of a sheep or scream of a buzzard disturbed a busy silence, made up of bee buzzes and breezes and the sound of a ton of grass growing every minute.

On either side of Tiffany the Nac Mac Feegles ran in a spread-out ragged line, staring grimly ahead.

They passed some of the mounds without

stopping, and ran up and down the sides of shallow valleys without a pause. And it was then that Tiffany saw a landmark ahead.

It was a small flock of sheep. There were only a few, freshly sheared, but there were always a handful of sheep at this place now. Strays would turn up there, and lambs would find their way to it when they'd lost their mothers.

This was a magic place.

There wasn't much to see now, just the iron wheels sinking into the turf and the pot-bellied stove with its short chimney . . .

On the day Granny Aching died, the men had cut and lifted the turf around the hut and stacked it neatly some way away. Then they'd dug a deep hole in the chalk, six feet deep and six feet long, lifting out the chalk in great damp blocks.

Thunder and Lightning had watched them carefully. They didn't whine or bark. They seemed more interested than upset.

Granny Aching had been wrapped in a woollen blanket, with a tuft of raw wool pinned to it. That was a special shepherd thing. It was there to tell any gods who might get involved that the person being buried there was a shepherd, and spent a lot of time on the hills, and what with lambing and one thing and another couldn't always take much time out for religion, there being no churches or temples up there, and therefore it was generally hoped that the gods would understand and look kindly on them. Granny Aching, it had to be said, had never been seen to pray to anyone or anything in her life, and it was agreed by all that, even now, she wouldn't have any time for a god who didn't understand that lambing came first.

The chalk had been put back over her and Granny Aching, who always said that the hills were in her bones, now had her bones in the hills.

Then they burned the hut. That wasn't usual, but her father had said that there wasn't a shepherd anywhere on the Chalk who'd use it now.

Thunder and Lightning wouldn't come when he called, and he knew better than to be angry, so they were left sitting quite contentedly by the glowing embers of the hut.

Next day, when the ashes were cold and blowing across the raw chalk, everyone went up onto the downs and with very great care put the turf back, so all that was left to see were the iron wheels on their axles, and the pot-bellied stove.

At which point – so everyone said – the two sheepdogs had looked up, their ears pricking, and had trotted away over the turf and were never seen again.

The pictsies carrying her slowed down gently, and Tiffany flailed her arms as they dropped her onto the grass. The sheep lumbered away slowly, then stopped and turned to watch her.

'Why're we stopping? Why're we stopping *here*? We've got to catch her!'

'Got to wait for Hamish, mistress,' said Rob Anybody.

'Why? Who's Hamish?'

'He might have the knowin' of where the Quin went with your wee laddie,' said Rob Anybody soothingly. 'We cannae just rush in, ye ken.'

A big, bearded Feegle raised his hand. 'Point o' order, Big Man. Ye *can* just rush in. We *always* just rush in.'

'Aye, Big Yan, point well made. But ye gotta know *where* ye're just gonna rush in. Ye cannae just rush in *anywhere*. It looks bad, havin' to rush oout again straight awa'.'

Tiffany saw that all the Feegles were staring intently upwards, and paying her no attention at all.

Angry and puzzled, she sat down on one of the rusty wheels and looked at the sky. It was better than looking around. There was Granny Aching's grave somewhere around here, although you couldn't find it now, not precisely. The turf had healed.

There were a few little clouds above her and nothing else at all, except the distant circling dots of the buzzards.

There were always buzzards over the Chalk. The shepherds had taken to calling them Granny Aching's chickens, and some of them called clouds like those up there today 'Granny's little lambs'. And Tiffany *knew* that even her father called the thunder 'Granny Aching cussin''.

And it was said that some of the shepherds, if wolves were troublesome in the winter, or a prize ewe had got lost, would go to the site of the old hut in the hills and leave an ounce of Jolly Sailor tobacco, just in case . . .

Tiffany hesitated. Then she shut her eyes. I want that to be true, she whispered to herself. I want to know that other people think she hasn't really gone too.

She looked under the wide rusted rim of the wheels and shivered. There was a brightly coloured little packet there.

She picked it up. It looked quite fresh, so it had probably been there for only a few days. There was the Jolly Sailor on the front, with his big grin and big yellow rain hat and big beard, with big blue waves crashing behind him.

Tiffany had learned about the sea from the Jolly Sailor wrappings. She'd heard it was big, and roared. There was a tower in the sea, which was a lighthouse that carried a big light on it at night to stop boats crashing into the rocks. In the pictures the beam of the lighthouse was a brilliant white. She knew about it so well she'd dreamed about it, and had woken up with the roar of the sea in her ears.

She'd heard one of her uncles say that if you looked at the tobacco label upside down then part of the hat and the sailor's ear and a bit of his collar made up a picture of a woman with no clothes on, but Tiffany had never been able to make it out and couldn't see what the point would be in any case.

She carefully pulled the label off the packet, and sniffed at it. It smelled of Granny. She felt her eyes begin to fill with tears. She'd never cried for Granny Aching before, never. She'd cried for dead lambs and cut fingers and for not getting her own way, but never for Granny. It hadn't seemed right.

And I'm not crying now, she thought, carefully putting the label in her apron pocket. Not for Granny being dead . . .

It was the smell. Granny Aching smelled of sheep, turpentine and Jolly Sailor tobacco. The three smells mixed together and became one smell which was, to Tiffany, the smell of the Chalk. It followed Granny Aching like a cloud, and it meant warmth, and silence, and a space around which the whole world revolved . . .

A shadow passed overhead. A buzzard was diving down from the sky towards the Nac Mac Feegle.

She leaped up and waved her arms. 'Run away! Duck! It'll kill you!'

They turned and looked at her for a moment as though she'd gone mad.

'Dinnae fash yersel', mistress,' said Rob Anybody.

The bird curved up at the bottom of its dive and as it climbed again a dot dropped from it. As it fell it seemed to grow two wings and start to spin like a sycamore bract, which slowed down the fall somewhat.

It was a pictsie, still spinning madly when he hit the turf a few feet away, where he fell over. He got up, swearing loudly, and fell over again. The swearing continued.

'A good landin', Hamish,' said Rob Anybody. 'The spinnin' certainly slows ye doon. Ye didnae drill right into the ground this time hardly at al'.'

Hamish got up more slowly this time, and managed

to stay upright. He had a pair of goggles over his eyes.

'I dinnae think I can tak' much more o' this,' he said, trying to untie a couple of thin bits of wood from his arms. 'I feel like a fairy wi' the wings on.'

'How can you survive that?' Tiffany asked.

The very small pilot tried to look her up and down, but only managed to look her up and further up.

'Who's the wee bigjob who knows sich a lot about aviation?' he said.

Rob Anybody coughed. 'She's the hag, Hamish. Spawn o' Granny Aching.'

Hamish's expression changed to a look of terror. 'I didnae mean to speak out o' turn, mistress,' he said, backing away. 'O' course, a hag'd have the knowing of anythin'. But 'tis nae as bad as it looks, mistress. I allus make sure I lands on my heid.'

'Aye, we're very resilient in the heid department,' said Rob Anybody.

'Have you seen a woman with a small boy?' Tiffany demanded. She hadn't much liked 'spawn'.

Hamish gave Rob Anybody a panicky look, and Rob nodded.

'Aye, I did,' said Hamish. 'Onna black horse. Riding up from the lowlan's goin' hell for—'

'We dinnae use bad language in front o' a hag!' Rob Anybody thundered.

'Begging your pardon, mistress. She was ridin' heck for leather,' said Hamish, looking more sheepish than the sheep. 'But she kenned I was spyin' her and called up a mist. She's gone to the other side, but I dinnae ken where.'

''Tis a perilous place, the other side,' said Rob Anybody slowly. 'Evil things there. A cold place. Not a place to tak' a wee babbie.'

It was hot on the downs, but Tiffany felt a chill. However bad it is, she thought, I'm going to have to go there. I know it. I don't have a choice.

'The *other* side?' she said.

'Aye. The magic world,' said Rob Anybody. 'There's . . . bad things there.'

'Monsters?' said Tiffany.

'As bad as ye can think of,' said Rob Anybody. '*Exactly* as bad as ye can think of.'

Tiffany swallowed hard, and closed her eyes. 'Worse than Jenny? Worse than the headless horseman?' she said.

'Oh, aye. They were wee pussycats compared to the scunners over there. 'Tis an ill-fared country that's come callin', mistress. 'Tis a land where dreams come true. That's the Quin's world.'

'Well, that doesn't sound too—' Tiffany began. Then she remembered some of the dreams she'd had, the ones where you were so glad to wake up . . . 'We're not talking about nice dreams, are we?' she said.

Rob Anybody shook his head. 'Nay, mistress. The other kind.'

And me with my frying pan and *Diseases of the Sheep*, thought Tiffany. And she had a mental picture of Wentworth among horrible monsters. They probably wouldn't have any sweeties at all.

She sighed. 'All right,' she said, 'how do I get there?'

'Ye dinnae ken the way?' said Rob Anybody.

It wasn't what she'd been expecting. What she *had* been expecting was more like 'Ach, ye cannae do that, a wee lass like you, oh dearie us no!' She wasn't so much expecting that as hoping it, in fact. But, instead, they were acting as if it were a perfectly reasonable idea—

'No!' she said. 'I don't dinnae any ken at all! I haven't done this before! Please help me!'

'That's true, Rob,' said a Feegle. 'She's new to the haggin'. Tak' her to the kelda.'

'Not e'en Granny Aching ever went to see the kelda in her ain cave!' snapped Rob Anybody. 'It's no' a—'

'Quiet!' hissed Tiffany. 'Can't you hear that?'

The Feegles looked around.

'Hear what?' said Hamish.

'It's a susurration!'

It felt as though the turf was trembling. The sky looked as though Tiffany was inside a diamond. And there was the smell of snow.

Hamish pulled a pipe out of his waistcoat and blew it. Tiffany couldn't hear anything, but there was a scream from high above.

'I'll let ye know what's happenin'!' cried the pictsie, and started to run across the turf. As he ran, he raised his arms over his head.

He was moving fast by then but the buzzard sped down and across the turf even faster and plucked him neatly into the air. As it beat at the air to rise again, Tiffany saw Hamish climbing up through the feathers.

The other Feegles had formed a circle around Tiffany, and this time they'd drawn their swords.

'Whut's the plan, Rob?' said one of them.

'OK, lads, this is what we'll do. As soon as we see somethin', we'll attack it. Right?'

This caused a cheer.

'Ach, 'tis a good plan,' said Daft Wullie.

Snow formed on the ground. It didn't fall, it . . . did the opposite of melting, rising up fast until the Nac Mac Feegles were waist deep, and then up to their necks. Some of the smaller ones began to disappear, and there was muffled cursing from under the snow.

And then the dogs appeared, lumbering towards Tiffany with a nasty purpose. They were big, black and heavily built, with orange eyebrows, and she could hear the growling from here.

She plunged her hand into her apron pocket and pulled out the toad. It blinked in the sharp light.

'Wazzup?'

Tiffany turned him round to face the things. 'What are *these*?' she said.

'Oh, doak! Grimhounds! Bad! Eyes of fire and teeth of razor blades!'

'What should I do about them?'

'Not be here?'

'Thank you! You've been very helpful!' Tiffany dropped him back into her pocket and pulled her frying pan out of her sack.

It wasn't going to be good enough, she knew that. The black dogs were big, and their eyes *were* flames, and when they opened their mouths to snarl she could see the light glint on steel. She'd never been afraid of dogs, but these dogs weren't from anywhere outside of a nightmare.

There were three of them, but they circled so that no matter how she turned she could only see two at once. She knew it would be the one behind her that attacked first.

'Tell me something more about them!' she said, turning the other way to the circle so that she could watch all three.

'Said to haunt graveyards!' said a voice from her apron.

'Why is there snow on the ground?'

'This has become the Queen's land. It's always winter there! When she puts out her power, it comes here too!'

But Tiffany could see green some way off, beyond the circle of snow.

Think, think . . .

The Queen's country. A magical place where there really were monsters. Anything you could dream of in nightmares. Dogs with eyes of flame and teeth of razors, yes. You didn't get them in the real world, they wouldn't work . . .

They were drooling now, red tongues hanging out, enjoying her fear. And part of Tiffany thought: It's amazing their teeth don't rust—

– and took charge of her legs. She dived between two of the dogs and ran towards the distant green.

There was a growl of triumph behind her and she heard the crunch of paws on snow.

The green didn't seem to be getting nearer.

She heard yells from the pictsies and a snarl that turned into a wail, but there was something behind her as she jumped over the last of the snow and rolled on the warm turf.

A grimhound leaped after her. She jerked herself away as it snapped, but it was already in trouble.

No eyes of fire, no teeth of razors. Not here, not in the *real* world, on the home turf. It was blind here and blood was already dripping from its mouth. You shouldn't jump with a mouthful of razors . . .

Tiffany almost felt sorry for it as it whined in pain, but the snow was creeping towards her and she hit the dog with the frying pan. It went down heavily, and lay still.

There was a fight going on back in the snow. It was flying up like a mist, but she could see two dark shapes in the middle, spinning around and snapping.

She banged on the pan and shouted, and a grimhound sprang from the whirling snow and landed in front of her, a Feegle hanging from each ear.

The snow flowed towards Tiffany. She backed away, watching the advancing, snarling dog. She held the pan like a bat.

'Come on,' she whispered. 'Jump!'

The eyes flamed at her, and then the dog looked down at the snow.

And vanished. The snow sank into the ground. The light changed.

Tiffany and the Wee Free Men were alone on the downs. Feegles were picking themselves up around her.

'Are you fine, mistress?' said Rob Anybody.

'Yes!' said Tiffany. 'It's easy! If you get them off the snow they're just dogs!'

'We'd best move on. We lost some of the lads.'

The excitement drained away.

'You mean they're dead?' Tiffany whispered. The sun was shining brightly again, the skylarks were back . . . and people were dead.

'Ach, no,' said Rob. 'We're the ones who's deid. Did ye not know that?'

CHAPTER 6

The Shepherdess

'You're *dead*?' said Tiffany. She looked around. Feegles were picking themselves up and grumbling, but no one was going 'Waily waily waily.' And Rob Anybody wasn't making any sense at all.

'Well, if you think you're dead, then what are they?' she went on, pointing to a couple of small bodies.

'Oh, they've gone back to the land o' the livin',' said Rob Anybody cheerfully. 'It's nae as good as this one, but they'll bide fine and come back before too long. No sense in grievin'.'

The Achings were not very religious, but Tiffany thought she knew how things ought to go, and they started out with the idea that you were alive and not dead yet.

'But you *are* alive!' she said.

'Ach, no, mistress,' said Rob, helping another pictsie to his feet. 'We *wuz* alive. And we wuz good boys back in the land o' the livin', and so when we died there we wuz borned into this place.'

'You mean . . . you think . . . that you sort of died somewhere else and then came here?' said Tiffany. 'You mean this is like . . . *heaven*?'

'Aye! Just as advertised!' said Rob Anybody. 'Lovely sunshine, good huntin', nice pretty flowers and wee burdies goin' cheep.'

'Aye, and then there's the fightin',' said another Feegle. And then they all joined in.

'An' the stealin'!'

'An' the drinkin' an' fightin'!'

'An' the kebabs!' said Daft Wullie.

'But there's bad things here!' said Tiffany. 'There's monsters!'

'Aye,' said Rob, beaming happily. 'Grand, isn't it? Everythin' laid on, even things to fight!'

'But *we* live here!' said Tiffany.

'Ach, well, mebbe all you humans wuz good in the Last World too,' said Rob Anybody generously. 'I'll just round up the lads, mistress.'

Tiffany reached into her apron and pulled out the toad as Rob walked away.

'Oh. We survived,' it said. 'Amazing. There are very definite grounds for an action against the owner of those dogs, by the way.'

'What?' said Tiffany, frowning. 'What are you *talking* about?'

'I . . . I . . . don't know,' said the toad. 'The thought

just popped into my head. Perhaps I knew something about dogs when I was human?'

'Listen, the Feegles think they're in heaven! They think they died and came here!'

'And?' said the toad.

'Well, that can't be right! You're supposed to be alive here and then die and end up in some heaven somewhere else!'

'Well, that's just saying the same thing in a different way, isn't it? Anyway, lots of warrior tribes think that when they die they go to a heavenly land somewhere,' said the toad. 'You know, where they can drink and fight and feast for ever? So maybe this is theirs.'

'But this is a real place!'

'So? It's what they believe. Besides, they're only small. Maybe the universe is a bit crowded and they have to put heavens anywhere there's room? I'm a toad, so you'll appreciate that I'm having to guess a lot here. Maybe they're just wrong. Maybe you're just wrong. Maybe *I'm* just wrong.'

A small foot kicked Tiffany on the boot.

'We'd be best be moving on, mistress,' said Rob Anybody. He had a dead Feegle over his shoulder. Quite a few of the others were carrying bodies too.

'Er . . . are you going to bury them?' said Tiffany.

'Aye, they dinnae need these ol' bodies noo an' it's no' tidy to leave 'em lyin' aboot,' said Rob Anybody. 'Besides, if the bigjobs find little wee skulls and bones aroound they'll start to wonder, and we don't want anyone pokin' aboot. Savin' your presence, mistress,' he added.

114

'No, that's very, er ... practical thinking,' said Tiffany, giving up.

The Feegle pointed to a distant mound with a thicket of thorn trees growing on it. A lot of the mounds had thickets on them. The trees took advantage of the deeper soil. It was said to be unlucky to cut them down.

'It's nae very far noo,' he said.

'You live in one of the mounds?' Tiffany asked. 'I thought they were, you know, the graves of ancient chieftains?'

'Ach, aye, there's some ol' dead kingie in the chamber next door but he's nae trouble,' said Rob. 'Dinnae fret, there's nae skelingtons or any such in oour bit. It's quite roomy, we've done it up a treat.'

Tiffany looked up at the endless blue sky over the endlessly green downland. It was all so peaceful again, a world away from headless men and big savage dogs.

What if I hadn't taken Wentworth down to the river? she thought. What would I be doing now? Getting on with the cheese, I suppose ...

I never knew about all this. I never knew I lived in heaven, even if it's only heaven to a clan of little blue men. I didn't know about people who flew on buzzards.

I never killed monsters before.

'Where do they come from?' she said. 'What's the name of the place the monsters *come* from?'

'Ach, ye prob'ly ken the place well,' said Rob Anybody. As they drew nearer the mound, Tiffany thought she could smell smoke in the air.

'Do I?' she said.

'Aye. But it's a no' a name I'll say in open air. It's a name to be whispered in a safe place. I'll not say it under this sky.'

It was too big to be a rabbit hole and badgers didn't live up here, but the entrance to the mound was tucked amongst the thorn roots and no one would have thought it was anything but the home of some kind of an animal.

Tiffany was slim, but even so she had to take off her apron and crawl on her stomach under the thorns to reach it. And it still needed several Feegles to push her through.

At least it didn't smell bad and, once you were through the hole, it opened up a lot. Really, the entrance was just a disguise. Underneath, the space was the size of quite a large room, open in the centre but with Feegle-sized galleries around the walls from floor to ceiling. They were crowded with pictsies of all sizes, washing clothes, arguing, sewing and, here and there, fighting, and doing everything as loudly as possible. Some had hair and beards tinged with white. Much younger ones, only a few inches tall, were running around with no clothes on, and yelling at one another at the tops of their little voices. After a couple of years of helping to bring up Wentworth, Tiffany knew what *that* was all about.

There were no girls, though. No Wee Free Women.

No . . . there was one.

The squabbling, bustling crowds parted to let her

116

through. She came up to Tiffany's ankle. She was prettier than the male Feegles, although the world was full of things prettier than, say, Daft Wullie. But, like them, she had red hair and an expression of determination.

She curtsied, then said, 'Are ye the bigjob hag, mistress?'

Tiffany looked around. She was the only person in the cavern who was over seven inches tall.

'Er, yes,' she said. 'Er . . . more or less. Yes.'

'I am Fion. The kelda says to tell you the wee boy will come to nae harm yet.'

'She's found him?' said Tiffany quickly. 'Where is he?'

'Nae, nae, but the kelda knows the way of the Quin. She didnae want you to fash yersel' on that score.'

'But she stole him!'

'Aye. 'Tis comp-li-cat-ed. Rest a wee while. The kelda will see you presently. She is . . . not strong now.'

Fion turned round with a swirl of skirts, strode back across the chalk floor as if she was a queen herself, and disappeared behind a large round stone that leaned against the far wall.

Tiffany, without looking down, carefully lifted the toad out of her pocket and held it close to her lips. 'Am I fashing myself?' she whispered.

'No, not really,' said the toad.

'You would tell me if I was, wouldn't you?' said Tiffany urgently. 'It'd be terrible if everyone could see I was fashing and I didn't know.'

'You haven't a clue what it means, have you . . . ?' said the toad.

'Not exactly, no.'

'She just doesn't want you to get upset, that's all.'

'Yes, I thought it was probably something like that,' lied Tiffany. 'Can you sit on my shoulder? I think I might need some help here.'

The ranks of the Nac Mac Feegle were watching her with interest, but at the moment it appeared that she had nothing to do but hurry up and wait. She sat down carefully, drumming her fingers on her knees.

'Whut d'ye think of the wee place, eh?' said a voice from below. 'It's great, yeah?'

She looked down. Rob Anybody Feegle and a few of the pictsies she'd already met were lurking there, watching her nervously.

'Very . . . cosy,' said Tiffany, because that was better than saying 'How sooty' or 'How delightfully noisy'. She added: 'Do you cook for all of you on that little fire?'

The big space in the centre held a small fire, under a hole in the roof which let the smoke get lost in the bushes above and in return brought in a little extra light.

'Aye, mistress,' said Rob Anybody.

'The small stuff, bunnies an' that,' added Daft Wullie. 'The big stuff we roasts in the chalk pi— mmph mmph . . .'

'Sorry, what was that?' said Tiffany.

'What?' said Rob Anybody innocently, his hand firmly over the mouth of the struggling Wullie.

'What was Wullie saying about roasting "big stuff"?' Tiffany demanded. 'You roast "big stuff" in the chalk pit? Is this the kind of big stuff that goes "baa"? Because that's the only big stuff you'll find in these hills!'

She kneeled down on the grimy floor and brought her face to within an inch of Rob Anybody's face, which was grinning madly and sweating.

'*Is it?*'

'Ach . . . ah . . . weel . . . in a manner o' speakin' . . .'

'*It is?*'

' 'Tis not thine, mistress!' shrieked Rob Anybody. 'We ne'er took an Aching ship wi'out the leave o' Granny!'

'Granny Aching let you have sheep?'

'Aye, she did, did that! As p-payment!'

'Payment? For what?'

'No Aching ship ever got caught by wolves!' Rob Anybody gabbled. 'No foxes took an Aching lamb, right? Nor no lamb e'er had its een pecked out by corbies, not wi' Hamish up in the sky!'

Tiffany looked sideways at the toad.

'Crows,' said the toad. 'They sometimes peck out the eyes of—'

'Yes, yes, I know what they do,' said Tiffany. She calmed down a little. 'Oh. I see. You kept away the crows and wolves and foxes for Granny, yes?'

'Aye, mistress! No' just kept 'em awa', neither!' said Rob Anybody triumphantly. 'There's good eatin' on a wolf.'

'Aye, they kebabs up a treat, but they're no' as

good as a ship, tho . . . mmph mmph . . .' Wullie managed, before a hand was clamped over his mouth again.

'From a hag ye only tak' what ye's given,' said Rob Anybody, holding his struggling brother firmly. 'Since she's gone, though, weel . . . we tak' the odd old ewe that would've deid anywa', but ne'er one wi' the Aching mark, on my honour.'

'On your honour as a drunken rowdy thief?' said Tiffany.

Rob Anybody beamed. 'Aye!' he said. 'An' I got a lot of good big reputation to protect there! That's the truth o' it, mistress. We keeps an eye on the ships of the hills, in mem'ry o' Granny Aching, an' in return we tak' what is hardly worth a thing.'

'And the baccy too, o' course . . . mmph mmph . . .' and then, once again, Daft Wullie was struggling to breathe.

Tiffany took a deep breath, not a wise move in a Feegle colony. Rob Anybody's nervous grin made him look like a pumpkin man faced with a big spoon.

'*You take the tobacco?*' hissed Tiffany. '*The tobacco the shepherds leave for . . . my grandmother?*'

'Ach, I forgot about that,' squeaked Rob Anybody. 'But we allus wait a few days in case she comes to collect it hersel'. Ye can ne'er tell wi' a hag, after all. And we do mind the ships, mistress. And she wouldna grudge us, mistress! Many's a night she'd share a pipe wi' the kelda outside o' her house on the wheelies! She'd no' be one to let good baccy get all rainy! Please, mistress!'

Tiffany felt intensely angry, and what made it worse was that she was angry with herself.

'When we find lost lambs and suchlike we drives 'em here for when the shepherds come lookin',' Rob Anybody added anxiously.

What did I think happened? Tiffany thought. Did I think she'd come back for a packet of Jolly Sailor? Did I think she was still somehow walking the hills, looking after the sheep? Did I think she . . . was still here, watching for lost lambs?

Yes! I want that to be true. I don't want to think she's just . . . gone. Someone like Granny Aching can't just . . . not be there any more. And I want her back so much, because she didn't know how to talk to me and I was too scared to talk to her, and so we never talked and we turned silence into something to share.

I know *nothing* about her. Just some books, and some stories she tried to tell me, and things I didn't understand, and I remember big red soft hands and that smell. I never knew who she really was. I mean, she must have been nine too, once. She was Sarah Grizzel. She got married and had children, two of them in the shepherding hut. She must've done all sorts of things I don't know about.

And into Tiffany's mind, as it always did sooner or later, came the figure of the blue and white china shepherdess, swirling in red mists of shame . . .

Tiffany's father took her to the fair at the town of Yelp one day not long before her seventh birthday, when the farm had some rams to sell. That was a ten-mile journey, the furthest she'd ever been. It was off the Chalk. Everything looked different. There were far more fenced fields and lots of cows and the buildings had tiled roofs instead of thatch. She considered that this was foreign travel.

Granny Aching had never been there, said her father on the way. She hated leaving the Chalk, he said. She said it made her dizzy.

It was a great day. Tiffany was sick on candyfloss, had her fortune told by a little old lady who said that many, many men would want to marry her, and won the shepherdess, which was made of china painted in white and blue.

She was the star prize on the hoop-la stall but Tiffany's father had said that it was all cheating, because the base was so wide that not one throw in a million could ever drop the hoop right over it.

She'd thrown the ring any old how, and it had been the one in a million. The stallholder hadn't been very happy about it landing over the shepherdess rather than the gimcrack rubbish on the rest of the stall. He handed it over when her father spoke sharply to him, though, and she'd hugged it all the way home on the cart, while the stars came out.

Next morning she'd proudly presented it to Granny Aching. The old woman had taken it very carefully in her wrinkled hands and stared at it for some time.

Tiffany was sure, now, that it had been a cruel thing to do.

Granny Aching had probably never heard of shepherdesses. People who cared for sheep on the Chalk were all called shepherds, and that was all there was to it. And this beautiful creature was as much unlike Granny Aching as anything could be.

The china shepherdess had an old-fashioned long dress, with the bulgy bits at the side that made it look as though she had saddlebags in her knickers. There were blue ribbons all over the dress, and all over the rather showy straw bonnet, and on the shepherd's crook, which was a lot more curly than any crook Tiffany had ever seen.

There were even blue bows on the dainty foot poking out from the frilly hem of her dress.

This wasn't a shepherdess who'd ever worn big old boots stuffed with wool, and tramped the hills in the howling wind with the sleet being driven along like nails. She'd never tried in that dress to pull out a ram who'd got his horns tangled in a thorn patch. This wasn't a shepherdess who'd kept up with the champion shearer for seven hours, sheep for sheep, until the air was hazy with grease and wool and blue with cussing, and the champion gave up because he couldn't cuss sheep as well as Granny Aching. No self-respecting sheepdog would ever 'come by' or 'walk up' for a simpering girl with saddlebags in her pants. It was a lovely thing but it was a joke of a shepherdess, made by someone who'd probably never seen a sheep up close.

What had Granny Aching thought about it? Tiffany couldn't guess. She'd seemed happy, because it's the job of grandmothers to be happy when grandchildren give them things. She'd put it up on her shelf, and then taken Tiffany on her knee and called her 'my little jiggit' in a *nervous sort of way, which she did when she was trying to be grandmotherly.*

Sometimes, in the rare times Granny was down at the farm, Tiffany would see her take down the statue and stare at it. But if she saw Tiffany watching she'd put it back quickly, and pretend she'd meant to pick up the sheep book.

Perhaps, Tiffany thought wretchedly, the old lady had seen it as a sort of insult. Perhaps she thought she was being told that this was what a shepherdess should look like. She shouldn't be an old lady in a muddy dress and big boots, with an old sack around her shoulders to keep the rain off. A shepherdess should sparkle like a starry night. Tiffany hadn't meant to, she'd never meant to, but perhaps she had been telling Granny that she wasn't . . . right.

And then a few months after that Granny had died, and in the years since then everything had gone wrong. Wentworth had been born, and then the Baron's son had vanished, and then there had been that bad winter when Mrs Snapperly died in the snow.

Tiffany kept worrying about the statue. She couldn't talk about it. Everyone else was busy, or not interested. Everyone was edgy. They'd have said that worrying about a silly statue was . . . silly.

Several times she nearly smashed the shepherdess, but she didn't because people would notice.

She wouldn't have given something as wrong as that to Granny Aching now, of course. She'd grown up.

She remembered that the old lady would smile oddly, sometimes, when she looked at the statue. If only she'd said something. But Granny liked silence.

*

And now it turned out that she'd made friends with a lot of little blue men, who walked the hills looking after the sheep, because they liked her too. Tiffany blinked.

It made a kind of sense. In memory of Granny Aching, the men left the tobacco. And in memory of Granny Aching, the Nac Mac Feegle minded the sheep. It all worked, even if it wasn't magic. But it took Granny away.

'Daft Wullie?' she said, staring hard at the struggling pictsie and trying not to cry.

'Mmph?'

'Is it true what Rob Anybody told me?'

'Mmph!' Daft Wullie's eyebrows went up and down furiously.

'Mr Feegle, you can please take your hand away from his mouth,' said Tiffany. Daft Wullie was released. Rob Anybody had looked worried, but Daft Wullie was terrified. He dragged his bonnet off and stood holding it in his hands, as if it was some kind of shield.

'Is all that true, Daft Wullie?' said Tiffany.

'Oh waily waily—'

'Just a simple yes or— A simple aye or nay, please.'

'Aye! It is!' blurted out Daft Wullie. 'Oh waily waily—'

'Yes, thank you,' said Tiffany, sniffing and trying to blink the tears away. 'All right. I understand.'

The Feegles eyed her cautiously.

'Ye're nae gonna get nasty aboot it?' said Rob Anybody.

'No. It all . . . works.'

She heard it echo around the cavern, the sound of hundreds of little men sighing with relief.

'She didnae turn me intae a pismire!' said Daft Wullie, grinning happily at the rest of the pictsies. 'Hey, lads, I talked wi' the hag and she didnae e'en look at me crosswise! She *smiled* at me!' He beamed at Tiffany and went on: 'An' d'ye ken, mistress, that if'n you hold the baccy label upside-doon then part o' the sailor's bonnet and his ear became a lady wi' nae mmph mmph . . .'

'Ach, there I goes again, accidentally nearly throttlin' ye,' said Rob Anybody, his hand clamping over Wullie's mouth.

Tiffany opened her mouth, but stopped when her ears tickled strangely.

In the roof of the cave, several bats woke up and hastily flew out of the smoke hole.

Some of the Feegles were busy on the far side of the chamber. What Tiffany had thought was a strange round stone was being rolled aside, revealing a large hole.

Now her ears squelched and felt as though all the wax was running out. The Feegles were forming up in two rows, leading to the hole.

Tiffany prodded the toad. 'Do I want to know what a pismire is?' she whispered.

'It's an ant,' said the toad.

'Oh? I'm . . . slightly surprised. And this sort of high-pitched noise?'

'I'm a toad. We're not good at ears. But it's probably him over there.'

There was a Feegle walking out of the hole from which came, now that Tiffany's eyes had become accustomed to the gloom, a faint golden light.

The newcomer's hair was white instead of red and, while he was tall for a pictsie, he was as skinny as a twig. He was holding some sort of fat skin bag, bristling with pipes.

'Now there's a sight I don't reckon many humans have seen and lived,' said the toad. 'He's playing the mousepipes!'

'They make my ears tingle!' Tiffany tried to ignore the two little ears still on the bag of pipes.

'High-pitched, see?' said the toad. 'Of course, the pictsies hear sounds differently than humans do. He's probably their battle poet too.'

'You mean he makes up heroic songs about famous battles?'

'No, no. He recites poems that frighten the enemy. Remember how important words are to the Nac Mac Feegle? Well, when a well-trained gonnagle starts to recite, the enemy's ears explode. Ah, it looks as though they're ready for you . . .'

In fact Rob Anybody was tapping politely on Tiffany's toecap. 'The kelda will see you now, mistress,' he said.

The piper had stopped playing and was standing respectfully beside the hole. Tiffany felt hundreds of bright little eyes watching her.

'Special Sheep Liniment,' whispered the toad.

'Pardon?'

'Take it in with us,' the toad said insistently. 'It'd be a good gift!'

The pictsies watched her carefully as she lay down again and crawled through the hole behind the stone, the toad hanging on tightly. As she got closer she realized that what she'd thought was a stone was an old round shield, green-blue and corroded with age. The hole it had covered was indeed wide enough for her to go through, but she had to leave her legs outside because it was impossible to get all of her into the room beyond. One reason was the bed, small though it was, which held the kelda. The other reason was that what the room was mostly full of, piled up around the walls and spilling across the floor, was gold.

CHAPTER 7

First Sight and
Second Thoughts

Glint, glisten, glitter, gleam . . .
Tiffany thought a lot about words, in the long hours of churning butter. 'Onomatopoeic', she'd discovered in the dictionary, meant words that sounded like the noise of the thing they were describing, like 'cuckoo'. But she thought there should be a word meaning 'a word that sounds like the noise a thing would make if that thing made a noise even though, actually, it doesn't, but would if it did'.

Glint, for example. If light made a noise as it reflected off a distant window, it'd go 'glint!' And the light of tinsel, all those little glints chiming together, would make a noise like 'glitterglitter'. 'Gleam' was a clean, smooth noise from a surface that intended to shine all day. And 'glisten' was the soft, almost greasy sound of something rich and oily.

The little cave contained all of these at once. There was only one candle, which smelled of sheep fat, but gold plates and cups gleamed, glistened, glinted and glittered the light back and forth until the one little flame filled the air with a light that even *smelled* expensive.

The gold surrounded the bed of the kelda, who was sitting up against a pile of pillows. She was much, much fatter than the male pictsies; she looked as if she'd been made of round balls of slightly squashy dough, and was the colour of chestnuts.

Her eyes were closed as Tiffany slid in, but they flicked open the moment she'd stopped pulling herself forward. They were the sharpest eyes she'd ever seen, much sharper even than Miss Tick's.

'So-o . . . you'll be Sarah Aching's wee girl?' said the kelda.

'Yes. I mean, aye,' said Tiffany. It wasn't very comfortable lying on her stomach. 'And you're the kelda?'

'Aye. I mean, yes,' said the kelda, and the round face became a mass of lines as the kelda smiled. 'What was your name, now?'

'Tiffany, er, Kelda.' Fion had turned up from some other part of the cave and was sitting down on a stool by the bed, watching Tiffany intently with a disapproving expression.

'A good name. In our tongue you'd be Tir-far-thóinn, Land Under Wave,' said the kelda. It sounded like 'Tiffan'.

'I don't think anyone *meant* to name—'

'Ach, what people mean to do and what is done are two different things,' said the kelda. Her little eyes shone. 'Your wee brother is . . . safe, child. Ye could say he's safer where he is noo than he has ever been. No mortal ills can touch him. The Quin wouldnae harm a hair o' his heid. And there's the evil o' it. Help me up here, girl.'

Fion leaped up immediately and helped the kelda struggle up higher amongst her cushions.

'Where wuz I?' the kelda continued. 'Ah, the wee laddie. Aye, ye could say he bides well where he is, in the Quin's own country. But I daresay there's a mother grievin'?'

'And his father too,' said Tiffany.

'An' his wee sister?' said the kelda.

Tiffany felt the words 'Yes, of course' trot automatically onto her tongue. She also knew that it would be very stupid to let them go any further. The little old woman's dark eyes were seeing right into her head.

'Aye, you're a born hag, right enough,' said the kelda, holding her gaze. 'Ye've got that little bitty bit inside o' you that holds on, right? The bitty bit that watches the rest o' ye. 'Tis the First Sight and Second Thoughts ye have, and 'tis a wee gift an' a big curse to ye. You see and hear what others canna', the world opens up its secrets to ye, but ye're always like the person at the party with the wee drink in the corner who cannae join in. There's a little bitty bit inside ye that willnae melt and flow. Ye're Sarah Aching's line, right enough. The lads fetched the right one.'

Tiffany didn't know what to say to that, so she didn't say anything. The kelda watched her, eyes twinkling, until Tiffany felt awkward.

'Why would the Queen take my brother?' she asked eventually. 'And why is she after me?'

'Ye think she is?'

'Well, yes, actually! I mean, Jenny might have been a coincidence, but the horseman? And the grimhounds? And taking Wentworth?'

'She's bending her mind to ye,' said the kelda. 'When she does, something of her world passes into this one. Mebbe she just wants to test you.'

'*Test* me?'

'To see how good you are. Ye're the hag noo, the witch that guards the edges and the gateways. So wuz yer granny, although she wouldnae ever call hersel' one. And so wuz I until noo, and I'll pass the duty to ye. She'll ha' to get past ye, if she wants this land. Ye have the First Sight and the Second Thoughts, just like yer granny. That's rare in a bigjob.'

'Don't you mean second sight?' Tiffany queried. 'Like people who can see ghosts and stuff?'

'Ach, no. That's typical bigjob thinking. *First Sight* is when you can see what's really there, not what your heid tells you *ought* to be there. Ye saw Jenny, ye saw the horseman, ye saw them as real thingies. Second sight is dull sight, it's seeing only what you expect to see. Most bigjobs ha' that. Listen to me, because I'm fadin' noo and there's a lot ye dinnae ken. Ye think this is the only world? That is a good thought for sheep and mortals who dinnae open their eyes. Because in truth there are more worlds than stars in the sky. Understand? They are everywhere, big and small, close as your skin. They are *everywhere*. Some ye can see an' some ye cannae but there are doors, Tiffan. They might be a hill or a tree or a stone or a turn in the road or they might e'en be a thought in yer heid, but they are there, all aroound ye. You'll have to learn to see 'em, because you walk amongst them and dinnae know it. And some of them . . . is poisonous.'

The kelda stared at Tiffany for a moment and then continued: 'Ye asked why the Quin should take your boy? The Quin likes children. She has none o' her own. She dotes on them. She'll give the wee boy everything he wants too. *Only* what he wants.'

'He only wants sweets!' said Tiffany.

'Is that so? An' did ye gi' them to him?' said the kelda, as if she was looking into Tiffany's mind. 'But what he *needs* is love an' care an' teachin' an' people sayin' "no" to him sometimes an' things o' that nature. He needs to be growed up strong. He willnae get that fra' the Quin. He'll get sweeties. For ever.'

Tiffany wished the kelda would stop looking at her like that.

'But I see he has a sister willin' to take any pains to bring him back,' said the little old woman, taking her eyes away from Tiffany. 'What a lucky wee boy he is, to be so fortunate. Ye ken how to be strong, do ye?'

'Yes, I think so.'

'Good. D'ye ken how to be weak? Can ye bow to the gale, can ye bend to the storm?' The kelda smiled again. 'Nay, ye neednae answer that. The wee burdie always has tae leap from the nest to see if it can fly. Anyway, ye have the feel o' Sarah Aching about ye, and no word e'en o' mine could turn her once she had set her mind to something. Ye're no' a woman yet, and that's no bad thing, because where ye'll be goin' is easy for children, hard for adults.'

'The world of the Queen?' ventured Tiffany, trying to keep up.

'Aye. I can feel it noo, lyin' over this one like a fog, as far awa' as the other side o' a mirror. I'm weakenin', Tiffan. I cannae defend this place. So here is my bargain, child. I'll point ye towards the Quin an', in return, ye'll tak' over as kelda.'

That surprised Fion as much as Tiffany. Her head shot up sharply and her mouth opened, but the kelda had raised a wrinkled hand.

'When *ye* are a kelda somewhere, my girl, ye'll expect people to do your biddin'. So dinnae give me the argument. That's my offer, Tiffan. Ye won't get a better.'

'But she *cannae*—' Fion began.

'Can she not?' said the kelda.

'She's nae a *pictsie*, Mother!'

'She's a bit on the large side, aye,' said the kelda. 'Dinnae fret, Tiffan. It willnae be for long. I just need ye to mind things for a wee while. Mind the land like yer granny did, and mind my boys. Then when yer wee boy is back home, Hamish'll fly up to the mountains and let it be known that the Chalk Hill clan has want o' a kelda. We've got a good place here, and the girls'll come flockin'. What d'ye say?'

'She disnae know our ways!' Fion protested. 'Ye're overtired, Mother!'

'Aye, I am,' said the kelda. 'But a daughter cannae run her mother's clan, ye know that. Ye're a dutiful girl, Fion, but it's time ye were pickin' your bodyguard and going awa' seeking a clan of your own. Ye cannae stay here.' The kelda looked up at Tiffany again. 'Will ye, Tiffan?' She held up a thumb the size of a match head and waited.

'What will I have to do?' said Tiffany.

'The thinkin',' said the kelda, still holding up her thumb. 'My lads are good lads, there's none braver. But they think their heids is most useful as weapons. That's lads for ye. We pictsies aren't like you big folk, ye ken. Ye have many sisters? Fion here has none. She's my only daughter. A kelda might be blessed wi' only one daughter in her whole life, but she'll have hundreds and hundreds o' sons.'

'They are *all* your sons?' said Tiffany, aghast.

'Oh aye,' said the kelda, smiling. 'Except for a few o' my brothers who travelled here with me when I came to be kelda. Oh, dinna look so astonished. The bairns are really wee when they're borned, like little peas in a pod. And they grow up fast.' She sighed. 'But sometimes I think all the brains is saved for the daughters. They're good boys, but they're no' great thinkers. You'll have to help them help ye.'

'Mother, she cannae carry oot the *duties* o' a kelda!' Fion protested.

'I don't see why not, if they're explained to me,' said Tiffany.

'Oh, do you not?' said Fion sharply. 'Weel, that's gonna be most *interesting*!'

'I recall Sarah Aching talkin' aboot ye,' said the kelda. 'She said ye were a strange wee one, always watchin' and listenin'. She said ye had a heid full o' words that ye ne'er spoke aloud. She wondered what'd become o' ye. Time for ye to find out, aye?'

Aware of Fion glaring at her, and maybe *because* of Fion glaring at her, Tiffany licked her thumb and touched it gently against the kelda's tiny thumb.

'It is done, then,' said the kelda. She lay back suddenly, and just as suddenly seemed to shrink. There were more lines in her face now. 'Never let it be said I left my sons wi'oot a kelda to mind them,' she muttered. 'Now I can go back to the Last World. Tiffan is the kelda for now, Fion. In her hoose, ye'll do what she says.'

Fion looked down at her feet. Tiffany could see that she was angry.

The kelda sagged. She beckoned Tiffany closer, and in a weaker voice said: 'There. 'Tis done. And now for my part o' the bargain. Listen. Find . . . the place where the time disnae fit. There's the way in. It'll shine out to ye. Bring him back to ease yer puir mother's heart and mebbe also your ain head—'

Her voice faltered, and Fion leaned quickly towards the bed.

The kelda sniffed.

She opened one eye.

'Not quite yet,' she murmured to Fion. 'Do I smell a wee drop of Special Sheep Liniment on yez, Kelda?'

Tiffany looked puzzled for a moment and then said: 'Oh, me. Oh. Yes. Er . . . here . . .'

The kelda struggled to sit up again. 'The best thing humans ever made,' she said. 'I'll just have a large wee drop, Fion.'

'It puts hairs on your chest,' Tiffany warned.

'Ach, weel, for a drop of Sarah Aching's Special Sheep Liniment I'll risk a curl or two,' said the old kelda. She took from Fion a leather cup about the size of a thimble, and held it up.

'I dinnae think it would be good for ye, Mother,' said Fion.

'I'll be the judge o' that at this time,' said the kelda. 'One drop afore I go, please, Kelda Tiffan.'

Tiffany tipped the bottle slightly. The kelda shook the cup irritably.

'It was a larger drop I had in mind, Kelda,' she said. 'A kelda has a generous heart.'

She took something too small to be a gulp but too large to be a sip.

'Aye, it's a lang time since I tasted this brose,' she said. 'Your granny and I used to ha' a sip or two in front o' the fire on cold nights . . .'

Tiffany saw it clearly in her head, Granny Aching and this little fat woman, sitting around the pot-bellied stove in the hut on wheels, while the sheep grazed under the stars . . .

'Ah, ye can see it,' said the kelda. 'I can feel yer eyes on me. That's the First Sight workin'.' She lowered the cup. 'Fion, go and fetch Rob Anybody and William the gonnagle.'

'The bigjob is blockin' the hole,' said Fion sulkily.

'I dare say there's room to wriggle past,' said the old kelda in the kind of calm voice that said a stormy voice could follow if people didn't do what they were told.

With a smouldering glance at Tiffany, Fion squeezed past.

'Ye ken anyone who keeps bees?' said the kelda. When Tiffany nodded the little old woman went on, 'Then you'll know why we dinnae have many daughters. You cannae ha' two quins in one hive wi'oot a big fight. Fion must take her pick o' them that will follow her and seek a clan that needs a kelda. That is our way. She thinks there's another way, as gels sometimes do. Be careful o' her.'

Tiffany felt something move past her, and Rob Anybody and the bard came into the room. There was more rustling and whispering too. An unofficial audience was gathering outside.

When things had settled down a little, the old kelda said: 'It is a bad thing for a clan to be left wi'oot a kelda to watch o'er it e'en for an hour. So Tiffan will be your kelda until a new one can be fetched . . .'

There was a murmur beside and behind Tiffany. The old kelda looked at William the gonnagle.

'Am I right that this has been done before?' she said.

'Aye. The songs say twice before,' said William. He frowned, and added: 'Or you could say it was three times if you include the time when the Quin was—'

He was drowned out by the cry that went up behind Tiffany:

'*Nae quin! Nae king! Nae laird! Nae master! We willna' be fooled again!*'

The old kelda raised a hand. 'Tiffan is the spawn of Granny Aching,' she said. 'Ye all ken of her.'

'Aye, and ye saw the wee hag stare the heidless horseman in the eyes he hasnae got,' said Rob Anybody. 'Not many people can do that!'

'And I have been your kelda for seventy years and my words cannae be gainsaid,' said the old kelda. 'So the choice is made. I tell ye, too, that ye'll help her steal back her wee baby brother. That is the fate I lay on you all in memory of me and Sarah Aching.'

She lay back in her bed, and in a quieter voice added, 'An' now I would have the gonnagle play *The Bonny Flowers*, and hope to see yez all again in the Last World. To Tiffan, I say, be wary.' The kelda took a deep breath. 'Somewhere, a' stories are real, a' songs are true . . .'

The old kelda fell silent. William the gonnagle inflated the bag of his mousepipes and blew into one of the tubes. Tiffany felt the bubbling in her ears of music too high-pitched to hear.

After a few moments Fion leaned over the bed to look at her mother, then started to cry.

Rob Anybody turned and looked up at Tiffany, his eyes running with tears. 'Could I just ask ye to go out intae the big chamber, Kelda?' he said, quietly. 'We ha' things to do, ye ken how it is . . .'

Tiffany nodded and, with great care, feeling pictsies scuttle out of her way, backed out of the room. She found a corner where she didn't seem to be in anyone's way and sat there with her back to the wall.

She'd expected a lot of 'waily waily waily' but it seemed the death of the kelda was too serious for that. Some Feegles were crying, and some were staring at nothing and, as the news spread, the tiered hall filled up with a wretched, sobbing silence . . .

. . . the hills had been silent on the day Granny Aching died.

Someone went up every day with fresh bread and milk and scraps for the dogs. It didn't need to be quite so often, but Tiffany had heard her parents talking and her father had said, 'We ought to keep an eye on Mam now.'

Today had been Tiffany's turn, but she'd never thought of it as a chore. She liked the journey.

But she'd noticed the silence. It was no longer the silence of many little noises, but a dome of quiet all around the hut.

She knew then, even before she went in at the open door and found Granny lying on the narrow bed.

She'd felt coldness spread though her. It even had a sound – it was like a thin, sharp musical note. It had a voice too. Her own voice. It was saying: It's too late, tears are no good, no time to say anything, there are things to be done . . .

And . . . then she fed the dogs, who were waiting patiently for their breakfast. It would have helped if they'd done something soppy, like whine or lick Granny's face, but they hadn't. And still Tiffany heard the voice in her mind: No tears, don't cry. Don't cry for Granny Aching.

Now, in her head, she watched the slightly smaller Tiffany move around the hut like a little puppet . . .

She'd tidied up the shed. Besides the bed and the stove there really wasn't much there. There was the clothes sack and the big water barrel and the food box, and that was it. Oh, stuff to do with sheep was all over the place – pots and bottles and sacks and knives and shears – but there was nothing there that said a person lived here, unless you counted the hundreds of blue and yellow Jolly Sailor wrappers pinned on one wall.

She'd taken one of them down – it was still underneath her mattress at home – and she remembered the Story.

It was very unusual for Granny Aching to say more than a sentence. She used words as if they cost money. But there'd been one day when she'd taken food up to the hut, and Granny had told her a story. A sort of a story. She'd unwrapped the tobacco, and looked at the wrapper, and then looked at Tiffany with that slightly puzzled look she used, and said: 'I must've looked at a thousand o' these things, and I never once saw his bo-ut.' That was how she pronounced 'boat'.

Of course Tiffany had rushed to have a look at this label, but she couldn't see any boat, any more than she could see the naked lady.

'That's 'cos the bo-ut is just where you can't see it,' Granny had said. 'He's got a bo-ut for chasin' the great white whale fish on the salt sea. He's always chasing it, all round the world. It's called Mopey. It's a beast like a big cliff of chalk, I heard tell. In a book.'

'Why's he chasing it?' Tiffany had asked.

'To catch it,' Granny had said. 'But he never will, the reason being, the world is round like a big plate and so is the sea and so they're chasing one another, so it is almost like he is chasing hisself. Ye never want to go to sea, jiggit. That's where worse things happen. Everyone says that. You stop along here, wheres the hills is in yer bones.'

And that was it. It was one of the very few times Granny Aching had ever said anything to Tiffany that wasn't, in some way, about sheep. It was the only time she ever acknowledged that there was a world beyond the Chalk. Tiffany used to dream about the Jolly Sailor chasing the whale fish in his boat. And sometimes the whale fish would chase her, but the Jolly Sailor always arrived in his mighty ship just in time and their chase would start again.

Sometimes she'd run to the lighthouse, and wake up just as the door swung open. She'd never seen the sea, but one of the neighbours had an old picture on the wall that showed a lot of men clinging to a raft in what looked like a huge lake full of waves. She hadn't been able to see the lighthouse at all.

And Tiffany had sat by the narrow bed and thought about Granny Aching, and about the little girl Sarah Grizzel very carefully painting the flowers in the book, and about the world losing its centre.

She missed the silence. What there was now wasn't the same kind of silence there had been before. Granny's silence was warm, and brought you inside. Granny Aching might sometimes have had trouble remembering the difference between children and lambs, but in her *silence you were welcome and belonged. All you had to bring was a silence of your own.*

Tiffany wished that she'd had a chance to say sorry about the shepherdess.

Then she'd gone home and told everyone that Granny was dead. She was seven, and the world had ended.

Someone was tapping politely on her boot. She opened her eyes and saw the toad. It was holding a small rock in its mouth. It spat it out.

'Sorry about that,' it said. 'I'd have used my arms but we're a very soggy species.'

'What am I supposed to *do*?' said Tiffany.

'Well, if you hit your head on this low ceiling you would have a definite claim for damages,' said the toad. 'Er . . . did I just say that?'

'Yes, and I hope you wish you hadn't,' said Tiffany. 'Why did you say it?'

'I don't know, I don't know,' moaned the toad. 'Sorry, what were we talking about?'

'I *meant*, what do the pictsies want me to *do* now?'

'Oh, I don't think it works like that,' said the toad. 'You're the kelda. *You* say what's to be done.'

'Why can't Fion be kelda? She's a pictsie!'

'Can't help you there,' said the toad.

'Can I be of serrrvice?' said a voice by Tiffany's ear.

She turned her head and saw, on one of the galleries that ran around the cave, William the gonnagle.

Up close, he was noticeably different from the other Feegles. His hair was neater, and plaited into one pigtail. He didn't have as many tattoos. He spoke differently too, more clearly and slowly than the others, sounding his 'R's like a drumroll.

'Er, yes,' said Tiffany. 'Why can't Fion be kelda here?'

William nodded. 'A good question,' he said politely. 'But, ye ken, a kelda cannot wed her brrrrotherrrr. She must go to a new clan and wed a warrrrior there.'

'Well, why couldn't that warrior come here?'

'Because the Feegles here would not know him. They'd have no rrrrespect for him.' William made 'respect' sound like an avalanche.

'Oh. Well . . . what was that about the Queen? You were going to say something and they stopped you.'

William looked embarrassed. 'I don't think I can tell you aboout—'

'I *am* the temporary kelda,' said Tiffany stiffly.

'Aye. Well . . . there was a time when we lived in the Queen's world and served her, before she grew so cold. But she tricked us, and we rrrrebelled. It was a dark time. She does not like us. And that is all I will say,' William added.

Tiffany watched Feegles going in and out of the kelda's chamber. Something was going on in there.

'They're burying her in the other part of the mound,' said William, without being asked. 'Wi' the other keldas o' this clan.'

'I thought they would be more . . . noisy,' said Tiffany.

'She was their motherrr,' said William. 'They do not want to shout. Their hearts are too full for worrrrds.

In time we will hold a wake to help her back to the land o' the living, and that'll be a loud one, I can promise ye. We'll dance the FiveHundredAnd-Twelvesome Reel to the tune o' "The Devil Among The Lawyers" and eat and drink, and I dare say my nephews will ha' headaches the size o' a sheep.' The old Feegle smiled briefly. 'But, for now, each Feegle remembers her in silence. We dinnae mourn like ye do, ye ken. We mourn for them that has tae stay behind.'

'Was she your mother too?' said Tiffany quietly.

'Nay. She was my sister. Did she no' tell ye that when a kelda goes to a new clan she takes a few o' her brothers with her? To be alone amongst strangers would be too much for a heart to bear.' The gonnagle sighed. 'Of course, in time, after the kelda weds, the clan is full of her sons and is no' so lonely for her.'

'It must be for you, though,' said Tiffany.

'You're a quick one, I'll grant ye that,' said William. 'I am the last o' those who came. When this is o'er I'll seek the leave of the next kelda to return to my ain folk in the mountains. This is a fiiine fat country and this is a fiiine bonny clan my nephews have, but I would like to die in the heather where I was borrrned. If you will excuse me, Kelda . . .'

He walked away and was lost in the shadows of the mound.

Tiffany suddenly wanted to go home. Perhaps it was just William's sadness, but now she felt shut up in the mound.

'I've got to get out of here,' she muttered.

'Good idea,' said the toad. 'You've got to find the place where the time is different, for one thing.'

'But how can I do that?' wailed Tiffany. 'You can't *see* time!'

She stuck her arms through the entrance hole and pulled herself up into the fresh air . . .

There was a big old clock in the farmhouse, and the time on it got set once a week. That is, when her father went to the market in Creel Springs he made a note of the position of the hands on the big clock there, and when he got home he moved the hands on their clock to the same position. It was really just for show, anyway. Everyone took their time from the sun, and the sun couldn't go wrong.

Now Tiffany lay amongst the trunks of the old thorn bushes, whose leaves rustled continuously in the breeze. The mound was like a little island in the endless turf; late primroses and even a few ragged foxgloves grew up here in the shelter of the thorn roots. Her apron lay beside her where she had left it earlier.

'She could have just told me where to look,' she said.

'But she didn't know where it would be,' said the toad. 'She just knew the signs to look for.'

Tiffany rolled over carefully and stared up at the sky between the low branches. It'll shine out, the kelda had said . . .

'I think I ought to talk to Hamish,' she said.

'Right ye are, mistress,' said a voice by her ear. She turned her head.

'How long have you been there?' she said.

'A' the time, mistress,' said the pictsie. Others poked their heads around the trees and out from under leaves. There were at least twenty on the mound.

'You've been watching me all the time?'

'Aye, mistress. 'Tis oour task to watch o'er our kelda. I'm up here most o' the time anyway, because I'm studying to become a gonnagle.' The young Feegle flourished a set of mousepipes. 'An' they willnae let me play doon there on account o' them sayin' my playin' sounds like a spider tryin' to fart through its ears, mistress.'

'But what happens if I want to spend a— have a— go to the— What happens if I say I don't want you to guard me?'

'If it's a wee call o' nature ye're talkin' aboout, mistress, the cludgie is o'er there in the chalk pit. Ye'll just sing oot to us where ye're goin' and no one'll go peeking, ye'll have oour word on it,' said the attendant Feegle.

Tiffany glared at him as he stood in the primroses, beaming with pride and anxious duty. He was younger than most of them, without as many scars and lumps. Even his nose wasn't broken.

'What's your name, pictsie?' she said.

'No'-as-big-as-Medium-Sized-Jock-but-bigger-than-Wee-Jock-Jock, mistress. There's no' that many Feegle names, ye ken, so we ha' to share.'

'Well, Not-as-big-as-Little-Jock—' Tiffany began.

'That'd be Medium-Sized Jock, mistress,' said Not-as-big-as-Medium-Sized-Jock-but-bigger-than-Wee-Jock-Jock.

'Well, Not-as-big-as-Medium-Sized-Jock-but-bigger-than-Wee-Jock, I can—'

'That's No'-as-big-as-Medium-Sized-Jock-but-bigger-than-Wee-Jock-*Jock*, mistress,' said Not-as-big-as-Medium-Sized-Jock-but-bigger-than-Wee-Jock-Jock. 'Ye were one jock short,' he added helpfully.

'You wouldn't be happier with, say, Henry?' said Tiffany helplessly.

'Ach, nay, mistress.' Not-as-big-as-Medium-Sized-Jock-but-bigger-than-Wee-Jock-Jock wrinkled his face. 'There's nay history tae the name, ye ken. But there have been a number o' brave warriors called No'-as-big-as-Medium-Sized-Jock-but-bigger-than-Wee-Jock-Jock. Why 'tis nearly as famous a name as Wee Jock itself! An', o' course, should Wee Jock hisself be taken back to the Last World then I'll get the name o' Wee Jock, which isnae to say that I mislike the name o' No'-as-big-as-Medium-Sized-Jock-but-bigger-than-Wee-Jock-Jock, ye ken. There's been many a fine story o' the exploits o' No'-as-big-as-Medium-Sized-Jock-but-bigger-than-Wee-Jock-Jock,' the pictsie added, looking so earnest that Tiffany didn't have the heart to say that they must have been very long stories.

Instead she said: 'Well, er, please, I want to talk to Hamish the aviator.'

'Nae problem,' said Not-as-big-as-Medium-Sized-Jock-but-bigger-than-Wee-Jock-Jock. 'He's up there right noo.'

He vanished. A moment later Tiffany heard – or, rather, felt with her ears – the bubbling sensation of a Feegle whistle.

Tiffany pulled *Diseases of the Sheep*, which was now looking very battered, out of her apron. There was a blank page at the back. She tore it out, feeling like a criminal for doing so, and took out her pencil.

Dear Mum and Dad,
How are you, I am well. Wentworth is also well but I have to go and fetch him from ~~the Qu~~ where he is staying. Hope to be back soon.
Tiffany
PS I hope the cheese is all right.

She was just considering this when she heard a rush of wings overhead. There was a whirring noise, a moment of silence and then a small, weary and rather muffled voice said: 'Ach, crivens . . .'

She looked out onto the turf. The body of Hamish was upside down a few feet away. His arms with their twirlers were still outstretched.*

It took some time to get him out. If he landed headfirst and spinning, Tiffany was told, he had to be unscrewed in the opposite direction so that his ears didn't come off.

When he was upright and swaying unsteadily, Tiffany said: 'Can you wrap this letter round a stone

---

* No words could describe what a Feegle in a kilt looks like upside down, so they won't try.

and drop it in front of the farmhouse where people will see it?'

'Aye, mistress.'

'And . . . er . . . does it hurt when you land headfirst like that?'

'Nay, mistress, but it is awfu' embarrassing.'

'Then there's a sort of toy we used to make that might help you,' said Tiffany. 'You make a kind of . . . bag of air—'

'Bag o' air?' said the aviator, looking puzzled.

'Well, you know how things like shirts billow out on a washing line when it's windy? Well, you just make a cloth bag and tie some strings to it and a stone to the strings, and when you throw it up the bag fills with air and the stone floats down.'

Hamish stared at her.

'Do you understand me?' said Tiffany.

'Oh, aye. I wuz just waitin' to see if you wuz goin' to tell me anything else,' said Hamish politely.

'Do you think you could, er, *borrow* some fine cloth?'

'Nay, mistress, but I ken well where I can steal some,' said Hamish.

Tiffany decided not to comment on this. She said: 'Where was the Queen when the mist came down?'

Hamish pointed. 'Aboot a half mile yonder, mistress.'

In the distance Tiffany could see some more mounds, and a few stones from the old days.

Trilithons, they were called, which just meant 'three stones'. The only stones found naturally on the downs were flints, which were never very big. But the stones of the trilithons had been dragged from at least ten miles away, and were stacked like a child stacks toy bricks. Here and there the big stones had been stood in circles; sometimes one stone had been placed all alone. It must have taken a lot of people a long time to do all that. Some people said there'd been human sacrifices up there. Some said they were part of some old religion. Some said they marked ancient graves.

Some said they were a warning: avoid this place.

Tiffany hadn't. She'd been there with her sisters a few times, as a dare, just in case there were any skulls. But the mounds around the stones were thousands of years old. All that you found there now were rabbit holes.

'Anything else, mistress?' said Hamish politely. 'Nay? Then I'll just be goin' . . .'

He raised his arms over his head and started to run across the turf. Tiffany jumped as the buzzard skimmed down a few yards away from her and snatched him back up into the sky.

'How can a man six inches high train a bird like that?' she asked as the buzzard circled again for height.

'Ach, all it takes is a wee drop o' kindness, mistress,' said Not-as-big-as-Medium-Sized-Jock-but-bigger-than-Wee-Jock-Jock.

'Really?'

'Aye, an' a big dollop o' cruelty,' Not-as-big-as-Medium-Sized-Jock-but-bigger-than-Wee-Jock-Jock

151

went on. 'Hamish trains 'em by runnin' aroound in a rabbit skin until a bird pounces on him.'

'That sounds awful!' said Tiffany.

'Ach, he's not too nasty aboot it. He just knocks them out wi' his heid, and then he's got a special oil he makes which he blows up their beak,' Not-as-big-as-Medium-Sized-Jock-but-bigger-than-Wee-Jock-Jock went on. 'When they wakes up, they thinks he's their mammy and'll do his biddin'.'

The buzzard was already a distant speck.

'He hardly seems to spend any time on the ground!' said Tiffany.

'Oh, aye. He sleeps in the buzzard's nest at night, mistress. He says it's wunnerfully warm. An' he spends all his time in the air,' Not-as-big-as-Medium-Sized-Jock-but-bigger-than-Wee-Jock-Jock added. 'He's ne'er happy unless he's got the wind under his kilt.'

'And the birds don't mind?'

'Ach, no, mistress. All the birds and beasts up here know it's good luck to be friends wi' the Nac Mac Feegle, mistress.'

'They do?'

'Well, to tell ye the truth, mistress, it's more that they know it's unlucky not to be friends wi' the Nac Mac Feegle.'

Tiffany looked at the sun. It was only a few hours away from setting.

'I must find the way in,' she said. 'Look, Not-as-small-as—'

'No'-as-big-as-Medium-Sized-Jock-but-bigger-than-Wee-Jock-Jock, mistress,' said the pictsie patiently.

'Yes, yes, thank you. Where is Rob Anybody? Where is *everybody*, in fact?'

The young pictsie looked a bit embarrassed.

'There's a bit o' a debate goin' on down below, mistress,' he said.

'Well, we have got to find my brother, OK? I *am* the kelda in this vicinity, yes?'

'It's a wee bit more comp-li-cat-ed than that, mistress. They're, er, discussin' ye . . .'

'Discussing *what* about me?'

Not-as-big-as-Medium-Sized-Jock-but-bigger-than-Wee-Jock-Jock looked as if he really didn't want to be standing there.

'Um, they're discussing . . . er . . . they . . .'

Tiffany gave up. The pictsie was blushing. Since he was blue to begin with, this turned him an unpleasant violet colour. 'I'll go back down the hole. Give my boots a push, will you, please?'

She slid down the dry dirt and Feegles scattered in the cave below as she landed.

When her eyes got accustomed to the gloom once more she saw that the galleries were crowded with pictsies again. Some of them were in the middle of washing, and many of them had, for some reason, smoothed down their red hair with grease. They all started at her as if caught in the act of something dreadful.

'We ought to be going if we're to follow the Queen,' she said, looking down at Rob Anybody, who'd been washing his face in a basin made of half a walnut shell. Water dripped off his beard, which he'd plaited up. There were three plaits in his long hair now too. If he turned suddenly he could probably whip somebody to death.

'Ach, weel,' he said, 'there's a wee matter we got tae sort oout, Kelda.' He twiddled the tiny facecloth in his hands. When Rob Anybody twiddled, he was worried.

'Yes?' said Tiffany.

'Er . . . will ye no' ha' a cup o' tea?' said Rob Anybody, and a pictsie staggered forward with a big gold cup that, once, must have been made for a king.

Tiffany took it. She *was* thirsty, after all. There was a sigh from the crowd when she sipped the tea. It was actually quite good.

'We stole a bag o' it fra' a pedlar who was asleep down by the high road,' said Rob Anybody. 'Good stuff, eh?' He patted down his hair with his wet hands.

Tiffany's cup stopped halfway to her lips. Perhaps the pictsies didn't realize how loudly they whispered, because her ear was on a level with a conversation.

'*Ach, she's a bit on the big side, no offence to her.*'

'*Aye, but a kelda has to be big, ye ken, to have lots of wee babbies.*'

'*Aye, fair enough, big wimmin is a' very well, but if a laddie was to try tae cuddle this one he'd had tae leave a chalk mark to show where he left off yesterday.*'

'*An' she's a bit young.*'

'*She neednae have any babbies yet, then. Or mebbe not too many at a time, say. Nae more than ten, mebbe.*'

'*Crivens, lads, what're ye talkin' aboout? 'Tis Rob*'

Anybody she'll choose anyway. Ye can see the big man's poor wee knees knocking fra' here!'

Tiffany lived on a farm. Any little beliefs that babies are delivered by storks or found under bushes tend to get sorted out early on if you live on a farm, especially when a cow is having a difficult calving in the middle of the night. And she'd helped with the lambing, when small hands could be very useful in difficult cases. She knew all about the bags of red chalk the rams had strapped to their chests, and why you knew later on that the ewes with the red smudges on their backs were going to be mothers in the spring. It's amazing what a child who is quiet and observant can learn, and this includes things people don't think she is old enough to know.

Her eye spotted Fion, on the other side of the hall. She was smiling in a worrying way.

'What's happening, Rob Anybody?' she said, laying the words down carefully.

'Ah, weel ... it's the clan rules, ye ken,' said the Feegle awkwardly. 'Ye being the new kelda an', an', weel, we're bound to ask ye, see, nae matter what we feel, we gotta ask ye mutter mutter mutter ...' He stepped back quickly.

'I didn't quite catch that,' said Tiffany.

'We've scrubbed up nice, ye ken,' Rob Anybody said. 'Some o' the lads actually had a bath in the dewpond, e'en though 'tis only May, and Big Yan washed under his arms for the first time ever, and Daft Wullie has picked ye a bonny bunch of flowers ...'

Daft Wullie stepped forward, swollen with nervous pride, and thrust the aforesaid bouquet into the air. They probably *had* been nice flowers, but he didn't have much idea of what a bunch was or how you picked one. Stems and leaves and dropping petals stuck out of his fist in all directions.

'Very nice,' said Tiffany, taking another sip of the tea.

'Guid, guid,' said Rob Anybody, wiping his forehead. 'So mebbe you'd like tae tell us mutter mutter mutter . . .'

'They want to know which one of them you're going to marry,' said Fion loudly. 'It's the rules. Ye have to choose, or quit as kelda. Ye have to choose yer man an' name the day.'

'Aye,' said Rob Anybody, not meeting Tiffany's eye.

Tiffany held the cup perfectly steady, but only because suddenly she couldn't move a muscle. She was thinking: *Aaargh! This is not happening to me! I can't— He couldn't— We wouldn't— They're not even— This is ridiculous! Run away!*

But she was aware of hundreds of nervous faces in the shadows. How you deal with this is going to be important, said her Second Thoughts. They're all watching you. And Fion wants to see what you'll do. You really didn't ought to dislike a girl four feet shorter than you, but you do.

'Well, this is very unexpected,' she said, forcing herself to smile. 'A big honour, of course.'

'Aye, aye,' said Rob Anybody, looking at the floor.

'And there's so many of you it'd be so hard to

choose,' Tiffany went on, still smiling. And her Second Thoughts said: He's not happy about it either!

'Aye, it will that,' said Rob Anybody.

'I'd just like to have a little fresh air while I think about it,' said Tiffany, and didn't let the smile fade until she was out on the mound again.

She crouched down and peered among the primrose leaves. 'Toad!' she yelled.

The toad crawled out, chewing something. 'Hm?' it said.

'They want to *marry* me!'

'Mm phmm ffm mm?'

'What are you eating?'

The toad swallowed. 'A very undernourished slug,' it said.

'I said they want to marry me!'

'And?'

'And? Well, just— Just *think*!'

'Oh, right, yeah, the height thing,' said the toad. 'It might not seem much now, but when you're five feet seven he'll still be six inches high—'

'Don't laugh at me! I'm the kelda!'

'Well, of course, that's the point, isn't it,' said the toad. 'As far as they're concerned, there's rules. The new kelda marries the warrior of her choice and settles down and has lots and lots of Feegles. It'd be a terrible insult to refuse—'

'I am not going to marry a Feegle! I can't have hundreds of babies! Tell me what to do!'

'Me? Tell the kelda what to do? I wouldn't dare,' said the toad. 'And I don't like being shouted at. Even toads have their pride, you know.' It crawled back into the leaves.

Tiffany took a deep breath, ready to shout, and then closed her mouth.

The old kelda must've known about this, she thought. So . . . she must have thought I'd be able to deal with it. It's just the rules, and they didn't know what to do about them. None of them wanted to marry a big girl like her, even if none of them would admit it. It was just the rules.

There must be a way round it. There had to be. But she had to accept a husband and she had to name the day. They'd told her that.

She stared at the thorn trees for a moment. Hmm, she thought.

She slid back down the hole.

The pictsies were waiting nervously, every scarred and bearded face watching hers.

'I accept *you*, Rob Anybody,' she said.

Rob Anybody's face became a mask of terror. She heard him mutter, 'Aw crivens!' in a tiny voice.

'But of course, it's the bride who names the day, isn't it?' said Tiffany cheerfully. 'Everyone knows that.'

'Aye,' Rob Anybody quavered. 'That's the tradition, right enough.'

'Then I shall.' Tiffany took a deep breath. 'At the end of the world is a great big mountain of granite rock a mile high,' she said. 'And every year, a tiny bird flies all the way to the rock and wipes its beak on it. Well, when the little bird has worn the mountain down to the size of a grain of sand . . . that's the day I'll marry you, Rob Anybody Feegle!'

Rob Anybody's terror turned to outright panic, but then he hesitated and, very slowly, started to grin.

'Aye, guid idea,' he said slowly. 'It doesnae do tae rush these things.'

'Absolutely,' said Tiffany.

'And that'd gi' us time tae sort ooout the guest list an' a' that,' the pictsie went on.

'That's right.'

'Plus there's a' that business wi' the wedding dress and buckets o' flowers and a' that kind of stuff,' said Rob Anybody, looking more cheerful by the second. 'That sort o' thing can tak' for ever, ye ken.'

'Oh yes,' said Tiffany.

'But she's really just said no!' Fion burst out. 'It'd take millions of years for the bird to—'

'She said aye!' Rob Anybody shouted. 'Ye al' heard her, lads! An' she's named the day! That's the rules!'

'Nae problem aboot the mountain, neither,' said Daft Wullie, still holding out the flowers. 'Just ye tell us where it is and I reckon we could ha' it doon a lot faster than any wee burdie—'

'It's got to be the bird!' yelled Rob Anybody desperately. 'OK? The wee burdie! Nae more arguin'! Anyone feelin' like arguin' will feel ma boot! Some o' us ha' got a wee laddie to steal back fra' the Quin!' He drew his sword and waved it in the air. 'Who's coming wi' me?'

That seemed to work. The Nac Mac Feegle liked clear goals. Hundreds of swords and battleaxes, and one bunch of battered flowers in the case of Daft Wullie, were thrust into the air and the war cry of the Nac Mac Feegle echoed around the chamber. The period of time it takes a pictsie to go from normal to mad fighting mood is so tiny it can't be measured on the smallest clock.

Unfortunately, since the pictsies were very individualistic, each one had his own cry and Tiffany could only make out a few over the din:

'*They can tak' oour lives but they cannae tak' oour troousers!*'

'*Bang went saxpence!*'

'*Ye'll tak' the high road an' I'll tak' yer wallet!*'

'*There can only be one t'ousand!*'

'*Ach, stick it up yer trakkans!*'

. . . but the voices gradually came together in one roar that shook the walls:

'*Nae king! Nae quin! Nae laird! Nae master! We willnae be fooled again!*'

This died away, a cloud of dust dropped from the roof, and there was silence.

'Let's gae!' cried Rob Anybody.

As one Feegle, the pictsies swarmed down the galleries and across the floor and up the slope to the hole. In a few seconds the chamber was empty, except for the gonnagle and Fion.

'Where have they gone?' said Tiffany.

'Ach, they just go,' said Fion, shrugging. 'I'm going tae stay here and look after the fire. *Someone* ought to act like a proper kelda.' She glared at Tiffany.

'I do hope you find a clan for yourself soon, Fion,'

said Tiffany sweetly. The pictsie scowled at her.

'They'll run arroound for a while, mebbe stun a few bunnies and fall over a few times,' said William. 'They'll slow down when they find oout they don't ken what they're supposed to do yet.'

'Do they always just run off like this?' said Tiffany.

'Ach, well, Rob Anybody disnae want too much talk about marryin',' said William, grinning.

'Yes, we have a lot in common in that respect,' said Tiffany.

She pulled herself out of the hole, and found the toad waiting for her.

'I listened in,' it said. 'Well done. Very clever. Very diplomatic.'

Tiffany looked around. There were a few hours to sunset, but the shadows were already lengthening.

'We'd better be going,' she said, tying on her apron. 'And you're coming, toad.'

'Well, I don't know much about how to get into—' the toad began, trying to back away. But toads can't back up easily, and Tiffany grabbed it and put it in her apron pocket.

She headed for the mounds and stones. My brother will never grow up, she thought, as she ran across the turf. That's what the old lady said. How does that work? What kind of a place is it where you never grow up?

The mounds got nearer. She saw William and Not-as-big-as-Medium-Sized-Jock-but-bigger-than-Wee-Jock-Jock running along beside her, but there was no sign of the rest of the Nac Mac Feegle.

And then she was among the mounds. Her sisters had told her that there were more dead kings buried under there, but it had never frightened her. Nothing on the downs had ever frightened her.

But it was cold here. She'd never noticed that before.

Find a place where the time doesn't fit. Well, the mounds were history. So were the old stones. Did they fit here? Well, yes, they belonged to the past, but they'd ridden on the hills for thousands of years. They'd grown old here. They were part of the landscape.

The low sun made the shadows lengthen. That was when the Chalk revealed its secrets. At some places, when the light was right, you could see the edges of old fields and tracks. The shadows showed up what brilliant noonlight couldn't see.

Tiffany had made up 'noonlight'.

She couldn't even see hoofprints. She wandered around the trilithons, which looked a bit like huge stone doorways, but even when she tried walking through them both ways nothing happened.

This wasn't according to plan. There should have been a magic door. She was sure of that.

A bubbling feeling in her ear suggested that someone was playing the mousepipes. She looked around, and saw William the gonnagle standing on a fallen stone. His cheeks were bulging and so was the bag of the mousepipes.

She waved at him. 'Can you see anything?' she called.

William took the pipe out of his mouth and the bubbling stopped. 'Oh, aye,' he said.

'The way to the Queen's land?'

'Oh, aye.'

'Well, would you care to *tell* me?'

'I dinnae need to tell a kelda,' said William. 'A kelda would see the clear way hersel'.'

'But you *could* tell me!'

'Aye, and you coulda said "please",' said William. 'I'm ninety-six years old. I'm nae a dolly in yer dolly hoose. Yer granny was a fiiine wuman, but I'll no' be ordered about by a wee chit of a girl.'

Tiffany stared for a moment and then lifted the toad out of her apron pocket.

'Chit?' she said.

'It means something very small,' said the toad. 'Trust me.'

'*He's* calling *me* small—!'

'I'm biggerrr on the inside!' said William. 'And I dare say your da' wouldnae be happy if a big giant of a wee girl came stampin' aroound ordering *him* aboout!'

'The old kelda ordered people about!' said Tiffany.

'Aye! Because she'd earned rrrespect!' The gonnagle's voice seemed to echo around the stones.

'Please, I don't know what to *do*!' wailed Tiffany.

William stared at her. 'Ach, weel, yer no' doin' too badly so far,' he said, in a nicer tone of voice. 'Ye got Rob Anybody out of marryin' ye wi'oout breakin' the rules, and ye're a game lass, I'll gi' ye that. Ye'll find the way if ye tak' yer time. Just don't stamp yer foot and expect the world to do yer biddin'. Al' ye're doing is shoutin' for sweeties, yer ken. Use yer eyes. Use yer heid.'

He put the pipe back in his mouth, puffed his cheeks until the skin bag was full, and made Tiffany's ears bubble again.

'What about you, toad?' said Tiffany, looking into the apron pocket.

'You're on your own, I'm afraid,' said the toad. 'Whoever I used to be, I didn't know much about finding invisible doors. And I resent being press-ganged too, I may say.'

'But . . . I don't know what to do! Is there a magic word I should say?'

'I don't know, *is* there a magic word you should say?' said the toad, and turned over.

Tiffany was aware that the Nac Mac Feegle were turning up. They had a nasty habit of being really quiet when they wanted to.

Oh, no, she thought. They think I know what to do! This isn't *fair*! I've not got any training for this. I haven't been to the witch school! I can't even find *that*! The opening must be somewhere around here and there must be clues but I don't know what they are!

They're watching me to see if I'm any good. And I'm good at cheese, and that's all. *But a witch Deals With Things . . .*

She shifted the toad around in her pocket and felt the weight of the book *Diseases of the Sheep*.

When she pulled it out, she heard a sigh go up from the assembled pictsies.

They think words are magical . . .

She opened the book at random, and frowned.

'Cloggets,' she said aloud. Around her, the pictsies nodded their heads and nudged one another.

'Cloggets are a trembling of the greebs in hoggets,' she read, 'which can lead to inflammation of the lower pasks. If untreated, it may lead to the more serious condition of Sloke. Recommended treatment is daily dosing with turpentine until there is no longer either any trembling, or turpentine, or sheep.'

She risked looking up. Feegles were watching her from every stone and mound. They looked impressed.

However, the words in *Diseases of the Sheep* cut no ice with magic doorways.

'Scrabbity,' read Tiffany. There was a ripple of anticipation.

'Scrabbity is a flaky skin condition, particularly around the lollets. Turpentine is a useful remedy—'

And then she saw, out of the corner of her eye, the teddy bear.

It was very small, and the kind of red you don't quite get in nature. Tiffany knew what it was. Wentworth loved the teddy-bear sweets. They tasted like glue mixed with sugar and were made of 100% Artificial Additives.

'Ah,' she said aloud. 'My brother was certainly brought here . . .'

This caused a stir.

She walked forward, reading aloud about Garget of the Nostrils and the Staggers but keeping an eye on the ground. And there was another teddy-bear sweet, green this time and quite hard to see against the turf.

O-K, Tiffany thought.

There was one of the three-stone arches a little way away; two big stones with another one laid across the top of them. She'd walked through it before, and nothing had happened,

But nothing *should* happen, she thought. You can't leave a doorway into your world that *anyone* can walk through, otherwise people would wander in and out by accident. You'd have to know it was there.

Perhaps that's the only way it would work.

Fine. Then I'll believe that this is the entrance.

She stepped through, and saw an astonishing sight: green grass, blue sky becoming pink around the setting sun, a few little white clouds late for bed, and a general warm, honey-coloured look to everything. It was amazing that there could be a sight like this. The fact that Tiffany had seen it nearly every day of her life didn't make it any less fantastic. As a bonus, you didn't even have to look through any kind of stone arch to see it. You could see it by standing practically *anywhere*.

Except . . .

. . . something was wrong. Tiffany walked through the arch several times, and still wasn't quite sure. She held up a hand at arm's length, trying to measure the sun's height against the horizon.

And then she saw the bird. It was a swallow, hunting flies, and a swoop took it behind the stones.

The effect was . . . odd, and almost upsetting. It passed behind the stone and she felt her eyes move to follow the swoop . . . but it was late. There was a moment when the swallow should have appeared, and it didn't.

Then it passed across the gap *and for a moment was on both sides of the other stone at the same time.*

Seeing it made Tiffany feel that her eyeballs had been pulled out and turned round.

Look for a place where the time doesn't fit . . .

'The world seen through that gap is at least one second behind the time here,' she said, trying to sound as certain as possible. 'I thi— I *know* this is the entrance.'

There was some whooping and clapping from the Nac Mac Feegles, and they surged across the turf towards her.

'That was *great*, al' that reading' ye did!' said Rob Anybody. 'I didnae understand a single word o' it!'

'Aye, it must be powerful language if you cannae make oout what the heel it's goin' on aboot!' said another pictsie.

'Ye definitely ha' got the makin's of a kelda, mistress,' said Not-as-big-as-Medium-Sized-Jock-but-bigger-than-Wee-Jock-Jock.

'Aye!' said Daft Wullie. 'It was smashin' the way you spotted them sweeties and didnae let on! We didnae think you'd see the wee green one too!'

The rest of the pictsies stopped cheering and glared at him.

'What did I say? What did I say?' he said.

Tiffany sagged. 'You all knew that was the way through, didn't you?' she said.

'Oh, aye,' said Rob Anybody. 'We ken that kind of stuff. We used tae live in the Quin's country, ye ken, but we rebelled against her evil rule—'

'An' we did that, an' then she threw us oout on account o' bein' drunk an' stealin' and fightin' al' the time,' said Daft Wullie.

'It wasnae like that at al'!' roared Rob Anybody.

'And you were waiting to see if I *could* find the way, right?' said Tiffany, before a fight could start.

'Aye. Ye did well, lassie.'

Tiffany shook her head. 'No, I didn't,' she said. 'I didn't do any real magic. I don't know how. I just looked at things and worked them out. It was cheating, really.'

The pictsies looked at one another.

'Ah, weel,' said Rob Anybody. 'What's magic, eh? Just wavin' a stick an' sayin' a few wee magical words. An' what's so clever aboot that, eh? But lookin' at things, really *lookin'* at 'em, and then workin' 'em oout, now, that's a *real* skill.'

'Aye, it is,' said William the gonnagle, to Tiffany's surprise. 'Ye used yer eyes and used yer heid. That's what a real hag does. The magicking is just there for advertisin'.'

'Oh,' said Tiffany, cheering up. 'Really? Well, then . . . there's our door, everyone!'

'Right,' said Rob Anybody. 'Now show us the way through.'

Tiffany hesitated and then thought: I can feel myself thinking. I'm *watching* the way I'm thinking. And what am I thinking? I'm thinking: I walked through this arch before, and nothing happened.

But I wasn't looking then. I wasn't thinking, either. Not properly.

The world I can see through the arch isn't actually real. It just looks as though it is. It's a sort of . . . magical picture, put there to disguise the entrance. And if you don't pay attention, well, you just walk in and out of it and you don't realize it.

Aha . . .

She walked through the arch. Nothing happened. The Nac Mac Feegles watched her solemnly.

O-K, she thought. I'm still being fooled, aren't I . . . ?

She stood in front of the stones, and stretched out her hand on either side of her, and shut her eyes. Very slowly she stepped forward . . .

Something crunched under her boots, but she didn't open her eyes until she couldn't feel the stones any more. When she did open them . . .

. . . it was a black and white landscape.

CHAPTER 8

Land of Winter

'Aye, she's got First Sight, sure enough,' said William's voice behind Tiffany as she stared into the world of the Queen. 'She's seein' what's *really* there . . .'

Snow stretched away under a sky so dirty white that Tiffany might have been standing inside a ping-pong ball. Only black trunks and scribbly branches of the trees, here and there, told her where the land stopped and the sky began . . .

. . . those, and of course, the hoofprints. They stretched away towards a forest of black trees, boughed with snow.

The cold was like little needles all over her skin.

She looked down, and saw the Nac Mac Feegles pouring through the gate, waist deep in the snow. They spread out, without speaking. Some of them had drawn their swords.

They weren't laughing and joking now. They were watchful.

'Right, then,' said Rob Anybody. 'Well done. You wait here for us and we'll get your wee brother back, nae problemo—'

'I'm coming too!' snapped Tiffany.

'Nay, the kelda disnae—'

'This one dis!' said Tiffany, shivering. 'I mean *does*! He's my brother. And *where* are we?'

Rob Anybody glanced up at the pale sky. There was no sun anywhere. 'Ye're here noo,' he said, 'so mebbe there's nae harm in tellin' ye. This is what ye call Fairyland.'

'*Fairyland?* No, it's not! I've seen pictures! Fairyland is . . . is all trees and flowers and sunshine and, and tinklyness! Dumpy little babies in romper suits with horns! People with wings! Er . . . and weird people! I've seen pictures!'

'It isnae always like this,' said Rob Anybody shortly. 'An' ye cannae come wi' us because ye ha' nae weapon, mistress.'

'What happened to my frying pan?' said Tiffany.

Something bumped against her heels. She looked around and saw Not-as-big-as-Medium-Sized-Jock-but-bigger-than-Wee-Jock-Jock hold up the pan triumphantly.

'OK, ye have the pan,' said Rob Anybody, 'but what ye need here is a sword of thunderbolt iron. That's like the, you know, official weapon for invadin' Fairyland . . .'

'I know how to use the use the pan,' said Tiffany. 'And I'm—'

'Incomin'!' yelled Daft Wullie.

Tiffany saw a line of black dots in the distance, and felt someone climb up her back and stand on her head.

'It's the black dogs,' Not-as-big-as-Medium-Sized-Jock-but-bigger-than-Wee-Jock-Jock announced. 'Dozens o' 'em, big man.'

'We'll never outrun the dogs!' Tiffany cried, grabbing her pan.

'Dinnae need to,' said Rob Anybody. 'We got the gonnagle wi' us this time. Ye might like to stick yer fingers in yer ears, though.'

William, with his eyes fixed on the approaching pack, was unscrewing some of the pipes from the mousepipes and putting them in a bag he carried hanging from his shoulder.

The dogs were much closer now. Tiffany could see the razor teeth and the burning eyes.

Slowly, William took out some much shorter, smaller pipes that had a silvery look to them, and screwed them in place. He had the look of someone who wasn't going to rush.

Tiffany gripped the handle of her pan. The dogs weren't barking. It would have been slightly less scary if they were.

William swung the mousepipes under his arm and blew into one until the bag bulged.

'I shall play,' he announced, as the dogs got close enough for Tiffany to see the drool, 'that firrrrm favourite, "The King Underrrr Waterrrr".'

As one pictsie, the Nac Mac Feegles dropped

their swords and put their hands over their ears.

William put the mouthpiece to his lips, tapped his foot once or twice and, as a dog gathered itself to leap at Tiffany, began to play.

A lot of things happened at more or less the same time. All Tiffany's teeth started to buzz. The pan vibrated in her hands and dropped onto the snow. The dog in front of her went cross-eyed and, instead of leaping, tumbled forward.

The grimhounds paid no attention to the pictsies. They howled. They spun around. They tried to bite their own tails. They stumbled, and ran into one another. The line of panting death broke into dozens of desperate animals, twisting and writhing and trying to escape from their own skins.

The snow was melting in a circle around William, whose cheeks were red with effort. Steam was rising.

He took the pipe from his mouth. The grimhounds, struggling in the slush, raised their heads. And then, as one dog, they put their tails between their legs and ran like greyhounds back across the snow.

'Weel, they ken we're here noo,' said Rob Anybody, wiping tears from his eyes.

'Ot aggened?' said Tiffany, touching her teeth to check that they were all still there.

'He played the notes o' pain,' Rob Anybody explained. 'Ye cannae hear 'em 'cos they're pitched so high, but the doggies can. Hurts 'em in their heids. Now we'd better get movin' before she sends somethin' else.'

'The Queen sent them? But they're like something out of nightmares!' said Tiffany.

'Oh aye,' said Rob Anybody. 'That's where she got them.'

Tiffany looked at William the gonnagle. He was calmly replacing the pipes. He saw her staring at him, looked up, and winked.

'The Nac Mac Feegle tak' music verrrrrra' seriously,' he said. And then he nodded at the snow near Tiffany's foot.

There was a sugary yellow teddy bear in the snow, made of 100% Artificial Additives.

And the snow, all round Tiffany, was melting away.

Two pictsies carried Tiffany easily. She skimmed across the snow, the clan running beside her.

No sun in the sky. Even on the dullest days, you could generally see where the sun was, but not here. And there was something else that was strange, something she couldn't quite give a name to. This didn't feel like a real place. She didn't know why she felt that, but something was wrong with the horizon. It looked close enough to touch, which was silly.

And things were not . . . finished. Like the trees in the forest they were heading towards, for example. A tree is a tree, she thought. Close up or far away, it's a tree. It has bark and branches and roots. And you know they're *there*, even if the tree is so far away that it's a blob.

The trees here, though, were different. She had a strong feeling that they *were* blobs, and were growing the roots and twigs and other details as she got closer, as if they were thinking, 'Quick, someone's coming! Look real!'

It was like being in a painting where the artist hadn't bothered much with the things in the distance, but had quickly rushed a bit of realness anywhere you were looking.

The air was cold and dead, like the air in old cellars.

The light grew dimmer as they reached the forest. In between the trees it became blue and eerie.

No birds, she thought.

'Stop,' she said.

The pictsies lowered her to the ground, but Rob Anybody said: 'We shouldnae hang aroound here too long. Heids up, lads.'

Tiffany lifted out the toad. It blinked at the snow.

'Oh, shoap,' it muttered. 'This is not good. I should be hibernating.'

'Why is everything so . . . strange?'

'Can't help you there,' said the toad. 'I just see snow, I just see ice, I just see freezing to death. I'm listening to my inner toad here.'

'It's not that cold!'

'Feels cold . . . to . . . me . . .' The toad shut its eyes. Tiffany sighed, and lowered it into her pocket.

'I'll tell ye where ye are,' said Rob Anybody, his eyes still scanning the blue shadows. 'Ye ken them wee bitty bugs that clings onto the sheeps and suck themsel' full o' blood and then drop off again? This whole world is like one o' them.'

'You mean like a, a tick? A parasite? A *vampire*?'

'Oh, aye. It floats aroound until it finds a place that's weak on a world where no one's payin' attention, and opens a door. Then the Quin sends in her folk. For the stealin', ye ken. Raidin' o' barns, rustlin' of cattle—'

'We use' to like stealin' the coo beasties,' said Daft Wullie.

'Wullie,' said Rob Anybody, pointing his sword, 'you ken I said there wuz times you should *think* before opening yer big fat gob?'

'Aye, Rob.'

'Weel, that wuz one o' them times.' Rob turned and looked up at Tiffany rather bashfully. 'Aye, we wuz wild champion robbers for the Quin,' he said. 'People wouldnae e'en go a-huntin' for fear o' little men. But 'twas ne'er enough for her. She always wanted more. But we said it's no' *right* to steal an ol' lady's only pig, or the food from them as dinnae ha' enough to eat. A Feegle has nae worries about stealin' a golden cup from a rich bigjob, ye ken, but takin' awa' the—'

– cup an old man kept his false teeth in made them feel ashamed, they said. The Nac Mac Feegle would fight and steal, certainly, but who wanted to fight the weak and steal from the poor?

Tiffany listened, at the end of the shadowy wood, to the story of a little world where nothing grew, where no sun shone, and where everything had to come from somewhere else. It was a world that took, and gave nothing back except fear. It raided – and people learned to stay in bed when they heard strange noises at night, because if anyone gave her trouble the Queen could control their dreams.

Tiffany couldn't quite pick up how she did this, but that's where things like the grimhounds and the headless horseman came from. These dreams were . . . more real. The Queen could take dreams and make them more . . . solid. You could step inside them and vanish. And you didn't wake up before the monsters caught up with you . . .

The Queen's people wouldn't just take food. They'd take people too—

'– like pipers,' said William the gonnagle. 'Fairies can't make music, ye ken. She'll steal a man awa' for the music he makes.'

'And she takes children,' said Tiffany.

'Aye. Your wee brother's not the first,' said Rob Anybody. 'There's no' a lot of fun and laughter here, ye ken. She thinks she's good wi' children.'

'The old kelda said she wouldn't harm him,' said Tiffany. 'That's true, isn't it?'

You could read the Nac Mac Feegle like a book. And it would be a big, simple book with pictures of Spot the Dog and a Big Red Ball and one or two short sentences on each page. What they were thinking turned up right there on their faces and, now, they were all wearing a look that said: Crivens, I hope she disnae ask us the question we dinnae wantae answer . . .

'That *is* true, isn't it?' she said.

'Oh, aye,' said Rob Anybody slowly. 'She didnae lie to ye there. The Quin'll try to be kind to him, but she disnae know how. She's an elf. They're no' very good at thinking of other people.'

'What will happen to him if we don't get him back?'

Again, there was that 'we dinnae like the way this is going' look.

'I *said*—' Tiffany repeated.

'I darrresay she'll send him back, in due time,' said William. 'An' he willnae be any olderr. Nothing grows old here. Nothing grows. Nothing at all.'

'So he'll be all right?'

Rob Anybody made a noise in his throat. It sounded like a voice that was trying to say 'aye' but was being argued with by a brain that knew the answer was 'no'.

'Tell me what you're not telling me,' said Tiffany.

Daft Wullie was the first to speak. 'That's a lot o' stuff,' he said. 'For example, the meltin' point o' lead is—'

'Time passes slower the deeper you go intae this place,' said Rob Anybody quickly. 'Years pass like days. The Quin'll get tired o' the wee lad after a coupla months, mebbe. A coupla months *here*, ye ken, where the time is slow an' heavy. But when he comes back into the mortal world, you'll be an old lady, or mebbe you'll be deid. So if youse has bairns o' yer own, you'd better tell them to watch out for a wee sticky kid wanderin' the hills shoutin' for sweeties, 'cos that'll be their Uncle Wentworth. That wouldna be the worst o' it, neither. Live in dreams for too long and ye go mad, ye can never wake up prop'ly, ye can never get the hang o' reality again . . .'

Tiffany stared at him.

'It's happened before,' said William.

'I *will* get him back,' said Tiffany quietly.

'We doon't doubt it,' said Rob Anybody. 'An' wheree'er ye go, we'll come with ye. The Nac Mac Feegle are afeared o' nothing!'

A cheer went up, but it seemed to Tiffany that the blue shadows sucked all the sound away.

'Aye, nothin' exceptin' lawyers mmph mmph,' Daft Wullie tried to say, before Rob managed to shut him up.

Tiffany turned back to the line of hoofprints, and began to walk.

The snow squeaked unpleasantly underfoot.

She went a little way, watching the trees get realer as she approached them, and then looked around.

All the Nac Mac Feegles were creeping along behind her. Rob Anybody gave her a cheery nod. And all her footprints had become holes in the snow, with grass showing through.

The trees began to annoy her. The way things changed was more frightening than any monster. You could hit a monster, but you couldn't hit a forest. And she wanted to hit *something*.

She stopped and scraped some snow away from the base of a tree and, just for a moment, there was nothing but greyness where it had been. As she watched, the bark grew down to where the snow was. Then it just stayed there, pretending it had been there all the time.

It was a lot more worrying than the grimhounds.

They were just monsters. They could be beaten. This was . . . frightening . . .

She was second thinking again. She felt the fear grow, she felt her stomach become a red-hot lump, she felt her elbows begin to sweat. But it was . . . not connected. She *watched* herself being frightened, and that meant that there was still this part of herself, the watching part, that wasn't.

The trouble was, it was being carried on legs that were. It had to be very careful.

And that was where it went wrong. Fear gripped her, all at once. She was in a strange world, with monsters, being followed by hundreds of little blue thieves. And . . . Black dogs. Headless horsemen. Monsters in the river. Sheep whizzing backwards across fields. Voices under the bed . . .

The terror took her. But, because she was Tiffany, she ran towards it, raising the pan. She had to get through the forest, find the Queen, get her brother, leave this place!

Somewhere behind her, voices started to shout—

She woke up.

There was no snow, but there *was* the whiteness of the bedsheet and the plaster ceiling of her bedroom. She stared at it for a while, then leaned down and peered under the bed.

There was nothing there but the guzunder. When she flung open the door of the doll's house, there was no one inside but the two toy soldiers and the teddy bear and the headless dolly.

The walls were solid. The floor creaked like it

always did. Her slippers were the same as they always were: old, comfortable and with all the pink fluff worn off.

She stood in the middle of the floor and said, very quietly, 'Is there anybody there?'

Sheep baa'd on the distant hillside, but they probably hadn't heard her.

The door squeaked open and the cat Ratbag came in. He rubbed up against her legs, purring like a distant thunderstorm, and then went and curled up on her bed.

Tiffany got dressed thoughtfully, daring the room to do something strange.

When she got downstairs, breakfast was cooking. Her mother was busy at the sink.

Tiffany darted out through the scullery and into the dairy. She scrambled on hands and knees around the floor, peering under the sink and behind cupboards.

'You can come out now, honestly,' she said.

No one came. She was alone in the room. She'd often been alone in the room, and had enjoyed it. It was almost her private territory. But now, somehow, it was too empty, too clean . . .

When she wandered back into the kitchen her mother was still standing by the sink, washing dishes, but a plate of steaming porridge had been put down in the one set place on the table.

'I'll make some more butter today,' said Tiffany carefully, sitting down. 'I might as well while we're getting all this milk.'

Her mother nodded, and put a plate on the draining board beside the sink.

'I haven't done anything wrong, have I?' said Tiffany.

Her mother shook her head.

Tiffany sighed. 'And then she woke up and it was all a dream.' It was just about the worst ending you could have to any story. But it had all seemed so *real*. She could remember the smoky smell in the pictsies' cave, and the way . . . who was it? . . . oh, yes, he'd been called Rob Anybody . . . the way Rob Anybody had always been so nervous about talking to her.

It was strange, she thought, that Ratbag had rubbed up against her. He'd sleep on her bed if he could get away with it, but during the day he kept well out of Tiffany's way. How odd . . .

There was a rattling noise near the mantelpiece. The china shepherdess on Granny's shelf was moving sideways of its own accord and, as Tiffany watched with her porridge spoon halfway to her mouth, it slid off and smashed on the floor.

The rattling went on. Now it was coming from the big oven. She should see the door actually shaking on the hinges.

She turned to her mother, and saw her put another plate down by the sink. But it wasn't being held in a hand . . .

The oven door burst open and slid across the floor.

'*Dinnae eat the porridge!*'

Nac Mac Feegles spilled out into the room, hundreds of them, pouring across the tiles.

The walls were shifting. The floor moved. And now the thing turning round at the sink was not even human but just ... stuff, no more human than a gingerbread man, grey as old dough, changing shape as it lumbered towards Tiffany.

The pictsies surged past her in a flurry of snow.

She looked up at the thing's tiny black eyes.

The scream came from somewhere deep inside. There was no Second Thought, no first thought, just a scream. It seemed to spread out as it left Tiffany's mouth until it became a black tunnel in front of her, and as she fell into it she heard, in the commotion behind her:

'Who d'yer think ye're lookin' at, pal? Crivens, but ye're gonna get sich a kickin'!'

Tiffany opened her eyes.

She was lying on damp ground in the snowy, gloomy wood. Pictsies were watching her carefully but, she saw, there were others behind them staring outwards, into the gloom amongst the tree trunks.

There was ... stuff in the trees. Lumps of stuff. It was grey, and hung there like old cloth.

She turned her head and saw William standing beside her, looking at her with concern.

'That was a dream, wasn't it ...?' she said.

'Weel noo,' said William, 'it was, and therrre again, it wasnae ...'

Tiffany sat up suddenly, causing the pictsies to leap back.

'But that ... thing was in it, and then you all came

out of the oven!' she said. 'You were *in* my dream! What is— *was* that creature?'

William the gonnagle stared at her as if trying to make up his mind.

'That was what we call a drome,' he said. 'Nothing here really belongs here, remember? Everything is a reflection from outside, or something kidnapped from another worrrld, or mebbe something the Quin has made outa magic. It was hidin' in the trees, and ye was goin' so fast ye didnae see it. Ye ken spiders?'

'Of course!'

'Well, spiders spin webs. Dromes spin dreams. It's easy in this place. The world you come from is nearly real. This place is nearly unreal, so it's almost a dream anywa'. And the drome makes a dream for ye, wi' a trap in it. If ye eats anythin' in the dream, ye'll never wanta' leave it.'

He looked as though Tiffany should have been impressed.

'What's in it for the drome?' she asked.

'It likes watchin' dreams. It has fun watching ye ha' fun. An' it'll watch ye eatin' dream food, until ye starve to death. Then the drome'll eat ye. Not right away, o' course. It'll wait until ye've gone a wee bit runny, because it hasnae teeth.'

'So how can anyone get out?'

'The best way is to find the drome,' said Rob Anybody. 'It'll be in the dream with you, in disguise. Then ye just gives it a good kickin'.'

'By kicking you mean—?'

'Choppin' its heid off generally works.'

Now, Tiffany thought, I am impressed. I wish I wasn't. 'And this is Fairyland?' she said.

'Aye. Ye could say it's the bit the tourists dinnae see,' said William. 'An' ye did well. Ye were fightin' it. Ye knew it wasnae right.'

Tiffany remembered the friendly cat, and the falling shepherdess. She'd been trying to send messages to herself. She should have listened.

'Thank you for coming after me,' she said meekly. 'How did you do it?'

'Ach, we can generally find a way intae *anywhere*, even a dream,' said William, smiling. 'We're a stealin' folk, after all.' A piece of the drome fell out of the tree and flopped onto the snow.

'One of them won't get me again!' said Tiffany.

'Aye. I believe you. Ye have murrrder in yer eyes,' said William, with a touch of admiration. 'If I was a drome I'd be pretty fearful noo, if I had a brain. There'll be more of them, mark you, and some of 'em are cunning. The Quin uses 'em as guards.'

'I won't be fooled!' Tiffany remembered the horror of the moment when the thing had lumbered around changing shape. It was worse because it was in her house, her *place*. She'd felt real terror as the big shapeless thing crashed across the kitchen, but the anger had been there too. It was invading *her place*.

The thing wasn't just trying to kill her, it was *insulting* her . . .

William was watching her.

'Aye, ye're lookin' mighty fierce,' he said. 'Ye must

love your wee brother to face a' these monsters for him . . .'

And Tiffany couldn't stop her thoughts. I don't love him. I know I don't. He's just so . . . sticky, and can't keep up, and I have to spend too much time looking after him, and he's always screaming for things. I can't talk to him. He just *wants* all the time.

But her Second Thinking said: He's *mine*. My place, my home, my brother! How dare anything touch what's *mine*!

She'd been brought up not to be selfish. She knew she wasn't, not in the way people meant. She tried to think of other people. She never took the last slice of bread. This was a different feeling.

She wasn't being brave or noble or kind. She was doing this because it had to be done, because there was no way that she could not do it. She thought of:

. . . *Granny Aching's light, weaving slowly across the downs, on freezing, sparkly nights or in storms like a raging war, saving lambs from the creeping frost or rams from the precipice. She froze and struggled and tramped through the night for idiot sheep that never said thank you and would probably be just as stupid tomorrow, and get into the same trouble again. And she did it because not doing it was unthinkable.*

There had been the time when they met the pedlar and the donkey in the lane. It was a small donkey and could hardly be seen under the pack he'd piled on it. And he was thrashing it because it had fallen over.

Tiffany had cried to see that, and Granny had looked

at her and then said something to Thunder and Lightning . . .

The pedlar had stopped when he heard the growling. The sheepdogs had taken up position on either side of the man, so that he couldn't quite see them both at once. He raised his stick as if to hit Lightning, and Thunder's growl grew louder.

'I'd advise ye not to do that,' said Granny.

He wasn't a stupid man. The eyes of the dogs were like steel balls. He lowered his arm.

'Now throw down the stick,' said Granny. The man did so, dropping it into the dust as though it had suddenly grown red-hot.

Granny Aching walked forward and picked it up. Tiffany remembered that it was a willow twig, long and whippy.

Suddenly, so fast that her hand was a blur, Granny sliced it across the man's face twice, leaving two long red marks. He began to move and some desperate thought must have saved him, because now the dogs were almost frantic for the command to leap.

'Hurts, don't it,' said Granny pleasantly. 'Now, I knows who you are, and I reckon you knows who I am. You sell pots and pans and they ain't bad, as I recall. But if I put out the word you'll have no business in my hills. Be told. Better to feed your beast than whip it. You hear me?'

With his eyes shut and his hands shaking, the man nodded.

'That'll do,' said Granny Aching, and instantly the dogs became, once more, two ordinary sheepdogs, who *came and sat either side of her with their tongues hanging out.*

Tiffany watched the man unpack some of the load and strap it to his own back and then, with great care, urge the donkey on along the road. Granny watched him go while filling her pipe with Jolly Sailor. Then, as she lit it, she said, as if the thought had just occurred to her:

'Them as can do, has to do for them as can't. And someone has to speak up for them as has no voices.'

Tiffany thought: Is this what being a witch is? It wasn't what I expected! When do the *good* bits happen?

She stood up. 'Let's keep going,' she said.

'Aren't ye tired?' said Rob.

'We're going to keep going!'

'Aye? Weel, she's probably headed for her place beyond the wood. If we dinnae carry ye, it'll tak' aboout a coupla hours—'

'I'll walk!' The memory of the huge dead face of the drome was trying to come back into her mind, but fury gave it no space. 'Where's the frying pan? Thank you! Let's go!'

She set off through the strange trees. The hoofprints almost glowed in the gloom. Here and there other tracks crossed them, tracks that could have been birds' feet, rough round footprints that could have been made by anything, squiggly lines that a snake might make, if there were such things as snow snakes.

The pictsies were running in line with her on either side.

Even with the edge of the fury dying away, it was hard looking at things here without her head aching. Things that seemed far off got closer too quickly, trees changed shape as she passed them . . .

Almost unreal, William had said. Nearly a dream. The world didn't have enough reality in it for distances and shapes to work probably. Once again the magic artist was painting madly. If she looked hard at a tree it changed, and became more tree-like and less like something drawn by Wentworth with his eyes shut.

This is a made-up world, Tiffany thought. Almost like a story. The trees don't have to be very detailed because who looks at trees in a story?

She stopped in a small clearing, and stared hard at a tree. It seemed to know it was being watched. It became more real. The bark roughened, and proper twigs grew on the end of the branches.

The snow was melting around her feet too. Although 'melting' was the wrong word. It was just disappearing, leaving leaves and grass.

If I was a world that didn't have enough reality to go around, Tiffany thought, then snow would be quite handy. It doesn't take a lot of effort. It's just white stuff. Everything looks white and simple. But *I* can make it complicated. I'm more real than this place.

She heard a buzzing overhead, and looked up.

And suddenly the air was filling with small people, smaller than a Feegle, with wings like dragonflies. There was a golden glow around them. Tiffany, entranced, reached out a hand—

At the same moment what felt like the entire clan of Nac Mac Feegle landed on her back and sent her sliding into a snowdrift.

When she struggled out, the clearing was a battlefield. The pictsies were jumping and slashing at the flying creatures, which were buzzing around them like wasps. As she stared two of them dived onto Rob Anybody and lifted him off his feet by his hair.

He rose in the air, yelling and struggling. Tiffany leaped up and grabbed him around the waist, flailing at the creatures with her other hand. They let go of the pictsie and dodged easily, zipping through the air as fast as hummingbirds. One of them bit her on the finger before buzzing away.

Somewhere a voice went: 'Ooooooooooooooo-eeerrrrrr . . .'

Rob struggled in Tiffany's grip. 'Quick, put me doon!' he yelled. 'There's gonna be poetry!'

CHAPTER 9

Lost Boys

The moan rolled around the clearing, as mournful as a month of Mondays.

'. . . rrrrrraaaaaaaaaaaaooooooooo . . .'

It sounded like some animal in terrible pain. But it was, in fact, Not-as-big-as-Medium-Sized-Jock-but-bigger-than-Wee-Jock-Jock, who was standing on a snowdrift with one hand pressed to his heart and the other outstretched, very theatrically.

He was rolling his eyes too.

'. . . ooooooooooooooooooooooooo . . .'

'Ach, the muse is a terrible thing to have happen to ye,' said Rob Anybody, putting his hands over his ears.

'. . . oooooiiiiiit *is* with grreat lamentation and much worrying dismay,' the pictsie groaned, 'that we rrregard the doleful prospect of Fairyland in considerrrable decay . . .'

In the air, the flying creatures stopped attacking and began to panic. Some of them flew into one another.

'With quite a large number of drrrrrrreadful incidents happening everrry day,' Not-as-big-as-Medium-Sized-Jock-but-bigger-than-Wee-Jock-Jock recited. 'Including, I am sorrrry to say, an aerial attack by the otherwise quite attractive fey . . .'

The flyers screeched. Some crashed into the snow, but the ones still capable of flight swarmed off amongst the trees.

'Witnessed by all of us at this time, And celebrated in this hasty rhyme!' Not-as-big-as-Medium-Sized-Jock-but-bigger-than-Wee-Jock-Jock shouted after them.

And they were gone.

Feegles were picking themselves up off the ground. Some were bleeding where the fairies had bitten them. Several were lying curled up and groaning.

Tiffany looked at her own finger. The bite of the fairy had left two tiny holes.

'It isnae too bad,' Rob Anybody shouted up from below. 'No one taken by them, just a few cases where the lads didnae put their hands o'er their ears in time.'

'Are they all right?'

'Oh, they'll be fine wi' counsellin'.'

On the mound of snow, William clapped Not-as-big-as-Medium-Sized-Jock-but-bigger-than-Wee-Jock-Jock on the shoulder in a friendly way.

'That, lad,' he said proudly, 'was some of the worst poetry I have heard for a long time. It was offensive to the ear and a torrrture to the soul. The last couple of lines need some work but ye has the groanin' off fiiine. A' in a', a verrry commendable effort! We'll make a gonnagle out of ye' yet!'

Not-as-big-as-Medium-Sized-Jock-but-bigger-than-Wee-Jock-Jock blushed happily.

In Fairyland words *really* have power, Tiffany thought. And I am more real. I'll remember that.

The pictsies assembled into battle order again, although it was pretty disorderly, and set off. Tiffany didn't rush too far ahead this time.

'That's yer little people wi' wings,' said Rob, as Tiffany sucked at her finger. 'Are ye happier now?'

'Why were they trying to carry you away?'

'Ach, they carries their victims off to their nest, where their young ones—'

'Stop!' said Tiffany. 'This is going to be horrible, right?'

'Oh, aye. Gruesome,' said Rob, grinning.

'And you used to *live* here?'

'Ah, but it wasnae so bad then. It wasnae perfect, mark you, but the Quin wasnae as cold in them days. The King was still aroound. She was always happy then.'

'What happened? Did the King die?'

'No. They had words, if ye tak' my meanin',' said Rob.

'Oh, you mean like an argument—'

'A bit, mebbe,' said Rob. 'But they was *magical* words. Forests destroyed, mountains explodin', a few hundred deaths, that kind of thing. And he went off to his own world. Fairyland was never a picnic, ye ken, even in the old days. But it was fine if you kept alert, an' there was flowers and burdies and summertime. Now there's the dromes and the hounds and the stinging fey and such stuff creepin' in from their own worlds, and the whole place has gone doon the lavvy.'

Things taken from their own worlds, thought Tiffany, as she tramped through the snow. Worlds all squashed together like peas in a sack, or hidden inside one another like bubbles inside other bubbles.

She had a picture in her head of things creeping out of their own world and into another, in the same way that mice invaded the larder. Only, there were worse things than mice.

What would a drome do if it got into our world? You'd never know it was there. It'd sit in the corner and you'd never see it, because it wouldn't let you. And it'd change the way you saw the world, give you nightmares, make you want to die . . .

Her Second Thoughts added: *I wonder how many have got in already and we don't know?*

And I'm in Fairyland, where dreams can hurt. Somewhere all stories are real, all songs are true. I thought that was a strange thing for the kelda to say . . .

Tiffany's Second Thoughts said: Hang on, was that a First Thought?

And Tiffany thought: No, that was a Third Thought. I'm thinking about how I think about what I'm thinking. At least, I think so.

Her Second Thoughts said: Let's all calm down, please, because this is quite a small head.

The forest went on. Or perhaps it was a small forest and, somehow, moved around them as they walked. This was Fairyland, after all. You couldn't trust it.

And the snow still vanished where Tiffany walked, and she only had to look at a tree for it to smarten up and make an effort to look like a real tree.

The Queen is . . . well, a queen, Tiffany thought. She's got a world of her own. She could do *anything* with it. And all she does is steal things, mess up people's lives . . .

There was the thud of hoofbeats in the distance.

It's her! What shall I do? What shall I say?

The Nac Mac Feegles leaped behind the trees.

'Come away oot o' the path!' hissed Rob Anybody.

'She might still have him!' said Tiffany, gripping the pan handle nervously and staring at the blue shadows between the trees.

'So? We'll find a wa' to steal him! She's the *Quin*! Ye cannae beat the Quin face to face!'

The hoofbeats were louder, and now it sounded as though there was more than one animal.

A stag appeared through the trees, steam pouring off it. It stared at Tiffany with wild red eyes and then, bunching up, leaped over her. She smelled the stink of it as she ducked, she felt its sweat on her neck.

It was a real animal. You couldn't imagine a reek like that.

And here came the dogs—

The first one she caught with the edge of the pan, bowling it over. The other turned to snap at her, then looked down in amazement as pictsies erupted from the snow under each paw. It was hard to bite anyone when all four of your feet were moving away in different directions, and then other pictsies landed on its head and biting anything ever again soon became . . . impossible. The Nac Mac Feegle hated grimhounds.

Tiffany looked up at a white horse. That was real too, as far as she could tell. And there was a boy on it.

'Who are *you*?' he said. He made it sound like 'What sort of thing are you?'

'Who are you?' said Tiffany, pushing her hair out of her eyes. It was the best she could do right now.

'This is *my* forest,' said the boy. 'I command you to do what I say!'

Tiffany peered at him. The dull, second-hand light of Fairyland was not very good, but the more she looked, the more certain she was. 'Your name is Roland, isn't it?' she said.

'You will not speak to me like that!'

'Yes, it is. You're the Baron's son!'

'I demand that you stop talking!' The boy's expression was strange now, creased up and pink, as if he was trying not to cry. He raised his hand with a riding whip in it—

There was a very faint 'thwap'. Tiffany glanced down. The Nac Mac Feegles had formed a pile under the horse's belly and one of them, climbing upon their shoulders, had just cut through the saddle girth.

She held up a hand quickly. 'Stand still!' she shouted, trying to sound commanding. 'If you move you'll fall off your horse!'

'Is that a spell? Are you a witch?' The boy dropped the whip and pulled a long dagger from his belt. 'Death to witches!'

He urged the horse forward with a jerk and then there was one of those long moments, a moment when the whole universe said 'uh-oh', and, still holding the dagger, the boy swivelled round the horse and landed in the snow.

Tiffany knew what would happen next. Rob Anybody's voice echoed among the trees:

'You're in trouble noo, pal! *Get him!*'

'No!' Tiffany yelled. 'Get away from him!'

The boy scrambled backwards, staring at Tiffany in horror.

'I do know you,' she said. 'Your name *is* Roland. You're the Baron's son. They said you'd died in the forest—'

'You mustn't talk about that!'

'Why not?'

'Bad things happen!'

'They're already happening,' said Tiffany. 'Look, I'm here to rescue my—'

But the boy had got to his feet and was running back through the forest. He turned and shouted, 'Get away from me!'

Tiffany ran after him, jumping over snow-covered

logs, and saw him ahead, dodging from tree to tree. Then he paused, and looked back.

She ran up to him saying, 'I know how to get you out—'

– *and danced*.

She was holding the hand of a parrot, or at least someone with the head of a parrot.

Her feet moved under her, perfectly. They twirled her around, and this time her hand was caught by a peacock, or at least someone with the head of a peacock. She glanced over his shoulder and saw that she was now in a room, no, a *ballroom* full of masked people, dancing.

Ah, she thought. Another dream. I should have looked where I was going . . .

The music was strange. There was a kind of rhythm to it, but it sounded muffled and odd, as if it was being played backwards, underwater, by musicians who'd never seen their instruments before.

And she *hoped* the dancers were wearing masks. She realized she was looking through the eyeholes of one, and wondered what she was. She was also wearing a long dress, which glittered.

O-K, she thought carefully. There was a drome there, and I didn't stop to look. And now I'm in a dream. But it's not mine. It must make use of what it finds in your head, and I've never been to anything like this . . .

'Fwa waa fwah waa wha?' said the peacock. The voice was like the music. It sounded almost like a voice, but it wasn't.

'Oh, yes,' said Tiffany. 'Fine.'

'Fwaa?'

'Oh. Er . . . wuff fawf fwaff?'

This seemed to work. The peacock-headed dancer bobbed a little bow, said, 'Mwa waf waf' sadly, and wandered off.

Somewhere in here is the drome, said Tiffany to herself. And it must be a pretty good one. This is a *big* dream.

Little things were wrong, though. There were hundreds of people in the room, but the ones in the distance, although they were moving about in quite a natural way, seemed the same as the trees – blobs and swirls of colour. You had to look hard to notice this, though.

First Sight, Tiffany thought.

People in brilliant costumes and still more masks walked arm in arm past her, as if she were just another guest. Those that weren't joining the new dance were heading for the long tables at one side of the hall, which were piled with food.

Tiffany had only seen such food in pictures. People didn't starve on the farm, but even when food was plentiful, at Hogswatch or after harvest, it never looked like this. The farm food was mostly shades of white or brown. It was never pink and blue, and never wobbled.

There were things on sticks, and things that gleamed and glistened in bowls. Nothing was simple. Everything had cream on it, or chocolate whirls, or thousands of little coloured balls. Everything was spun or glazed or added to or mixed up. This wasn't food; it was what food became if it had been good and had gone to food heaven.

It wasn't just for eating, it was for show. It was piled up against mounds of greenery and enormous arrangements of flowers. Here and there huge transparent carvings were landmarks in this landscape of food. Tiffany reached up and touched a glittering cockerel. It was ice, damp under her fingertips. There were others too . . . a jolly fat man, a bowl of fruits all carved in ice, a swan . . .

Tiffany was, for a moment, tempted. It seemed a very long time since she had eaten anything. But the food was too obviously not food at all. It was bait. It was supposed to say: Hello, little kiddie. Eat me.

I'm getting the hang of this, thought Tiffany. Good job the creature didn't think of cheese—

– and there was cheese. Suddenly, *cheese had always been there.*

She'd seen pictures of lots of different cheeses in the Almanack. She was good at cheese and had always wondered what the others tasted like. They were faraway cheeses with strange-sounding names, cheeses like Treble Wibbley, Waney Tastey, Old Argg, Red Runny and the legendary Lancre Blue, which had to be nailed to the table to stop it attacking other cheeses.

Just a taste wouldn't hurt, surely. It wasn't the same as eating, was it? After all, she was in control, wasn't she? She'd seen right through the dream straight away, hadn't she? So it couldn't have any effect, could it?

And . . . well, *cheese* was hardly temptation for anyone . . .

OK, the drome must've put the cheese in as soon as she'd thought of it, but . . .

She was already holding the cheese knife. She didn't quite remember picking it up.

A drop of cold water landed on her hand. It made her glance up at the nearest glittering ice carving.

Now it was a shepherdess, with a saddlebag dress and a big bonnet. Tiffany was sure it had been a swan when she'd looked at it before.

The anger came back. She'd nearly been fooled! She looked at the cheese knife. 'Be a sword,' she said. After all, the drome was making her dream, but she was doing the dreaming. She was real. Part of her wasn't asleep.

There was a clang.

'Correction,' said Tiffany. 'Be a sword that isn't so heavy.' And this time she got something she could actually hold.

There was a rustling in the greenery and a red-haired face poked out.

'Psst,' it whispered. 'Dinnae eat the canapés!'

'You're a bit late!'

'Ach, weel, it's a cunnin' ol' drome ye're dealin' with here,' said Rob Anybody. 'The dream wouldnae let us in unless we wuz properly dressed . . .'

He stepped out, looking very sheepish in a black suit with a bow tie. There was more rustling and other pictsies pushed their way out of the greenery. They looked a bit like red-headed penguins.

'Properly dressed?' said Tiffany.

'Aye,' said Daft Wullie, who had a piece of lettuce on his head. 'An' these troosers are a wee bit chafin' around the nethers, I don't mind tellin' ye.'

'Have ye spotted the creature yet?' said Rob Anybody.

'No! It's so crowded!'

'We'll help ye look,' said Rob Anybody. 'The thing cannae hide if ye're right up close. Be careful, mind you! If it thinks ye're gonna whap it one, there's nae tellin' what it'll try! Spread oot, lads, and pretend ye're enjoying the cailey.'

'Whut? D'ye mean get drunk an' fight an' that?' said Daft Wullie.

'Crivens, ye wouldna' believe it,' said Rob Anybody, rolling his eyes. 'Nae, ye pudden'! This is a *posh* party, ye ken? That means ye mak' small talk an' mingle!'

'Ach, I'm a famous mingler! They won't even know we're here!' said Daft Wullie. 'C'mon!'

Even in a dream, even at a posh ball, the Nac Mac Feegle knew how to behave. You charged in madly, and you screamed . . . politely.

'*Lovely weather for the time o' year, is it not, ye wee scunner!*'

'*Hey, jimmy, ha' ye no got a pommes frites for an ol' pal?*'

'*The band is playin' divinely, I dinnae think!*'

'*Make my caviar deep-fried, willya?*'

There was something wrong with the crowd. No one was panicking or trying to run away, which was *certainly* the right response to an invasion of Feegles.

Tiffany set off again through the crowd. The masked people at the party paid her no attention, either. And that's because they're background people, she thought, just like the background trees. She walked along the room to a pair of double doors, and pulled them open.

There was nothing but blackness beyond it.

So . . . the only way out was to find the drome. She hadn't really expected anything else. It could be anywhere. It could be behind a mask, it could be a table. It could be anything.

Tiffany stared at the crowd. And it was then she saw Roland.

He was sitting at a table by himself. It was spread with food, and he had a spoon in his hand.

She ran over and knocked it onto the floor. 'Haven't you got any sense at all?' she said, pulling him upright. 'Do you want to stay here for ever?'

And then she felt the movement behind her. Later on, she was sure she hadn't heard anything. She'd just known. It was a dream, after all.

She glanced around, and there was the drome. It was almost hidden behind a pillar.

Roland just stared at her.

'Are you all right?' said Tiffany desperately, trying to shake him. 'Have you eaten anything?'

'Fwa fwa faff,' murmured the boy.

Tiffany turned back to the drome. It was moving towards her, but very slowly, trying to stay in the shadows. It looked like a little snowman made of dirty snow.

The music was getting louder. The candles were getting brighter. Out on the huge dance floor, the animal-headed couples whirled faster and faster. And the floor shook. The dream was in trouble.

The Nac Mac Feegles were running to her from every part of the floor, trying to be heard above the din.

The drome was lurching towards her, podgy white fingers grasping the air.

'First Sight,' breathed Tiffany.

She cut Roland's head off.

The snow had melted all across the clearing, and the trees looked real and properly tree-like.

In front of Tiffany, the drome fell backwards. She was holding the old frying pan in her hand, but it had cut beautifully. Odd things, dreams.

She turned and faced Roland, who was staring at her with a face so pale he might as well have been a drome.

'It was frightened,' she said. 'It wanted me to attack you instead. It tried to look like you and made *you* look like a drome. But it didn't know how to speak. You do.'

'You might have killed me!' he said hoarsely.

'No,' said Tiffany. 'I just explained. Please don't run away. Have you seen a baby boy here?'

Roland's face wrinkled. 'What?' he said.

'The Queen took him,' said Tiffany. 'I'm going to fetch him home. I'll take you too, if you like.'

'You'll never get away,' whispered Roland.

'I got in, didn't I?'

'Getting in is easy. No one gets out!'

'I mean to find a way,' said Tiffany, trying to sound a lot more confident than she felt.

'She won't let you!' Roland started to back away again.

'Please don't be so . . . so *stupid*,' said Tiffany. 'I'm going to find the Queen and get my brother back, whatever you say. Understand? I've got this far. And I've got help, you know.'

'Where?' said Roland.

Tiffany looked around. There was no sign of the Nac Mac Feegles.

'They always turn up,' she said. 'Just when I need them.'

It struck her that there was suddenly something very . . . empty about the forest. It seemed colder too.

'They'll be here any minute,' she added hopefully.

'They got trapped in the dream,' said Roland flatly.

'They can't have. I killed the drome!'

'It's more complicated than that,' said the boy. 'You don't know what it's like here. There's dreams inside dreams. There's . . . other things that live inside dreams, horrible things. You never know if you've really woken up. And the Queen controls them all. They're fairy people, anyway. You can't trust them. You can't trust anyone. I don't trust you. You're probably just another dream.'

He turned his back and walked away, following the line of hoofprints.

Tiffany hesitated. The only other real person was

going away, leaving her here with nothing but the trees, and the shadows.

And, of course, anything horrible that was running towards her through them . . .

'Er . . .' she said. 'Hello? Rob Anybody? William? Daft Wullie?'

There was no reply. There wasn't even an echo. She was alone, apart from her heartbeats.

Well, of *course* she'd fought things and won, hadn't she? But the Nac Mac Feegles had been there and, somehow, that'd made it easy. They never gave up, they'd attack absolutely anything and they didn't know the meaning of the word 'fear'.

Tiffany, who had read her way through the dictionary, had a Second Thought there. 'Fear' was only one of thousands of words the pictsies probably didn't know the meaning of. Unfortunately, she *did* know what it meant. And the taste and feel of fear too. She felt it now.

She gripped the pan. It didn't seem quite such a good weapon any more.

The cold blue shadows between the trees seemed to be spreading out. They were darkest ahead of her, where the hoofprints led. Strangely enough the wood behind her seemed almost light and inviting.

Someone doesn't want me to go on, she thought. That was . . . quite encouraging. But the twilight was misty and shimmered unpleasantly. Anything could be waiting.

She was waiting too. She realized that she was waiting for the Nac Mac Feegles, hoping against hope that she'd hear a sudden cry, even of 'Crivens!' (She was sure it was a swear word.)

She pulled out the toad, which lay snoring on the palm of her hand, and gave it a prod.

'Whp?' it croaked.

'I'm stuck in a wood of evil dreams and I'm all alone and I think it's getting darker,' said Tiffany. 'What should I do?'

The toad opened one bleary eye and said: 'Leave.'

'That is not a lot of help!'

'Best advice there is,' said the toad. 'Now put me back, the cold makes me lethargic.'

Reluctantly, Tiffany put the creature back in her apron pocket, and her hand touched *Diseases of the Sheep.*

She pulled it out and opened it at random. There was a cure for the Steams, but it had been crossed out in pencil. Written in the margin, in Granny Aching's big, round, *careful* handwriting was:

> *This dunt work. One desert spoonfull of terpentine do.*

Tiffany closed the book with care, and put it back gently so as not to disturb the sleeping toad. Then, gripping the pan's handle tightly, she stepped into the long blue shadows.

How do you get shadows when there's no sun in the sky? she thought, because it was better to think about things like this than all the other, much worse things that were on her mind.

But these shadows didn't need light to create them. They crawled around on the snow of their own accord, and backed away when she walked towards them. That, at least, was a relief.

They piled up behind her. They were following her. She turned and stamped her foot a few times and they scurried off behind the trees, but she knew they were flowing back when she wasn't looking.

She saw a drome in the distance ahead of her, standing half-hidden behind a tree. She screamed at it and waved the pan threateningly, and it lumbered off quickly.

When she looked round she saw two more behind her, a long way back.

The track led uphill a little, into what looked like a much thicker mist. It glowed faintly. She headed for it. There was no other way to go.

When she reached the top of the rise, she looked down into a shallow valley.

There were four dromes in it – big ones, bigger than any she'd seen so far. They were sitting down in a square, their dumpy legs stretched out in front of them. Each one had a gold collar around its neck, attached to a chain.

'Tame ones?' Tiffany wondered, aloud. 'But—'

. . . who could put a collar around the neck of a drome? Only someone who could dream as well as they could.

We tamed the sheepdogs to help us herd sheep, she

thought. The Queen uses dromes to herd dreams . . .

In the centre of the square formed by the dromes the air was full of mist. The hooftracks, and the tracks of Roland, led down past the tame dromes and into the cloud.

Tiffany spun round. The shadows darted back.

There was nothing else nearby. No birds sang, nothing moved in the woods. But she could make out three more dromes now, their big round soggy faces peering at her around tree trunks.

She was being herded now.

At a time like this it would be nice to have someone around to say something like 'No! It's too dangerous! Don't do it!'

Unfortunately, there wasn't. She was going to commit an act of extreme bravery and no one would know if it all went wrong. That was frightening, but also . . . annoying. That was it . . . *annoying*. This place annoyed her. It was all stupid and strange.

It was the same feeling she'd had when Jenny had leaped out of the river. Out of *her* river. And the Queen had taken *her* brother. Maybe it was selfish to think like that, but anger was better than fear. Fear was a damp cold mess, but anger had an edge. She could use it.

They were *herding* her! Like a – a sheep!

Well, an angry sheep could send a vicious dog away, whimpering.

So . . .

Four big dromes, sitting in a square.

It was going to be a big dream . . .

Raising the pan to shoulder height, to swipe at anything that came near, and suppressing a dreadful urge to go to the toilet, Tiffany walked slowly down the slope, across the snow, through the mist . . .

. . . and into summer.

CHAPTER 10

Master Stroke

The heat struck like a blowlamp, so sharp and sudden that she gasped.

She'd had sunstroke once, up on the downs, when she'd gone without a bonnet. And this was like that; the world around her was in worrying shades of dull green, yellow and purple, without shadows. The air was so full of heat that she felt she could squeeze smoke out of it.

She was in . . . reeds, they looked like, much taller than her.

. . . with sunflowers growing in them, except . . .

. . . the sunflowers were white . . .

. . . because they *weren't*, in fact, sunflowers at all.

They were daisies. She knew it. She'd stared at them dozens of times, in that strange picture in the Faerie Tales. They were daisies, and these weren't giant reeds around her, they were blades of grass and she was very, very small.

She was in the weird picture. The picture was the dream, or the dream was the picture. Which way round didn't matter, because she was right in the middle of it. If you fell off a cliff, it wouldn't matter if the ground was rushing up or you were rushing down. You were in trouble either way.

Somewhere in the distance there was a loud *crack!* and a ragged cheer. Someone clapped and said, in a sleepy sort of voice, 'Well done. Good man. Ver' well done . . .'

With some effort, Tiffany pushed her way between the blades of grass.

On a flat rock, a man was cracking nuts half as big as he was, with a two-handed hammer. He was being watched by a crowd of people. Tiffany used the word 'people' because she couldn't think of anything else that was suitable, but it was stretching the word a bit to make it fit all the . . . people.

They were different sizes, for one thing. Some of the men were taller than her, even if you allowed for the fact that *everyone* was shorter than the grass. But others were tiny. Some of them had faces that you wouldn't look at twice. Others had faces that no one would want to look at even *once*.

This is a dream, after all, Tiffany told herself. It doesn't have to make sense, or be nice. It's a dream, not a daydream. People who say things like 'may all your dreams come true' should try living in one for five minutes.

She stepped out into the bright, stiflingly hot

clearing just as the man raised his hammer again, and said, 'Excuse me?'

'Yes?' he said.

'Is there a Queen around here?' said Tiffany.

The man wiped his forehead, and nodded towards the other side of the clearing.

'Her Majesty has gone to her bower,' he said.

'That being a nook or resting place?' said Tiffany.

The man nodded and said, 'Correct again, Miss Tiffany.'

Don't ask how he knows your name, Tiffany told herself.

'Thank you,' she said, and because she had been brought up to be polite she added, 'Best of luck with the nut-cracking.'

'This one's the toughest yet,' said the man.

Tiffany walked off, trying to look as if this collection of strange nearly-people was just another crowd. Probably the scariest ones were the Big Women, two of them.

Big women were valued on the Chalk. Farmers liked big wives. Farmwork was hard and there was no call for a wife who couldn't carry a couple of piglets or a bale of hay. But these two could have carried a horse each. They stared haughtily at her as she walked past.

They had tiny, stupid little wings on their backs.

'Nice day for watching nuts being cracked!' said Tiffany cheerfully, as she went past. Their huge pale faces wrinkled, as if they were trying to work out what she was.

Sitting down near them, watching the nut-cracker

with an expression of concern, was a little man with a large head, a fringe of white beard and pointy ears. He was wearing very old-fashioned clothes, and his eyes followed Tiffany as she went past.

'Good morning,' she said.

'*Sneebs!*' he said, and in her head appeared the words: 'Get away from here!'

'Excuse me?' she said.

'*Sneebs!*' said the man, wringing his hands. And the words appeared, floating in her brain: 'It's terribly dangerous!'

He waved a pale hand, as if to brush her away. Shaking her head, Tiffany walked on.

There were lords and ladies, people in fine clothes and even a few shepherds. But some of them had a pieced-together look. They looked, in fact, like a picture book back in her bedroom.

It was made of thick card, worn raggedy-edged by generations of Aching children. Each page showed a character, and each was cut into four strips that could be turned over independently. The point of the whole thing was that a bored child could turn over parts of the pages and change the way the characters were dressed. You could end up with a soldier's head on a baker's chest wearing a maid's dress and a farmer's big boots.

Tiffany had never been bored enough. She considered that even things that spend their whole lives hanging from the underside of branches would never be bored enough to spend more than five seconds with that book.

The people around her looked either as though

they'd been taken from that book, or had dressed for a fancy-dress party in the dark. One or two of them nodded to her as she passed, but didn't seem surprised to see her.

She ducked under a round leaf much bigger than she was and took out the toad again.

'Whap? It's sti' cooold,' said the toad, hunching down on her hand.

'Cold? The air's baking!'

'There's just snow,' said the toad. 'Put me back, I'm freezing!'

Just a minute, thought Tiffany. 'Do toads dream?' she said.

'No!'

'Oh . . . so it's not really hot?'

'No! You just think it is!'

'Psst,' said a voice.

Tiffany put the toad away and wondered if she dared to turn her head.

'It's me!' said the voice.

Tiffany turned towards a clump of daisies twice the height of a man. 'That's not a lot of help . . .'

'Are you mad?' said the daisies.

'I'm looking for my brother,' said Tiffany sharply.

'The horrible child who screams for sweeties all the time?'

The daisy stems parted and the boy Roland darted out and joined her under the leaf.

'Yes,' she said, edging away, and feeling that only a sister has a right to call even a brother like Wentworth 'horrible'.

'And threatens to go to the toilet if he's left alone?' said Roland.

'Yes! Where is he?'

'*That's* your brother? The one who's permanently sticky?'

'I told you!'

'And you really want him back?'

'Yes!'

'Why?'

He's my brother, Tiffany thought. What's 'why?' got to do with it?

'Because he's my brother! Now tell me where he is?'

'Are you sure you can get out of here?' said Roland.

'Of course,' Tiffany lied.

'And you can take me with you?'

'Yes.' Well, she hoped so.

'All right. I'll let you do that,' said Roland, relaxing.

'Oh, you'll *let* me, will you?' said Tiffany.

'Look, I didn't know what you were, all right?' said Roland. 'There's always weird things in the forest. Lost people, bits of dreams that're still lying around . . . you have to be careful. But if you really know the way, then I ought to get back before my father worries too much.'

Tiffany felt the Second Thoughts starting. They said: Don't change your expression. Just . . . check . . .

'How long have you been here?' she asked carefully. 'Exactly?'

'Well, the light doesn't really change much,' said the boy. 'It feels like I've been here . . . oh, hours. Maybe a day . . .'

216

Tiffany tried hard not to let her face give anything away, but it didn't work. Roland's eyes narrowed.

'I have, haven't I?' he said.

'Er . . . why do you ask?' said Tiffany, desperately.

'Because in a way it . . . feels like . . . longer. I've only been hungry two or three times, and been to the . . . you know . . . twice, so it can't be *very* long. But I've done all kinds of things . . . it's been a busy day . . .' His voice trailed off.

'Um. You're right,' said Tiffany. 'Time goes slowly here. It's been . . . a bit longer . . .'

'A hundred years? Don't tell me it's a hundred years! Something magical has happened and it's a hundred years, yes?'

'What? No! Um . . . nearly a year.'

The boy's reaction was surprising. This time he looked *really* frightened. 'Oh, no! That's worse than a hundred years!'

'How?' said Tiffany, bewildered.

'If it was a hundred years I wouldn't get a thrashing when I got home!'

Hmm, thought Tiffany. 'I don't think that's going to happen,' she said aloud. 'Your father has been very miserable. Besides, it's not your fault you were stolen by the Queen—' She hesitated, because this time it was *his* expression that gave it all away. 'Was it?'

'Well, there was this fine lady on a horse with bells all over its harness and she galloped past me when I was out hunting and she was laughing, so of *course* I spurred my horse and chased after her and . . .' He fell silent.

'That probably wasn't a good decision,' said Tiffany.

'It's not . . . *bad* here,' said Roland. 'It just keeps . . . changing. There's . . . doorways everywhere. I mean entrances into other . . . places . . .' His voice tailed off.

'You'd better start at the beginning,' said Tiffany.

'It was great at first,' said Roland. 'I thought it was, you know, an adventure? She fed me sweetmeats—'

'What are they, exactly?' said Tiffany. Her dictionary hadn't included that one. 'Are they like sweetbreads?'

'I don't know. What are sweetbreads?'

'The pancreas or thymus gland of a cow,' said Tiffany. 'Not a very good name, I think.'

Roland's face went red with the effort of thought. 'These were more like nougat.'

'Right. Go on,' said Tiffany.

'And then she told me to sing and dance and skip and play,' said Roland. 'She said that's what children were supposed to do.'

'Did you?'

'Would you? I'd feel like an idiot. I'm twelve, you know.' Roland hesitated. 'In fact, if what you say is true, I'm thirteen now, right?'

'Why did she want you to skip and play?' said Tiffany, instead of saying, 'No, you're still twelve and act like you're eight.'

'She just said that's what children do,' said Roland.

Tiffany wondered about this. As far as she could see, children mostly argued, shouted, ran around very

218

fast, laughed loudly, picked their noses, got dirty and sulked. Any seen dancing *and* skipping *and* singing had probably been stung by a wasp.

'Strange,' she said.

'And then when I wouldn't she gave me more sweets.'

'More nougat?'

'Sugar plums,' said Roland. 'They're, like, plums. You know? With sugar on? She's always trying to feed me sugar! She thinks I like it!'

A small bell rang in Tiffany's memory. 'You don't think she's trying to feed you up before she bakes you in an oven and eats you, do you?'

'Of course not. Only wicked witches do that.'

Tiffany's eyes narrowed. 'Oh yes,' she said carefully. 'I forgot. So you've been living on sweeties?'

'No, I know how to hunt! Real animals get in here. I don't know how. Sneebs thinks they find the doorways in by accident. And then they starve to death, because it's always winter here. Sometimes the Queen sends out robbing parties if a door opens into an interesting world too. This whole place is like . . . a pirate ship.'

'Yes, or a sheep tick,' said Tiffany, thinking aloud.

'What're they?'

'They're insects that bite sheep and suck blood and don't drop off until they're full,' said Tiffany.

'Yuck. I suppose that's the kind of thing peasants have to know about,' said Roland. 'I'm glad I don't. I've seen through the doorways to one or two worlds. They wouldn't let me out, though. We got potatoes from one, and fish from another. I think they frighten people into giving them stuff. Oh, and there was the world where the dromes come from. They laughed about that and said if I wanted to go in there I was welcome. I didn't! It's all red, like a sunset. A great huge sun on the horizon, and a red sea that hardly moves, and red rocks, and long shadows. And those horrible creatures sitting on the rocks, living off crabs and spidery things and little scribbity creatures. It was awful. There was this sort of ring of little claws and shells and bones around every one of them.'

'Who are they?' said Tiffany, who had noted the word 'peasants'.

'What do you mean?'

'You keep talking about "they",' said Tiffany. 'Who do you mean? The people out there?'

'Those? Most of them aren't even real,' said Roland. 'I mean the elves. The fairies. That's who she's Queen of. Didn't you know?'

'I thought they were small!'

'I think they can be any size they like,' said Roland. 'They're not . . . exactly real. They're like . . . dreams of themselves. They can be as thin as air or solid as a rock. Sneebs says.'

'Sneebs?' said Tiffany. 'Oh . . . the little man that just says *sneebs* but real words turn up in your head?'

'Yes, that's him. He's been here for *years*. That's how I knew about the time being wrong. Sneebs got back to his own world once, and it was all different. He was so miserable he found another doorway and came straight back.'

'He *came* back?' said Tiffany, astonished.

'He said it was better to belong where you don't belong than not to belong where you used to belong, remembering when you used to belong there,' said Roland. 'At least, I think that's what he said. He said it's not too bad here if you keep out of the Queen's way. He says you can learn a lot.'

Tiffany looked back at the hunched figure of Sneebs, who was still watching the nut-cracking. He didn't look as though he was learning anything. He just looked like someone who'd been frightened for so long it had become part of his life, like freckles.

'But you mustn't make the Queen angry,' said Roland. 'I've seen what happens to people who make her angry. She sets the Bumble-Bee women on them.'

'Are you talking about those huge women with the tiny wings?'

'Yes! They've vicious. And if the Queen gets really angry with someone, she just stares at them, and . . . they change.'

'What into?'

'Other things. I don't want to have to draw you a picture.' Roland shuddered. 'And if I did, I'd need a lot of red and purple crayons. Then they get dragged off and left for the dromes.' He shook his head. 'Listen, dreams are real here. *Really* real. When you're inside them you're not . . . exactly here. The nightmares are real too. You can *die*.'

This doesn't *feel* real, Tiffany told herself. This feels like a dream. I could almost wake up from it.

I must always remember what's real.

She looked down at her faded blue dress, with the bad stitching around the hem caused by it being let out and taken in as its various owners had grown. That was real.

And she was real. Cheese was real. Somewhere not far away was a world of green turf under a blue sky, and that was real.

The Nac Mac Feegle were real, and once again she wished they were here. There was something about the way they shouted 'Crivens!' and attacked everything in sight that was so very comforting.

Roland was probably real.

Almost everything else was really a dream, in a robber world that lived off the real worlds and where time nearly stood still and horrible things could happen at any moment. I don't want to know anything more about it, she decided. I just want to get my brother and go home, while I'm still angry.

Because when I stop being angry, that'll be the time to get frightened again, and I'll be *really* frightened this time. Too frightened to think. As frightened as Sneebs. And I must think . . .

'The first dream I fell into was like one of mine,' she said. 'I've had dreams where I wake up and I'm still asleep. But the ballroom, I've never—'

'Oh, that was one of mine,' said Roland. 'From when I was young. I woke up one night and went down to the big hall and there were all these people with masks on, dancing. It was just so . . . bright.' He looked wistful for a moment. 'That was when my mother was still alive.'

'This one's a picture from a book I've got,' said Tiffany. 'She must have got that from me—'

'No, she often uses it,' said Roland. 'She likes it. She picks up dreams from everywhere. She collects them.'

Tiffany stood up, and picked up the frying pan again. 'I'm going to see the Queen,' she said.

'Don't,' said Roland. 'You're the only other real person here except Sneebs, and he's not very good company.'

'I'm going to get my brother and go home,' said Tiffany flatly.

'I'm not going to come with you, then,' said Roland. 'I don't want to see what she turns you into.'

Tiffany stepped out into the heavy, shadowless light, and followed the path up the slope. Giant grasses arched overhead. Here and there more strangely dressed, strangely shaped people turned to watch her, but then acted as though she was just a passing wanderer, of no interest whatsoever.

She glanced behind her. In the distance the nut-cracker had found a bigger hammer, and was getting ready to strike.

'Wanna wanna *wanna* sweetie!'

Tiffany's head shot round like a weathercock in a tornado. She ran along the path, head down, ready to swing the pan at anything that stood in her way, and burst through a clump of grass into a space lined with daisies. It could well have been a bower. She didn't bother to check.

Wentworth was sitting on a large, flat stone, surrounded by sweets. Many of them were bigger than he was. Smaller ones were in piles, large ones lay like logs. And they were in every colour sweets can be, such as Not-Really-Raspberry Red, Fake-Lemon Yellow, Curiously-Chemical Orange, Some-Kind-of-Acidy Green and Who-Knows-What Blue.

Tears were falling off his chin in blobs. Since they were landing amongst the sweets, serious stickiness was already taking place.

Wentworth howled. His mouth was a big red tunnel with the wobbly thing that no one knows the name of bouncing up and down in the back of his throat. He only stopped crying when it was time either to breathe in or die, and even then it was only for one huge sucking moment before the howl came back again.

Tiffany knew what the problem was immediately. She'd seen it before, at birthday parties. Her brother was suffering from tragic sweet deprivation. Yes, he was surrounded by sweets. But the moment he took any sweet at all, said his sugar-addled brain, that meant he was *not taking all the rest*. And there were so many sweets *he'd never be able to eat them all*. It was too much to cope with. The only solution was to burst into tears.

The only solution at home was to put a bucket over his head until he calmed down, and take almost all the sweets away. He could deal with a few handfuls at a time.

Tiffany dropped the pan and swept him up in her arms. 'It's Tiffy,' she whispered. 'And we're going home.'

And this is where I meet the Queen, she thought. But there was no scream of rage, no explosion of magic . . . nothing.

There was just the buzz of bees in the distance, and the sound of wind in the grass, and the gulping of Wentworth, who was too shocked to cry.

She could see now that the far side of the bower contained a couch of leaves, surrounded by hanging flowers. But there was no one there.

'That's because I'm behind you,' said the voice of the Queen in her ear.

Tiffany turned round quickly.

There was no one there.

'*Still* behind you,' said the Queen. 'This is *my* world, child. You'll never be as fast as me, or as clever as me. Why are you trying to take my boy away?'

'He isn't yours! He's ours!' said Tiffany.

'You never loved him. You have a heart like a little snowball. I can see it.'

Tiffany's forehead wrinkled. 'Love?' she said. 'What's that got to do with it? He's my *brother*! *My* brother!'

'Yes, that's a very witchy thing, isn't it,' said the voice of the Queen. 'Selfishness. Mine, mine, mine. All a witch cares about is what's *hers*.'

'You stole him!'

'Stole? You mean you thought you *owned* him?'

Tiffany's Second Thoughts said: She's finding your weaknesses. Don't listen to her.

'Ah, you have Second Thoughts,' said the Queen. 'I expect you think that makes you very witchy, do you?'

225

'Why won't you let me see you?' said Tiffany. 'Are you frightened?'

'Frightened?' said the voice of the Queen. 'Of something like *you*?'

And the Queen was there, in front of her. She was much taller than Tiffany, but just as slim; her hair was long and black, her face pale, her lips cherry red, her dress black and white and red. And it was all, very slightly, wrong.

Tiffany's Second Thoughts said: It's because she's perfect. Completely perfect. Like a doll. No one real is as perfect as that.

'That's not you,' said Tiffany, with absolute certainty. 'That's just your dream of you. That's not you at all.'

The Queen's smile disappeared for a moment and came back all edgy and brittle.

'Such rudeness, and you hardly know me,' she said, sitting down on the leafy seat. She patted the space beside her. 'Do sit down,' she said. 'Standing there like that is so confrontational. I will put your bad manners down to simple disorientation.' She gave Tiffany a beautiful smile.

Look at the way her eyes move, said Tiffany's Second Thoughts. I don't think she's using them to see you with. They're just beautiful ornaments.

'You have invaded my home, killed some of my creatures and generally acted in a mean and despicable way,' said the Queen. 'This offends me. However, I understand that you have been badly led by disruptive elements—'

'You stole my brother,' said Tiffany, holding Wentworth tightly. 'You steal all sorts of things.' But her voice sounded weak and tinny in her ears.

'He was wandering around lost,' said the Queen calmly. 'I brought him home and comforted him.'

And what there was about the Queen's voice was this: it said, in a friendly, understanding way, that she was right and you were wrong. And this wasn't your fault, exactly. It was probably the fault of your parents, or your food, or something so terrible you've completely forgotten about it. It wasn't *your* fault, the Queen understood, because *you* were a nice person. It was just such a terrible thing that all these bad influences had made you make the wrong choices. If only you'd admit that, Tiffany, then the world would be a much happier place—

– this cold place, guarded by monsters, in a world where nothing grows older, or up, said her Second Thoughts. A world with the Queen in charge of everything. Don't listen.

She managed to take a step backwards.

'Am I a monster?' said the Queen. 'All I wanted was a little bit of company—'

And Tiffany's Second Thoughts, quite swamped by the Queen's wonderful voice, said: Miss Female Robinson . . .

She'd come to work as a maid at one of the farms many years ago. They said that she'd been brought up in a Home for the Destitute in Yelp. They said she'd been born there after her mother had arrived during a terrible storm and the master had written in his big black diary: 'To Miss Robinson, female infant', and her young mother hadn't been very bright and was dying in any case and had thought that was the baby's name. After all, it had been written down in an official book.

Miss Robinson was quite old now, never said much, never ate much, but you never saw her not doing something. No one could scrub a floor like Miss Female Infant Robinson. She had a thin, wispy face with a pointed red nose, and thin, pale hands with red knuckles, which were always busy. Miss Robinson worked hard.

Tiffany hadn't understood a lot of what was going on when the crime happened. The women talked about it in twos and threes at garden gates, their arms folded, and they'd stop and look indignant if a man walked past.

She picked up bits of conversation, though sometimes they seemed to be in a kind of code, like: 'Never really had anyone of her own, poor old soul. Wasn't her fault she was skinnier'n a rake,' and 'They say that when they found her she was cuddling it and said it was hers,' and 'The house was full of baby clothes she'd knitted!' That last one had puzzled Tiffany at the time, because it was said in the same tone of voice that someone'd use to say 'And the house was full of human skulls!'

But they all agreed on one thing: We can't have this. A crime's a crime. The Baron's got to be told.

Miss Robinson had stolen a baby, Punctuality Riddle, who had been much loved by his young parents even *though they'd named him 'Punctuality' (reasoning that if children could be named after virtues like Patience, Faith and Prudence, what was wrong with a little good timekeeping?).*

He'd been left in his crib in the yard, and had vanished. And there had been all the usual searchings and weepings, and then someone had mentioned that Miss Robinson had been taking home extra milk . . .

It was kidnapping. There weren't many fences on the Chalk, and very few doors with locks. Theft of all kinds was taken very seriously. If you couldn't turn your back on what was yours for five minutes, where would it all end? The law's the law. A crime's a crime . . .

Tiffany had overheard bits of arguments all over the village, but the same phrases cropped up over and over again. *Poor thing never meant no harm. She was a hard worker, never complained. She's not right in the head. The law's the law. A crime's a crime.*

And so the Baron was told, and he held a court in the Great Hall, and everyone who wasn't wanted up on the hills turned up, including Mr and Mrs Riddle, she looking worried, he looking determined, and Miss Robinson, who just stared at the ground with her red knuckly hands on her knees.

It was hardly a trial. Miss Robinson was confused about what she was guilty of, and it seemed to Tiffany that so was everyone else. They weren't certain why they were there, and they'd come to find out.

The Baron had been uneasy too. The law was clear. Theft was a dreadful crime, and stealing a human being was much worse. There was a prison in Yelp, right beside the Home for the Destitute; some said there was even a connecting door. That was where thieves went.

And the Baron wasn't a big thinker. His family had held the Chalk by not changing their mind about anything for hundreds of years. He sat and listened and drummed his fingers on the table and looked at people's faces and acted like a man sitting on a very hot chair.

Tiffany was in the front row. She was there when the man started to give his verdict, 'um'ing and 'ah'ing, trying not to say the words he knew he'd have to say, when the door at the back of the hall opened and the sheepdogs Thunder and Lightning trotted in.

They came down the aisle between the rows of benches and sat down in front of the Baron, looking bright-eyed and alert.

Only Tiffany craned to see back up the aisle. The doors were still slightly ajar. They were far too heavy even for a strong dog to push them open. And she could just make out someone looking through the crack.

The Baron stopped, and stared. He, too, looked at the other end of the hall.

And then, after a few moments, he pushed the law book aside and said: 'Perhaps we should do this a different way . . .'

And there was a different way, involving people paying a little more attention to Miss Robinson. It wasn't perfect, and not everyone was happy, but it worked.

Tiffany smelled the scent of Jolly Sailor outside the hall when the meeting was over, and thought about the

*Baron's dog. 'Remember this day,' Granny Aching had
said, and, 'Ye'll have cause to.'*

Barons needed reminding . . .

'Who will speak up for you?' Tiffany said aloud.

'Speak up for me?' answered the Queen, her fine
eyebrows arching.

And Tiffany's Third Thoughts said: Watch her face
when she is worried.

'There isn't anyone, is there?' said Tiffany, backing
away. 'Is there anyone you've been kind to? Anyone
who'll say you're not just a thief and a bully? Because
that's what you are. You've got a . . . you're like the
dromes, you've just got one trick . . .'

And there it was. Now she could see what her Third
Thoughts had spotted. The Queen's face *flickered* for a
moment.

'And that's not your body,' said Tiffany, plunging
on. 'That's just what you want people to see. It's not
real. It's just like everything else here, it's hollow and
empty—'

The Queen ran forward and slapped her much
harder than a dream should be able to. Tiffany landed
in the moss and Wentworth rolled away, yelling,
'Wanna go-a toy-lut!'

Good, said Tiffany's Third Thoughts.

'Good?' said Tiffany aloud.

'Good?' said the Queen.

Yes, said the Third Thoughts, because she doesn't
know you can have Third Thoughts and your hand is
only a few inches from the frying pan and things like

her hate iron, don't they? She's angry. Now make her furious, so that she doesn't think. Hurt her.

'You just live here in a land full of winter and all you do is dream of summers,' said Tiffany. 'No wonder the King went away.'

The Queen stood still for a moment, like the beautiful statue she so much resembled. Again, the walking dream flickered and Tiffany thought she saw . . . something. It was not much bigger than her, and almost human, and a little shabby and, just for a moment, shocked. Then the Queen was back, tall and angry, and she drew a deep breath—

Tiffany grabbed the pan and swung it as she rolled onto her feet. It hit the tall figure only a glancing blow, but the Queen wavered like air over a hot road, and screamed.

Tiffany didn't wait to see what else was going to happen. She grabbed her brother again, and ran away, down through the grass, past the strange figures looking round at the sound of the Queen's anger.

Now shadows moved in the shadowless grasses. Some of the people – the joke people, the ones that looked like a flaps-on-the-pages picture book – changed shape and started to move after Tiffany and her screaming brother.

There was a booming noise on the other side of the clearing. The two huge creatures that Roland had called the Bumble-Bee women were rising off the ground, their tiny wings blurring with the effort.

Somebody grabbed her and pulled her into the grasses. It was Roland.

'Can you get out now?' he demanded, his face red.

'Er . . .' Tiffany began.

'Then we'd better just run,' he said. 'Give me your hand. Come on!'

'Do *you* know a way out?' Tiffany panted, as they dashed through giant daisies.

'No,' Roland panted back. 'There isn't one. You saw . . . the dromes outside . . . this is a really *strong* dream . . .'

'Then why are we running?'

'To keep out . . . of her way. If you . . . hide long enough . . . Sneebs says she . . . forgets . . .'

I don't think she's going to forget me very quickly, Tiffany thought.

Roland had stopped, but she pulled her hand away and ran onward, with Wentworth clinging to her in silent amazement.

'Where are you going?' shouted Roland behind her.

'I *really* want to keep out of her way!'

'Come back! You're running right back!'

'No I'm not! I'm running in a straight line!'

'This is a dream!' Roland shouted, but it was louder now because he was catching her up. 'You're running right around—'

Tiffany burst into a clearing . . .

. . . *the* clearing.

The Bumble-Bee women landed on either side of her, and the Queen stepped forward.

'You know,' said the Queen, 'I really expected better of you, Tiffany. Now, give me back the boy, and I shall decide what to do next.'

'It's not a big dream,' mumbled Roland behind her. 'If you go too far you end up coming back—'

'I could make a dream for you that's even smaller than you are,' said the Queen pleasantly. 'That can be quite painful!'

The colours were brighter. And sounds were louder. Tiffany could smell something too, and what was strange about that was that up until now there had been no smells.

It was a sharp, bitter smell that you never forgot. It was the smell of snow. And underneath the insect buzzings in the grass, she heard the faintest of voices.

'Crivens! I cannae find the way oot!'

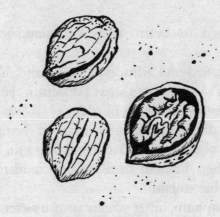

CHAPTER 11

Awakening

On the other side of the clearing, where the nut-cracking man had been at work, was the last nut, half as high as Tiffany. And it was rocking gently. The cracker took a swipe at it with the hammer, and it rolled out of the way.

See what's really there . . . said Tiffany to herself, and laughed.

The Queen gave her a puzzled look. 'You find this funny?' she demanded. 'What's funny about this? What is amusing about this situation?'

'I just had a funny thought,' said Tiffany. The Queen glared, as people without a sense of humour do when they're confronted with a smile.

You're not very clever, thought Tiffany. You've never needed to be. You can get what you want just by dreaming it. You believe in your dreams, so you never have to *think*.

She turned and whispered to Roland, 'Crack the nut! Don't worry about what I do, crack the nut!'

The boy looked at her blankly.

'What did you say to him?' snapped the Queen.

'I said goodbye,' said Tiffany, holding on tightly to her brother. 'I'm not handing my brother over, no matter what you do!'

'Do you know what colour your insides are?' said the Queen. Tiffany shook her head mutely.

'Well, now you'll find out,' said the Queen, smiling sweetly.

'You're not powerful enough to do anything like that,' said Tiffany.

'You know, you are right,' said the Queen. 'That kind of physical magic is, indeed, very hard. But I can make you *think* I've done the most . . . terrible things. And that, little girl, is all I need to do. Would you like to beg for mercy now? You may not be able to later.'

Tiffany paused. 'No-o,' she said at last. 'I don't think I will.'

The Queen leaned down. Her grey eyes filled Tiffany's world. 'People here will remember this for a long time,' she said.

'I hope so,' said Tiffany. 'Crack . . . the . . . nut.'

For a moment the Queen looked puzzled again. She was not good at dealing with sudden changes. 'What?'

'Eh? Oh . . . right,' muttered Roland.

'What did you say to him?' the Queen demanded, as the boy ran towards the hammer man.

Tiffany kicked her on the leg. It wasn't a witch thing. It was *so* nine years old, and she wished she could have thought of something better. On the other hand, she had hard boots and it was a good kick.

The Queen shook her. 'Why did you *do* that?' she said. 'Why won't you do what I say? Everyone could be so happy if only they'd do what I say!'

Tiffany stared at the woman's face. The eyes were grey now, but the pupils were like silver mirrors.

I know what you are, said her Third Thoughts. You're something that's never learned anything. You don't know *anything* about people. You're just . . . a child that's got old.

'Want a sweetie?' she whispered.

There was a shout behind her. She twisted in the Queen's grip, and saw Roland fighting for the hammer. As she watched he turned desperately and raised the heavy thing over his head, knocking over the elf behind him.

The Queen pulled her round savagely as the hammer fell. 'Sweetie?' she hissed. 'I'll show you swe—'

'*Crivens! It's the Quin! An' she's got oour kelda, the ol' topher!*'

'*Nae quin! Nae laird! Wee Free Men!*'

'*I could murrrder a kebab!*'

'*Get her!*'

Tiffany might have been the only person, in all the worlds that there are, to be happy to hear the sound of the Nac Mac Feegle.

They poured out of the smashed nut. Some were

still wearing bow ties. Some were back in their kilts. But they were all in a fighting mood and, to save time, were fighting with one another to get up to speed.

The clearing . . . cleared. Real or dreams, the people could see trouble when it rolled towards them in a roaring, cursing, red and blue tide.

Tiffany ducked out of the Queen's grasp and, still holding Wentworth, hurried into the grasses to watch.

Big Yan ran past, carrying a struggling full-sized elf over his head. Then he stopped suddenly, and tossed it high over the clearing.

'An' away he goes, right on his *heid*!' he yelled, then turned and ran back into the battle.

The Nac Mac Feegles couldn't be trodden on, or squeezed. They worked in groups, running up one another's backs to get high enough to punch an elf or, for preference, bash it with their heads. And once anyone was down, it was all over bar the kicking.

There was some method in the way the Nac Mac Feegle fought. For example, they always chose the biggest opponent because, as Rob Anybody said later, 'It makes them easier to hit, ye ken.' And they simply didn't *stop*. It was that which wore people down. It was like being attacked by wasps with fists.

It took them a little while to realize that they'd run out of people to fight. They carried on fighting one another for a bit anyway, since they'd come all this way, and then settled down and began to go through the pockets of the fallen in case there was any loose change.

Tiffany stood up.

'Ach, weel, no' a bad job tho' I says it mysel',' said Rob Anybody, looking around. 'A very neat fight an' we didnae e'en ha' to resort to usin' poetry.'

'How did you get into the nut?' said Tiffany. 'I mean, it was . . . a nut!'

'Only way we could find in,' said Rob Anybody. 'It's got to be a way that fits. 'Tis difficult work, navigatin' in dreams.'

'Especially when ye're a wee bittie pished,' said Daft Wullie, grinning broadly.

'What? You've been . . . drinking?' said Tiffany. 'I've been facing the Queen and you've been in a *pub*?'

'Ach, no!' said Rob Anybody. 'Ye ken that dream wi' the big party? When you had the pretty frock an' a'? We got stuck in it.'

'But I killed the drome!'

Rob looked a little shifty. 'Weeeel,' he said, 'we didnae get oout as easily as you. It took us a wee while.'

'Until we finished all the drink,' said Daft Wullie helpfully. Rob glared at him.

'Ye didnae ha' to put it like that!' he snapped.

'You mean the dream keeps on going?' said Tiffany.

'If you're thirsty enough,' said Daft Wullie. 'An' it wasnae just the drink, there was can-a-pays as well.'

'But I thought if you ate or drank in a dream you stayed there!' said Tiffany.

'Aye, for most creatures,' said Rob Anybody. 'Not for us, though. Hooses, banks, dreams, 'tis a' the same to us. There's nothing we cannae get in or oot of.'

'Except maybe pubs,' said Big Yan.

'Oh, aye,' said Rob Anybody cheerfully. 'Gettin' oot o' pubs sometimes causes us a cerrrtain amount o' difficulty, I'll grant ye that.'

'And where did the Queen go?' Tiffany demanded.

'Ach, she did an offski as soon as we arrived,' said Rob Anybody. 'An' so should we, lady, afore the dream changes.' He nodded at Wentworth. 'Is this the wee bairn? Ach, what a noseful o' bogeys!'

'Wanna sweetie!' shouted Wentworth, on automatic sweetie pilot.

'Weeel, ye cannae ha' none!' shouted Rob Anybody. 'An' stop snivellin' and come awa' wi' us and stop bein' a burden to your wee sister!'

Tiffany opened her mouth to protest, and shut it again when Wentworth, after a moment of shock, chuckled.

'Funny!' he said. 'Wee man! Weewee man!'

'Oh dear,' said Tiffany. 'You've got him started now.'

But she was very surprised, nonetheless. Wentworth never showed this much interest in anyone who wasn't a jelly baby.

'Rob, we've got a real one here,' a pictsie called out. To her horror, Tiffany saw that several of the Nac Mac Feegles were holding up Roland's unconscious head. He was full-length on the ground.

'Ah, that was the laddie who wuz rude to ye,' said Rob. 'An' he tried to hit Big Yan with a hammer too. That wasnae a clever thing to try. What shall we do with him?'

The grasses trembled. The light was fading from the sky. The air was growing colder too.

'We can't leave him here!' said Tiffany.

'OK, we'll drag him along,' said Rob Anybody. 'Let's move right *noo*!'

'Weewee man! Weewee man!' shouted Wentworth gleefully.

'He'll be like this all day, I'm afraid,' said Tiffany. 'Sorry.'

'Run for the door,' said Rob Anybody. 'Can ye no' see the door?'

Tiffany looked around desperately. The wind was bitter now.

'See the door!' Rob Anybody commanded. She blinked, and spun round.

'Er . . . er . . .' she said. The sense of a world beneath that had come to her when she was frightened of the Queen did not turn up so easily now. She tried to concentrate. The smell of snow . . .

It was ridiculous to talk about the smell of snow. It was just pure frozen water. But Tiffany always knew, when she woke up, if it had snowed in the night. Snow had a smell like the taste of tin. Tin *did* have a taste, although admittedly it tasted like the smell of snow.

She thought she heard her brain creak with the effort of thinking. If she was in a dream, she had to wake up. But it was no use running. Dreams were full of running. But there was one direction that looked . . . thin, and white.

She shut her eyes, and thought about snow, crisp and white as fresh bedsheets. She concentrated on the feel of it under her feet. All she had to do was wake up . . .

She *was* standing in snow.

'Right,' said Rob Anybody.

'I got out!' said Tiffany.

'Ach, sometimes the door's in yer ain heid,' said Rob Anybody. 'Noo let's move!'

Tiffany felt herself being lifted into the air. Nearby, a snoring Roland rose up on dozens of small blue legs as the Feegles got underneath him.

'Nae stoppin' until we get right oout o' here!' said Rob Anybody. 'Feegles wha hae!'

They skimmed over the snow, with parties of Feegles running on ahead. After a minute or two Tiffany looked behind them, and saw the blue shadows spreading. They were getting darker too.

'Rob—' she said.

'Aye, I ken,' said Rob. 'Run, lads!'

'They're moving *fast*, Rob!'

'I ken that too!'

Snow stung Tiffany's face. Trees blurred with the speed. The forest sped past. But the shadows were spreading across the path ahead and every time the party ran through them they seemed to have a certain solidity, like fog.

Now the shadows behind were night-black in the middle.

But the pictsies had passed the last tree, and the snowfields stretched ahead.

They stopped, so quickly that Tiffany almost toppled into the snow.

'What's happened?'

'Where's all oour old footprints gone?' said Daft

Wullie. 'They wuz there a moment ago! Which way *noo*?'

The trampled track that had led them on like a line had vanished.

Rob Anybody spun round and looked back at the forest. Darkness curled above it like smoke, spreading along the horizon.

'She's sendin' nightmares after us,' he growled. 'This is gonna be a toughie, lads.'

Tiffany saw shapes in the spreading night. She hugged Wentworth tightly.

'Nightmares,' repeated Rob Anybody, turning to her. 'Ye wouldnae want to know about *them*. We'll hold 'em off. Ye must mak' a run for it. Get awa' wi' ye, noo!'

'I've got nowhere to run to!' said Tiffany.

She heard a high-pitched noise, a sort of chittering, insect noise, coming from the forest. The pictsies had drawn together. Usually they grinned like anything if they thought a fight was coming up, but this time they looked deadly serious.

'Ach, she's a bad loser, the Quin,' said Rob.

Tiffany turned to look at the horizon behind her. The boiling blackness was there too, a ring that was closing in from all sides.

Doors everywhere, she thought. The old kelda said there's doors everywhere. I must find a door. But there's just snow and a few trees . . .

The pictsies drew their swords.

'What, er, kind of nightmares are coming?' said Tiffany.

'Ach, long-leggity things with muckle legs and huge teeth, and flappy wings and a hundred eyes, that kinda stuff,' said Daft Wullie.

'Aye, and wuss than that,' said Rob Anybody, staring at the speeding dark.

'What's worse than that?' said Tiffany.

'Normal stuff gone wrong,' said Rob.

Tiffany looked blank for a moment, and then shuddered. Oh yes, she knew about those nightmares. They didn't happen often, but they were horrible when they did. She'd woken up once shaking at the thought of Granny Aching's boots, which had been chasing her, and another time it was a box of sugar. Anything could be a nightmare.

She could put up with monsters. But she didn't want to face mad boots.

'Er . . . I have an idea,' she said.

'So do I,' said Rob Anybody. 'Dinnae be here, that's my idea!'

'There's a clump of trees over there,' said Tiffany.

'So what?' said Rob. He was staring at the line of nightmares. Things were visible in it, now – teeth, claws, eyes, ribs. From the way he was glaring it was obvious that, whatever happened later, the first few monsters were going to face a serious problem. If they had faces, anyway.

'Can you *fight* nightmares?' said Tiffany. The chittering noise was getting a lot louder.

'There's no' a thing we cannae fight,' growled Big Yan. 'If it's got a heid, we can gi' it a faceful o' dandruff. If it disnae have a heid, it's due a good kickin'!'

Tiffany stared at the onrushing . . . things.

'Some of them have got *more* than one head!' she said.

'It's oour lucky day, then,' said Daft Wullie.

The pictsies shifted their weight, ready to fight.

'Piper,' said Rob Anybody to William the gonnagle, 'play us a lament. We'll fight to the sound of the mousepipes—'

'No!' said Tiffany. 'I'm not standing for this! The way to fight nightmares is to wake up! I am your kelda! This is an order! We're heading for those trees right now! Do what I say!'

'Weewee man!' yelled Wentworth.

The pictsies glanced at the trees, and then at Tiffany.

'Do it!' she yelled, so loudly that some of them flinched. 'Right now! Do what I tell you! There's a better way!'

'Ye cannae cross a hag, Rob,' muttered William.

'I'm going to get you home!' snapped Tiffany. I hope, she added to herself. But she'd seen a small, round, pale face staring at them around a tree trunk. There was a drome in those trees.

'Ach, aye, but—' Rob Anybody glanced past Tiffany and added: 'Aw no, look at that . . .'

There was a pale dot in front of the racing line of monstrousness.

Sneebs was making a break for it. His arms pumped like pistons. His little legs seemed to spin. His cheeks were like balloons.

The tide of nightmares rolled over him and kept coming.

Rob sheathed his sword. 'Ye heard oour kelda, lads!' he shouted. 'Grab her! We'rrre offski!'

Tiffany was lifted up. Feegles raised the unconscious Roland. And everyone ran for the trees.

Tiffany pulled her hand out of her apron pocket, and opened up the crumpled wrapper of Jolly Sailor tobacco. It was something to focus on, to remind her of a dream . . .

People *said* you could see the sea from the very top of the downs, but Tiffany had stared hard on a fine winter's day, when the air was clear, and seen nothing but the hazy blue of distance. But the sea on the Jolly Sailor packet was deep blue, with white crests on the waves. It *was* the sea, for Tiffany.

It had looked like a *small* drome in the trees. That meant it wasn't very powerful. She hoped so. She had to hope so . . .

The trees got closer. So did the ring of nightmares. Some of the sounds were horrible, of cracking bones and crushing rocks and stinging insects and screaming cats, getting nearer and nearer and nearer—

CHAPTER 12

Jolly Sailor

There was sand around her, and white waves crashing, and water draining off the shingle and sounding like an old woman sucking a hard mint.

'Crivens! Where are we noo?' said Daft Wullie.

'Aye, and why're we all lookin' like yellow mushrooms?' Rob Anybody added.

Tiffany looked down, and giggled. Every pictsie was wearing a Jolly Sailor outfit, with an oilskin coat and a huge yellow oilskin rain hat that covered most of their faces. They started to wander about, bumping into one another.

My dream! Tiffany thought. The drome uses what it can find in your head . . . but this is *my* dream. I can *use* it.

Wentworth had gone quiet. He was staring at the waves.

There was a boat pulled up on the shingle. As one pictsie, or small yellow mushroom, the Nac Mac Feegles were flocking towards it and clambering up the sides.

'What are you doing?' said Tiffany.

'Best if we wuz leavin',' said Rob Anybody. 'It's a good dream ye've found us, but we cannae stay here.'

'But we should be safe here!'

'Ach, the Quin finds a way in everywhere,' said Rob, as a hundred pictsies raised an oar. 'Dinnae fash yersel', we know all about boats. Did ye no' see Not-totally-wee-Georgie pike fishin' wi' Wee Bobby in the stream the other day? We is no strangers to the piscatorial an' nautical arts, ye ken.'

And they did indeed seem to know about boats. The oars were heaved into the rowlocks, and a party of Feegles pushed it down the stones and into the waves.

'Now you just hand us the wee bairn,' shouted Rob Anybody from the stern. Uncertainly, her feet slipping on the wet stones, Tiffany waded through the cold water and handed Wentworth over.

He seemed to think it was very funny.

'Weewee mens!' he yelled, as they lowered him into the boat. It was his only joke, so he wasn't going to stop.

'Aye, that's right,' said Rob Anybody, tucking him under the seat. 'Noo just you bide there like a good boy and no yellin' for sweeties or Uncle Rob'll gi' ye a skelpin' across the earhole, OK?'

Wentworth chuckled.

Tiffany ran back up the beach and hauled Roland to his feet. He opened his eyes and looked blearily at her.

'W'a's happening?' he said. 'I had this strange drea—' and then he shut his eyes again, and sagged.

'Get in the boat!' Tiffany shouted, dragging him across the shingle.

'Crivens, are we takin' this wee streak o' uselessness?' said Rob, grabbing Roland's trousers and heaving him aboard.

'Of course!' Tiffany hauled herself in afterwards, and landed in the bottom of the boat as a wave took it. The oars creaked and splashed, and the boat jerked forward. It jolted once or twice as more waves hit it, and then began to plunge across the sea. The pictsies were strong, after all. Even though each oar was a battleground as pictsies hung from it, or piled up on one another's shoulders or just heaved anything they could grasp, both oars were almost bending as they were dragged through the water.

Tiffany picked herself up, and tried to ignore the sudden uncertain feeling in her stomach.

'Head for the lighthouse!' she said.

'Aye, I ken that,' said Rob Anybody. 'It's the only place there is! And the Quin disnae like light.' He grinned. 'It's a good dream, lady. Have ye no' looked at the sky?'

'It's just a blue sky,' said Tiffany.

'It's no' *exactly* a sky,' said Rob Anybody. 'Look behind ye.'

Tiffany turned. It was a blue sky. Very blue. But

above the retreating beach, halfway up the sky, was a band of yellow. It looked a long way away, and hundreds of miles across. And in the middle of it, looming over the world as big as a galaxy and grey-blue with distance, was a lifebelt.

On it, but spelled backwards in letters larger than the moon, were the words:

'We are in the label?' said Tiffany.

'Oh, aye,' said Rob Anybody.

'But the sea feels . . . real. It's salty and wet and cold. It's not like paint! I didn't dream it salty or so cold!'

'Nae kiddin'? Then it's a picture on the outside, and it's real on the inside.' Rob nodded. 'Ye ken, we've been robbin' an' runnin' aroound on all kinds o' worlds for a lang time, and I'll tell ye this: the universe is a lot more comp-li-cated than it looks from the ooutside.'

Tiffany took the grubby label out of her pocket and stared at it again. There was the lifebelt, and the lighthouse. But the Jolly Sailor himself wasn't there. What *was* there, so tiny as to be little bigger than a dot on the printed sea, was a tiny rowing boat.

She looked up. There were storm clouds in the sky, in front of the huge, hazy lifebelt. They were long and ragged, curling as they came.

'It didnae take her long to find a way in,' muttered William.

'No,' said Tiffany, 'but this is my dream. I know how it goes. Keep rowing!'

Tangling and tumbling, some of the clouds passed overhead and then swooped towards the sea. They vanished beneath the waves like a waterspout in reverse.

It began to rain hard, so hard that a haze of mist rose over the sea.

'Is that it?' Tiffany wondered. 'Is that all she can do?'

'I doot it,' said Rob Anybody. 'Bend them oars, lads!'

The boat shot forward, bouncing through the rain from wavetop to wavetop.

But, against all normal rules, it was now trying to go uphill. The water was mounding up and up, and the boat washed backwards in the streaming surf.

Something was rising. Something white was

pushing the seas aside. Great waterfalls poured off the shining dome that climbed towards the storm sky.

It rose higher, and still there was more. And, eventually, there was an eye. It was tiny compared to the mountainous head above it, and it rolled in its socket and focused on the tiny boat.

'Now, *that's* a heid that be a day's work e'en for Big Yan,' said Rob Anybody. 'I reckon we'd have to come back tomorrow! Row, boys!'

'It's a dream of mine,' said Tiffany, as calmly as she could manage. 'It's the whale fish.'

I never dreamed the smell, though, she added to herself. But here it is, a huge, solid, world-filling smell of salt and water and fish and ooze—

'Whut does it eat?' Daft Wullie asked.

'Ah, I know that,' said Tiffany, as the boat rocked on the swell. 'Whales aren't dangerous, because they just eat very small things . . .'

'*Row like the blazes, lads!*' Rob Anybody yelled.

'How d'ye ken it only eats wee stuff?' said Daft Wullie as the whale fish's mouth began to open.

'I paid a whole cucumber once for a lesson on Beasts of the Deep,' said Tiffany, as a wave washed over them. 'Whales don't even have proper teeth!'

There was a creaking sound and a gust of fishy halitosis about the size of a typhoon, and the view was full of enormous, pointy teeth.

'Aye?' said Wullie. 'Weel, no offence meant, but I dinnae think this beastie went to the same school as ye!'

The surge of water was pushing them away. And

Tiffany could see the whole of the head now and, in a way she couldn't possibly describe, the whale looked like the Queen. The Queen was *there*, somewhere.

The anger came back.

'This is *my* dream,' she shouted at the sky. 'I've dreamed it dozens of times! You're not allowed in here! And whales don't eat people! Everyone who isn't very stupid knows that!'

A tail the size of a field rose and slapped down on the sea. The whale shot forward.

Rob Anybody threw off his yellow hat and drew his sword.

'Ach, weel, we tried,' he said. 'This wee beastie's gonna get the worst belly ache there ever wuz!'

'Aye, we'll cut oour way out!' shouted Daft Wullie.

'No, keep rowing!' said Tiffany.

'It's ne'er been said that the Nac Mac Feegle turned their back on a foe!' Rob yelled.

'But you're rowing *facing* backwards!' Tiffany pointed out.

The pictsie looked crestfallen. 'Oh, aye, I hadnae thought o' it like that,' he said, sitting down again.

'Just row!' Tiffany insisted. 'We're nearly at the lighthouse!'

Grumbling, because even if they *were* facing the right way they were still going the wrong way, the pictsies hauled on the oars.

'That's a great big heid he's got there, ye ken,' said Rob Anybody. 'How big would you say that heid is, gonnagle?'

'Ach, I'd say it's *verrra* big, Rob,' said William, who

was with the team on the other oar. 'Indeed, I might commit myself to sayin' it's enorrrrmous.'

'Ye'd go as far as that, would ye?'

'Oh, aye. Enorrrrmous is fully justified . . .'

It's nearly on us, Tiffany thought.

This has got to work. It's my dream. Any moment. Any moment now . . .

'An' how near us would you say it is, then?' asked Rob conversationally, as the boat wallowed and jerked just ahead of the whale.

'That's a verrra good question, Rob,' said William. 'And I'd answer it by sayin' it's verrra close indeed.'

Any moment now, thought Tiffany. I know Miss Tick said you shouldn't believe in your dreams, but she meant you shouldn't just *hope*.

Er . . . any moment now, I . . . hope. He's never missed . . .

'In fact I'd go so farrr as to say *exceedingly* close—' William began.

Tiffany swallowed, and hoped that the whale wouldn't. There was only about thirty yards of water between the teeth and the boat.

And then it was filled with a wooden wall that blurred as it went past, making a zipzipzip noise.

Tiffany looked up, her mouth open. White sails flashed across the storm clouds, pouring rain like waterfalls. She looked up at rigging and ropes and sailors lined up on the spars, and cheered.

And then the stern of the Jolly Sailor's ship was disappearing into the rain and mist, but not before Tiffany saw the big bearded figure at the wheel, dressed in yellow oilskins. He turned and waved just once, before the ship vanished into the murk.

She managed to stand up again, as the boat rocked in the swell, and yelled at the towering whale: 'You've got to chase him! That's how it has to work! You chase him, he chases you! *Granny Aching said so!* You can't *not* do it and still be the whale fish! This is *my* dream! My rules! I've had more practice at it than you!'

'Big fishy!' yelled Wentworth.

That was more surprising than the whale. Tiffany stared at her little brother as the boat rocked again.

'Big fishy!' said Wentworth again.

'That's right!' Tiffany said, delighted. 'Big fishy! And what makes it *particularly* interesting it that a whale isn't a fish! It is in fact a mammal, just like a cow!'

Did you just say that? said her Second Thoughts, as all the pictsies stared at her and the boat spun in the surf. The first time he's ever said anything that wasn't about sweeties or weewee and you just *corrected* him?

Tiffany looked at the whale. It was having trouble. But it was *the* whale, the whale she'd dreamed about many times after Granny Aching had told her that story, and not even the Queen could control a story like that.

It turned reluctantly in the water and dived in the wake of the Jolly Sailor's ship.

'Big fishy gone!' said Wentworth.

'No, it's a mammal—' Tiffany's mouth said, before she could stop it.

The pictsies were still staring at her.

'It's just that he ought to get it right,' she mumbled, ashamed of herself. 'It's a mistake lots of people make . . .'

You're going to turn into somebody like Miss Tick, said her Second Thoughts. Do you really want that?

'Yes,' said a voice, and Tiffany realized that it was hers again. The anger rose up joyfully. 'Yes! I'm *me*! I am careful and logical and I look up things I don't understand! When I hear people use the wrong words I get edgy! I am good with cheese. I read books fast! I *think*! And I always have a piece of string! That's the kind of person I am!'

She stopped. Even Wentworth was staring at her now. He blinked.

'Big water cow gone . . .' he suggested meekly.

'That's right! Good boy!' said Tiffany. 'When we get home you can have *one* sweet!'

She saw the massed ranks of the Nac Mac Feegles still looking at her with worried expressions.

'Is it OK wi' you if we get on?' said Rob Anybody, holding up a nervous hand. 'Before yon whale fi— Before yon whale cow comes back?'

Tiffany looked past them. The lighthouse wasn't far. A little jetty stretched out from its tiny island.

'Yes, please. Er . . . thank you,' she said, calming down a bit. The ship and the whale had vanished into the rain and the sea was merely lapping at the shore.

A drome was sitting on the rocks with its pale, fat legs sticking out in front of it. It was staring out to sea and didn't appear to notice the approaching boat. It thinks it's home, Tiffany thought. I've given it a dream it likes.

Pictsies poured onto the jetty and tied up the boat.

'OK, we're here,' said Rob Anybody. 'We'll just chop yon creature's heid off and we'll be right oout o' here . . .'

'Don't!' said Tiffany.

'But it—'

'Leave it alone. Just . . . leave it alone, all right? It's not interested.' And it knows about sea, she added to herself. It's probably homesick for the sea. That's why it's such a *real* dream. I'd have never have got it right by myself.

A crab crawled out of the surf by the drome's feet, and settled down to dream crab dreams.

It looks as though a drome can get lost in its own dream, she thought. I wonder if it'll ever wake up?

She turned to the Nac Mac Feegles. 'In my dream I always wake up when I reach the lighthouse,' she said.

The pictsies looked up at the red and white tower and, as one Feegle, drew their swords.

'We dinnae trust the Quin,' said Rob. 'She'll let ye think ye're safe, and just when ye've dropped your guard she'll leap oout. She'll be waitin' behind the door, ye can bet on it. Ye'll let us go in first.'

It was an instruction, not a question. Tiffany nodded, and watched the Nac Mac Feegles swarm over the rocks towards the tower.

Alone on the jetty, except for Wentworth and the unconscious Roland, she lifted the toad out of her pocket. It opened its yellow eyes and stared at the sea.

'Either I'm dreaming, or I'm on a beach,' it said. 'And toads don't dream.'

'In my dream they can,' said Tiffany. 'And this is *my* dream.'

'Then it is an extremely dangerous one!' said the toad ungratefully.

'No, it's lovely,' said Tiffany. 'It's wonderful. Look at the way the light dances on the waves.'

'Where are the notices warning people they could drown?' complained the toad. 'No lifebelts or shark nets. Oh, dear. Do I see a qualified lifeguard? I think not. Supposing someone was to—'

'It's a beach,' said Tiffany. 'Why are you talking like this?'

'I – I don't know,' said the toad. 'Can you put me down, please? I feel a headache coming on.'

Tiffany put it down and it shuffled into some seaweed. After a while she heard it eating something.

The sea was calm.

It was peaceful.

It was exactly the moment anyone sensible should distrust.

But nothing happened. It was followed by nothing else happening. Wentworth picked up a pebble from the shingle and put it in his mouth, on the basis that anything might be a sweetie.

Then, suddenly, there were noises from the lighthouse. Tiffany heard muffled shouts, and thuds, and once or twice the sound of breaking glass. At one point there was a noise like something heavy falling down a long spiral staircase and hitting every step on the way.

The door opened. The Nac Mac Feegles came out. They looked satisfied.

'Nae problemo,' said Rob Anybody. 'No one there.'

'But there was a lot of noise!'

'Oh, aye. We had to make sure,' said Daft Wullie.

'Weewee men!' shouted Wentworth.

'I'll wake up when I go through the door,' said Tiffany, pulling Roland out of the boat. 'I always have. It must work. This is my dream.' She hauled the boy upright and turned to the nearest Feegle. 'Can you bring Wentworth?'

'Aye.'

'And you won't get lost or, or drunk or anything?'

Rob Anybody looked offended. 'We ne'er get lost!' he said. 'We always ken where we are! It's just sometimes mebbe we aren't sure where everything else is, but it's no' our fault if *everything else* gets lost! The Nac Mac Feegle are never lost!'

'What about drunk?' said Tiffany, dragging Roland towards the lighthouse.

'We've ne'er been lost in oour lives! Is that no' the case, lads?' said Rob Anybody. There was a murmur of resentful agreement. 'The words "lost" and "Nac Mac Feegle" shouldnae turn up in the same sentence!'

'And drunk?' said Tiffany again, laying Roland down on the shingle.

'Gettin' lost is something that happens to other people!' declared Rob Anybody. 'I want to make that point perrrfectly clear!'

'Well, at least there shouldn't have been anything to drink in a lighthouse,' said Tiffany. She laughed. 'Unless you drank the lamp oil, and *no one* would dare do that!'

The pictsies suddenly fell silent.

'What would that be, then?' said Daft Wullie, in a slow, careful voice. 'Would it be the stuff in a kind o' big bottle kind o' thingie?'

'Wi' a wee skull and crossbones on it?' said Rob Anybody.

'Yes, probably, and it's horrible stuff,' said Tiffany. 'It'd make you terribly ill if you drank it.'

'Really?' said Rob Anybody thoughtfully. 'That's verra . . . interesting. What sort o' ill would that be, kind o' thing?'

'I think you'd probably die,' said Tiffany.

'We're already dead,' said Rob Anybody.

'Well, you'd be very, very sick, then,' said Tiffany. She gave him a strong look. 'It's inflammable too. It's a good job you didn't drink it, isn't it . . .'

Daft Wullie belched loudly. There was a strong smell of paraffin.

'Aye,' he said.

Tiffany went and fetched Wentworth. Behind her, she heard some muffled whispering as the pictsies went into a huddle.

'*I told yez the wee skull on it meant we shouldnae touch it!*'

'*Big Yan said that showed it wuz strong stuff! An' things ha' come to a pretty pass, ye ken, if people are going to leave stuff like that aroound where innocent*' *people could accidentally smash the door doon and lever the bars aside and take the big chain off'f the cupboard and pick the lock and drink it!'*

'What's inflammable mean?'

'It means it catches fire!'

'OK, OK, dinnae panic. No belchin', and none of youse is to tak' a leak anywhere near any naked flames, OK? And act nat'ral.'

Tiffany smiled to herself. Pictsies seemed very hard to kill. Perhaps believing you were already dead made you immune. She turned and looked towards the lighthouse door. She had never actually seen it opened in her dream. She'd always thought that the lighthouse was full of light, on the basis that on the farm the cowshed was full of cows and the woodshed was full of wood.

'All right, all right,' she said, looking down at Rob Anybody. 'I'm going to carry Roland, and I want you to bring Wentworth.'

'Don't you want to carry the wee lad?' said Rob.

'Weewee man!' shouted Wentworth.

'You bring him,' said Tiffany shortly. She meant: I'm not sure this is going to work, and he might be safer with you than with me. I hope I'm going to wake up in my bedroom. Waking up in my bedroom would be nice . . .

Of course, if everyone else wakes up there too, there might be some difficult questions asked, but anything's better than the Queen—

There was a rushing, rattling noise behind her. She turned, and saw the sea disappearing, very quickly. It was pulling back down the shore. As she watched, rocks and clumps of seaweed rose above the surf and then were suddenly high and dry.

'Ah,' she said, after a moment. 'It's all right. I know what this is. It's the tide. The sea does this. It goes in and out every day.'

'Aye?' said Rob Anybody. 'Amazin'. It looks like it's pourin' awa' though a hole . . .'

About fifty yards away the last rivulets of sea water were disappearing over an edge, and some of the pictsies were already heading towards it.

Tiffany suddenly had a moment of something that wasn't exactly panic. It was a lot slower and nastier than panic. It began with just a nagging little doubt, that said: isn't the tide a bit slower?

The teacher (**Wonders of the Nattral Wurld, One Apple**) hadn't gone into much detail. But there were fish flapping on the exposed sea bed, and surely the fish in the sea didn't die every day?

'Er, I think we'd better be careful . . .' she said, trailing after Rob Anybody.

'Why? It's nae as though the water's risin',' he said. 'When does the tide come back?'

'Um, not for hours, I think,' said Tiffany, feeling the slow, nasty panic getting bigger. 'But I'm not sure this—'

'Tons o' time, then,' said Rob Anybody.

They'd reached the edge, where the rest of the pictsies were lined up. A little bit of water still trickled over their feet, pouring down into the gulf beyond.

It was like looking down into a valley. At the far

side, miles and miles away, the retreating sea was just a gleaming line.

Below them, though, were the shipwrecks. There were a lot of them. Galleons and schooners and clippers, masts broken, rigging hanging, hulls breached, lay strewn across the puddles in what had been the bay.

The Nac Mac Feegles, as one pictsie, sighed happily.

'Sunken treasure!'

'Aye! Gold!'

'Bullion!'

'Jools!'

'What makes you think they've got treasure in?' said Tiffany.

The Nac Mac Feegles looked amazed, as if she'd suggested that rocks could fly.

'There's *got* to be treasure in 'em,' said Daft Wullie. 'Otherwise what's the point of lettin' 'em sink?'

'That's right,' said Rob Anybody. 'There's got t'be gold in sunken ships, otherwise it wouldnae be worth fighting all them sharkies and octopussies and stuff. Stealin' treasure fra' the ocean's bed, that's aboout the biggest, best thievin' *ever*!'

And now what Tiffany felt was real, honest panic.

'That's a lighthouse!' she said, pointing. 'Can you see it? A lighthouse so ships don't run into the rocks! Right? Understand? This is a trap made just for you! The Queen's still around!'

'Mebbe just can we go down and look inside one wee ship?' said Rob Anybody meekly.

'No! Because—' Tiffany looked up. A gleam had

caught her eye. 'Because . . . the sea . . . is . . . coming . . . back . . .' she said.

What looked like a cloud on the horizon was getting bigger, and glittering as it came. Tiffany could already hear the roar.

She ran back up the beach and got her hands under Roland's armpits, so that she could drag him to the lighthouse. She looked back, and the pictsies were still watching the huge, surging wave.

And there was Wentworth, watching the wave happily, and bending down slightly so that, if *they* stood on tiptoe, he could hold hands with two Feegles.

The image branded itself on her eyes. The little boy, and the pictsies, all with their backs to her, and all staring with interest at the rushing, glittering, sky-filling wall of water.

'Come on!' Tiffany yelled. 'I was wrong, this isn't the tide, this is the Queen—'

Sunken ships were lifted up and spun around in the hissing mountain of surf.

'Come *on!*'

Tiffany managed to haul Roland across her shoulder and, staggering across the rocks, made it to the lighthouse door as the water crashed behind her—

– for a moment the world was full of white light—

– and snow squeaked underfoot.

It was the silent, cold land of the Queen. There was no one around and nothing to see except snow and, in the distance, the forest. Black clouds hovered over it.

Ahead of her, and only just visible, was a picture in

the air. It showed some turf, and a few stones, lit with moonlight.

It was the other side of the door back home.

She turned round desperately.

'Please!' she shouted. It wasn't a request to anyone special. She just needed to shout. 'Rob? William? Wullie? *Wentworth?*'

Away towards the forest there was the barking of the grimhounds.

'Got to get out,' muttered Tiffany. 'Got to get away . . .'

She grabbed Roland by the collar and dragged him towards the door. At least he slid better on snow.

No one and nothing tried to stop her. The snow spilled a little way through the doorway between the stones and onto the turf, but the air was warm and alive with night-time insect noises. Under a real moon, under a real sky, she pulled the boy over to a fallen stone and sat him up against it. She sat down next to him, exhausted to the bone, and tried to get her breath back.

Her dress was soaked, and smelled of the sea.

She could hear her own thoughts, a long way off:

They could still be alive. It was a dream, after all. There must be a way back. All I have to do is find it. I've got to go back in there.

The dogs sounded very loud . . .

She stood up again, although what she really wanted to do was sleep.

The three stones of the door were a black shape against the stars.

And as she watched, they fell down. The one on the left slipped over, slowly, and the other two ended up leaning against it.

She ran over and hauled at the tons of stone. She prodded the air around them in case the doorway was still there. She squinted madly, trying to see it.

Tiffany stood under the stars, alone, and tried not to cry.

'What a shame,' said the Queen. 'You've let everybody down, haven't you . . . ?'

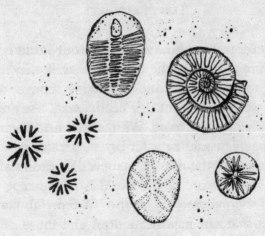

CHAPTER 13

Land Under Wave

The Queen walked over the turf towards Tiffany. Where she'd trodden, frost gleamed for a moment. The little part of Tiffany that was still thinking thought: That grass will be dead in the morning. She's killing *my* turf.

'The whole of life is but a dream, when you come to think of it,' said the Queen in the same infuriatingly calm, pleasant voice. She sat down on the fallen stones. 'You humans are such dreamers. You dream that you're clever. You dream that you're important. You dream that you're special. You know, you're almost better than dromes. You're certainly more imaginative. I have to thank you.'

'What for?' said Tiffany, looking at her boots. Terror clamped her body in red-hot wires. There wasn't anywhere to run to.

'I never realized how wonderful your world *is*,' said the Queen. 'I mean, the dromes . . . well, they're not much more than a kind of walking sponge, really. Their world is ancient. It's nearly dead. They're not really *creative* any more. With a little help from me, your people could be a lot better. Because, you see, you dream all the time. *You*, especially, dream all the time. Your picture of the world is a landscape with you in the middle of it, isn't it? Wonderful. Look at you, in that rather horrible dress and those clumpy boots. You dreamed you could invade my world with a frying pan. You had this dream about Brave Girl Rescuing Little Brother. You thought you were the heroine of a *story*. And then you left him behind. You know, I think being hit by a billion tons of sea water must be like having a mountain of iron drop on your head, don't you?'

Tiffany couldn't think. Her head was full of hot, pink fog. It *hadn't* worked.

Her Third Thoughts were somewhere in the fog, trying to make themselves heard.

'Got Roland out,' she muttered, still staring at her boots.

'But he's not yours,' said the Queen. 'He is, let us face it, a rather stupid boy with a big red face and brains made of pork, just like his father. You left your little brother behind with a bunch of little thieves and you rescued a spoiled little fool.'

There was no *time*! shrieked the Third Thoughts. You wouldn't have got to him *and* got back to the lighthouse! You nearly didn't get away as it was! You got Roland out! It was the logical thing to do! You don't have to be guilty about it! What's better, to try to save your brother and be brave, courageous, stupid and dead, or save the boy and be brave, courageous, sensible and alive?

But something kept saying that stupid and dead would have been more . . . right.

Something kept saying: Would you say to Mum that you could see there wasn't time to rescue your brother so you rescued someone else instead? Would she be *pleased* that you'd worked that out? Being right doesn't always work.

It's the Queen! yelled the Third Thoughts. It's her voice! It's like hypnotism! You've got to stop listening!

'I expect it's not your fault you're so cold and heartless,' said the Queen. 'It's probably all to do with your parents. They probably never gave you enough time. And having Wentworth was a very cruel thing to do, they really should have been more careful. And they let you read too many words. It can't be good for a young brain, knowing words like paradigm and eschatological. It leads to behaviour such as using your own brother as monster bait.' The Queen sighed. 'Sadly, that kind of thing happens all the time. I think you should be proud of not being worse than just deeply introverted and socially maladjusted.'

She walked around Tiffany.

'It's so sad,' she continued. 'You dream that you are strong, sensible, logical . . . the kind of person who always has a bit of string. But that's just your excuse for not being really, properly human. You're just a brain, no heart at all. You didn't even cry when Granny Aching died. You *think* too much, and now your precious thinking has let *you* down. Well, *I* think it's best if I just kill you, don't you?'

Find a stone! the Third Thoughts screamed. Hit her!

Tiffany was aware of other figures in the gloom. There were some of the people from the summer pictures, but there were also dromes and the headless horseman and the Bumble-Bee women.

Around her, frost crept over the ground.

'I think we'll like it here,' said the Queen.

Tiffany felt the cold creeping up her legs. Her Third Thoughts, hoarse with effort, shouted: Do *something*!

She should have been better organized, she thought dully. She shouldn't have relied on dreams. Or . . . perhaps I should have been a real human being. More . . . feeling. But I couldn't help not crying! It just . . . wouldn't come! And how can I stop thinking? And thinking about thinking? And even thinking about thinking about thinking?

She saw the smile in the Queen's eyes, and thought: Which one of all those people doing all that thinking is *me*?

Is there really any *me* at all?

Clouds poured across the sky like a stain. They covered the stars. They were the inky clouds from the frozen world, the clouds of nightmare. It began to rain, rain with ice in it. It hit the turf like bullets, turning it into chalky mud. The wind howled like a pack of grimhounds.

Tiffany managed to take a step forward. The mud sucked at her boots.

'A bit of spirit at last?' said the Queen, stepping back.

Tiffany tried another step, but things were not working any more. She was too cold and too tired. She could feel her *self* disappearing, getting lost . . .

'So sad, to end like this,' said the Queen.

Tiffany fell forward, into the freezing mud.

The rain grew harder, stinging like needles, hammering on her head and running like icy tears down her cheeks. It struck so hard it left her breathless.

She felt the cold drawing all the heat out of her. And that was the only sensation left, apart from a musical note.

It sounded like the smell of snow, or the sparkle of frost. It was high and thin and drawn out.

She couldn't feel the ground under her and there was nothing to see, not even the stars. The clouds had covered everything.

She was so cold she couldn't *feel* the cold any more, or her fingers. A thought managed to trickle through her freezing mind. Is there any me at all? Or do my thoughts just dream of me?

The blackness grew deeper. Night was never as black as this, and winter never as cold. It was colder than the deep winters when the snow came down and Granny Aching would plod from snowdrift to snowdrift, looking for warm bodies. The sheep could survive the snow if the shepherd had some wits,

Granny used to say. The snow kept the cold away, the sheep surviving in warm hollows under roofs of snow while a bitter wind blew harmlessly over them.

But this was as cold as those days when even the snow couldn't fall, and the wind was pure cold itself, blowing ice crystals across the turf. Those were the killer days in early spring, when the lambing had begun and winter came howling down one more time . . .

There was darkness everywhere, bitter and starless.

There was a speck of light, a long way off.

One star. Low down. Moving . . .

It got bigger in the stormy night.

It zigzagged as it came.

Silence covered Tiffany, and drew her into itself.

The silence smelled of sheep, and turpentine, and tobaccco.

And then . . . came movement, as if she was falling through the ground, very fast.

And gentle warmth, and, just for a moment, the sound of waves.

And her own voice, inside her head.

This land is in my bones.

Land under wave.

Whiteness.

It tumbled through the warm, heavy darkness around her, something like snow but as fine as dust. It piled up somewhere below her, because she could see a faint whiteness.

A creature like an ice-cream cone with lots of tentacles shot past her and jetted away.

I'm underwater, thought Tiffany.

I remember . . .

This is the million-year rain under the sea, this is the new land being born underneath an ocean. It's not a dream. It's . . . a memory. The land under wave. Millions and millions of tiny shells . . .

This land was *alive.*

All the time there was the warm, comforting smell of the shepherding hut, and the feeling of being held in invisible hands.

The whiteness below her rose up and over her head, but it didn't seem uncomfortable. It was like being in a mist.

Now I'm inside the chalk, like a flint, like a calkin . . .

She wasn't sure how long she spent in the warm deep water, or if indeed any time really had passed, or if the millions of years went past in a second, but she felt movement again, and a sense of rising.

More memories poured into her mind.

There's always been someone watching the borders. They didn't decide to. It was decided for them. Someone has to care. Sometimes, they have to fight. Someone has to speak for that which has no voice . . .

She opened her eyes. She was still lying in the mud, and the Queen was laughing at her and, overhead, the storm still raged.

But she felt warm. In fact, she felt hot, red-hot with anger . . . anger at the bruised turf, anger at her own stupidity, anger at this beautiful creature whose only talent was control.

This . . . creature was trying to take her *world.*

All witches are selfish, the Queen had said. But Tiffany's Third Thoughts said: Then turn selfishness into a weapon! Make all things yours! Make other lives and dreams and hopes yours! Protect them! Save them! Bring them into the sheepfold! Walk the gale for them! Keep away the wolf! My dreams! My brother! My family! My land! My world! How dare you try to take these things, because *they are mine*!

I have a duty!

The anger overflowed. She stood up clenched her fists and screamed at the storm, putting into the scream all the rage that was inside her.

Lightning struck the ground on either side of her. It did so twice.

And it stayed there, crackling, and two dogs formed.

Steam rose from their coats, and blue light sparked from their ears as they shook themselves. They looked attentively at Tiffany.

The Queen gasped, and vanished.

'Come by, Lightning!' shouted Tiffany. 'Away to me, Thunder!' And she remembered the time when she'd run across the downs, falling over, shouting all the wrong things, while the two dogs had done exactly what needed to be done . . .

Two streaks of black and white sped away across the turf and up towards the clouds.

They herded the storm.

Clouds panicked and scattered, but always there was a comet streaking across the sky and they were turned. Monstrous shapes writhed and screamed in

the boiling sky, but Thunder and Lightning had
worked many flocks; there was an occasional snap of
lightning-sparked teeth, and a wail. Tiffany stared
upwards, rain pouring off her face, and shouted
commands that no dog could possibly have heard.

Jostling and rumbling and screaming, the storm
rolled off the hills and away towards the mountains,
where there were deep canyons that could pen it.

Out of breath, glowing with triumph, Tiffany
watched until the dogs came back and settled, once
again, on the turf. And then she remembered
something else: it *didn't* matter *what* orders she gave
those dogs. They were not her dogs. They were
working dogs.

Thunder and Lightning didn't take orders from a
little girl.

And the dogs weren't looking at her.

They were looking just behind her.

She'd have turned if someone had told her a
horrible monster was behind her. She'd have turned if
they'd said it had a thousand teeth. She didn't want to
turn round now. Forcing herself was the hardest thing
she'd ever done.

She was not afraid of what she might see. She was
terribly, mortally frightened, afraid to the centre of
her bones of what she might not see. She shut her eyes
while her cowardly boots shuffled her round and
then, after a deep breath, she opened them again.

There was a gust of Jolly Sailor tobacco, and sheep,
and turpentine.

Sparkling in the dark, light glittering off the white

shepherdess dress and every blue ribbon and silver buckle of it, was Granny Aching, smiling hugely, glowing with pride. In one hand she held the huge ornamental crook, hung with blue bows.

She pirouetted slowly, and Tiffany saw that while she was a brilliant, glowing shepherdess from hat to hem, she still had her huge old boots on.

Granny Aching took her pipe out of her mouth, and gave Tiffany the little nod that was, from her, a round of applause. And then – she wasn't.

Real starlit darkness covered the turf, and the night-time sounds filled the air. Tiffany didn't know if what had just happened was a dream or had happened somewhere that wasn't quite *here* or had only happened in her head. It didn't matter. It had *happened*. And now—

'But I'm still here,' said the Queen, stepping in front of her. 'Perhaps it *was* all a dream. Perhaps you have gone a little mad, because you are after all a very strange child. Perhaps you had help. How good are *you*? Do you really think that *you* can face me alone? I can make you think whatever I please—'

'Crivens!'

'Oh no, not *them*,' said the Queen, throwing up her hands.

It wasn't just the Nac Mac Feegles, but also Wentworth, a strong smell of seaweed, a lot of water and a dead shark. They appeared in mid-air and landed in a heap between Tiffany and the Queen. But a pictsie was always ready for a fight, and they bounced, rolled and came up drawing their swords and shaking sea water out of their hair.

'Oh, 'tis you, izzut?' said Rob Anybody, glaring up at the Queen. 'Face to face wi' ye at last, ye bloustie ol' callyack that ye are! Ye canna' come here, unnerstan? Be off wi' ye! Are ye goin' to go quietly?'

The Queen stamped heavily on him. When she took her foot away, only the top of his head was visible above the turf.

'Well, are ye?' he said, pulling himself out as if nothing had happened. 'I don't wantae havtae lose my temper wi' ye! An' it's no good sendin' your pets against us, 'cos you ken we can take 'em tae the cleaners!' He turned to Tiffany, who hadn't moved. 'You just leave this tae us, Kelda. Us an' the Quin, we go way back!'

The Queen snapped her fingers. 'Always leaping into things you don't understand,' she hissed. 'Well, can you face these?'

Every Nac Mac Feegle sword suddenly glowed blue.

Back in the crowd of eerily lit pictsies a voice that sounded very much like that of Daft Wullie said:

'Ach, we're in *real* trouble noo . . .'

Three figures had appeared in the air, a little way away. The middle one, Tiffany saw, had a long red gown, a strange long wig and black tights with buckles on his shoes. The others were just ordinary men, it seemed, in ordinary grey suits.

'Oh, ye are a harrrrrd wumman, Quin,' said William the gonnagle, 'to set the lawyers ontae us . . .'

'See the one on the left there,' whimpered a pictsie.

'See, he's got a briefcase! It's a *briefcase*! Oh, waily, waily, a briefcase, waily . . .'

Reluctantly, a step at a time, pressing together in terror, the Nac Mac Feegles began to back away.

'Oh, waily waily, he's snappin' the clasps,' groaned Daft Wullie. 'Oh, waily waily waily, 'tis the sound o' Doom when a lawyer does that!'

'Mister Rob Anybody Feegle and sundry others?' said one of the figures in a voice of dread.

'There's naebody here o' that name!' shouted Rob Anybody. 'We dinnae know anythin'!'

'We have heard a list of criminal and civil charges totalling nineteen thousand, seven hundred and sixty-three separate offences—'

'We wasnae there!' yelled Rob Anybody desperately. 'Isn't that right, lads?'

'– including more than two thousand cases of Making an Affray, Causing a Public Nuisance, Being Found Drunk, Being Found Very Drunk, Using Offensive Language (taking into account ninety-seven counts of Using Language That Was Probably Offensive If Anyone Else Could Understand It), Committing a Breach of the Peace, Malicious Lingering—'

'It's mistaken identity!' shouted Rob Anybody. 'It's no' oour fault! We wuz only standing there an' someone else did it and ran awa'!'

'– Grand Theft, Petty Theft, Burglary, House-breaking, Loitering With Intent To Commit a Felony—'

'We wuz misunderstood when we was wee bairns!'

yelled Rob Anybody. 'Ye're only pickin' on us cuz we're blue! We always get blamed for everythin'! The polis hate us! We wasnae even in the country!'

But, to groans from the cowering pictsies, one of the lawyers produced a big roll of paper from his briefcase. He cleared his throat and read out: 'Angus, Big; Angus, No'-As-Big-As-Big-Angus; Angus, Wee; Archie, Big; Archie, One-Eyed; Archie, Wee Mad—'

'They've got oour names!' sobbed Daft Wullie. 'They've got oour *names*! It's the pris'n hoose for us!'

'Objection! I move for a writ of *Habeas Corpus*,' said a small voice. 'And enter a plea of *Vis-ne faciem capite repletam*, without prejudice.'

There was absolute silence for a moment. Rob Anybody turned to look at the frightened Nac Mac Feegles and said: 'OK, OK, which of youse said that?'

The toad crawled out of the crowd, and sighed. 'It suddenly all came back to me,' it said. 'I remember what I was now. The legal language brought it all back. I'm a toad now but . . .' it swallowed, 'once I was a lawyer. And this, people, is illegal. These charges are a complete tissue of lies based on hearsay evidence.'

It raised yellow eyes towards the Queen's lawyers. 'I further move that the case is adjourned *sine die* on the basis of *Potest-ne mater tua suere, amice*.'

The lawyers had pulled large books out of nowhere and were thumbing through them hastily.

'We're not familiar with counsel's terminology,' said one of them.

'Hey, they're sweatin',' said Rob Anybody. 'You mean we can have lawyers on *oour* side as well?'

'Yes, of course,' said the toad. 'You can have defence lawyers.'

'Defence?' said Rob Anybody. 'Are you tellin' me we could get awa' wi' it 'cos of a tishoo o' lies?'

'Certainly,' said the toad. 'And with all the treasure you've stolen you can pay enough to be very innocent indeed. My fee will be—'

It gulped as a dozen glowing swords were swung towards him.

'I've just remembered *why* that fairy godmother turned me into a toad,' it said. 'So, in the circumstances, I'll take this case *pro bono publico.*'

The swords didn't move.

'That means for free,' it added.

'Oh, right, we like the sound o' that,' said Rob Anybody, to the sound of swords being sheathed. 'How come ye're a lawyer *an*' a toad?'

'Oh, well, it was just bit of an argument,' said the toad. 'A fairy godmother gave my client three wishes – the usual health, wealth and happiness package – and when my client woke up one wet morning and didn't feel *particularly* happy she got me to bring an action for breach of contract. It was a definite first in the history of fairy godmothering. Unfortunately, as it turned out, so was turning the client into a small hand mirror and her lawyer, as you see before you, into a toad. I think the worst part was when the judge applauded. That was hurtful, in my opinion.'

'But ye can still remember all that legal stuff? *Guid,*' said Rob Anybody. He glared at the other lawyers.

'Hey, youse scunners, we got a cheap lawyer and we no' afraid tae use him wi' prejudice!'

The other lawyers were pulling more and more paperwork out of the air now. They looked worried, and a little frightened. Rob Anybody's eyes gleamed as he watched them.

'What does all that Viznee-facey-em stuff mean, my learned friend?' he said.

'*Vis-ne faciem capite repletam,*' said the toad. 'It was the best I could do in a hurry, but it means, approximately,' he gave a little cough, ' "would you like a face which is full of head?" '

'And tae think we didnae know legal talkin' was that simple,' said Rob Anybody. 'We could all be lawyers, lads, if we knew the fancy words! Let's *get* them!'

The Nac Mac Feegle could change mood in a moment, especially at the sound of a battle cry. They raised their swords in the air.

'*Twelve hundred angry men!*' they shouted.

'*Nae more courtroom drama!*'

'*We ha' the law on oour side!*'

'*The law's made to tak' care o' raskills!*'

'No,' said the Queen, and waved her hand.

Lawyers and pictsies faded away. There was just her and Tiffany, facing one another on the turf at dawn, the wind hissing around the stones.

'What have you done with them?' Tiffany shouted.

'Oh, they're around . . . somewhere,' said the Queen airily. 'It's all dreams, anyway. And dreams within dreams. You can't rely on anything, little girl. Nothing is real. Nothing lasts. Everything goes. All you can do is learn to dream. And it's too late for that. And I . . . I have had longer to learn.'

Tiffany wasn't sure which of her thoughts was operating now. She was tired. She felt as though she was watching herself from above and a little behind. She saw herself set her boots firmly on the turf, and then . . .

. . . and then . . .

. . . and then, like someone rising from the clouds of a sleep, she felt the deep, deep Time below her. She sensed the breath of the downs and the distant roar of ancient, ancient seas trapped in millions of tiny shells. She thought of Granny Aching, under the turf, becoming part of the chalk again, part of the land under wave. She felt as if huge wheels, of time and stars, were turning slowly around her.

She opened her eyes and then, somewhere inside, opened her eyes again.

She heard the grass growing, and the sound of worms below the turf. She could feel the thousands of little lives around her, smell all the scents on the breeze, and see all the shades of the night . . .

The wheels of stars and years, of space and time, locked into place. She knew exactly where she was, and who she was, and what she was.

She swung a hand. The Queen tried to stop her, but she might as well have tried to stop a wheel of years. Tiffany's hand caught her face and knocked her off her feet.

'I never cried for Granny because there was no need to,' she said. 'She has never left me!'

She leaned down, and centuries bent with her.

'The secret is not to dream,' she whispered. 'The secret is to wake up. Waking up is harder. I have woken up and I am real. I know where I come from and I know where I'm going. You cannot fool me any more. Or touch me. Or anything that is mine.'

I'll never be like this again, she thought, as she saw the terror in the Queen's face. I'll never again feel as tall as the sky and as old as the hills and as strong as the sea. I've been given something for a while, and the price of it is that I have to give it back.

And the *reward* is giving it back too. No human could live like this. You could spend a day looking at a flower to see how wonderful it is, and that wouldn't get the milking done. No wonder we dream our way through our lives. To be awake, and see it all as it really is . . . no one could stand that for long.

She took a deep breath, and picked the Queen up. She was aware of things happening, of dreams roaring around her, but they didn't affect her. She was real and she was awake, more awake than she'd ever been. She had to concentrate even to think against the storm of sensations pouring into her mind.

The Queen was as light as a baby and changed shape madly in Tiffany's arms – into monsters and mixed-up beasts, things with claws and tentacles. But, at last, she was small and grey, like a monkey, with a large head and big eyes and a little downy chest that went up and down as she panted.

She reached the stones. The arch still stood. It was

never down, Tiffany thought. She had no strength, no magic, just one trick. The worst one.

'Stay away from here,' said Tiffany, stepping though the stone doorway. 'Never come back. Never touch what is mine.' And then, because the thing was so weak and baby-like, she added: 'But I hope there's someone who'll cry for you. I hope the King comes back.'

'You *pity* me?' growled the thing that had been the Queen.

'Yes. A bit,' said Tiffany. Like Miss Robinson, she thought.

She put the creature down. It scampered across the snow, turned, and became the beautiful Queen again.

'You won't win,' the Queen said. 'There's always a way in. People dream.'

'Sometimes we waken,' said Tiffany. 'Don't come back . . . or there *will be* a reckoning . . .'

She concentrated, and now the stones framed nothing more – or less – than the country beyond.

I shall have to find a way of sealing that, said her Third Thoughts. Or her twentieth thoughts, perhaps. Her head was *full* of thoughts.

She managed to walk a little way and then sat down, hugging her knees. Imagine getting stuck like this, she thought. You'd have to wear earplugs and noseplugs and a big black hood over your head, and *still* you'd see and hear too much . . .

She closed her eyes, and closed her eyes again.

She felt it all draining away. It *was* like falling asleep, sliding from that strange wide-awakeness into just normal, everyday . . . well, being awake. It felt as if everything was blurred and muffled.

This is how we always feel, she thought. We sleepwalk through our lives, because how could we live if we were always that awake—

Someone tapped her on the boot.

CHAPTER 14

Small, Like Oak Trees

'Hey, where did you get to?' shouted Rob Anybody, glaring up at her. 'One minute we was just aboout to give them lawyers a good legal seein'-to, next minute you and the Quin wuz gone!'

Dreams within dreams, Tiffany thought, holding her head. But they were over, and you couldn't look at the Nac Mac Feegle and not know what was real.

'It's over,' she said.

'Didja kill her?'

'No.'

'She'll be back, then,' said Rob Anybody. 'She's awfu' stupid, that one. Clever with the dreaming, I'll grant ye, but not a brain in her heid.'

Tiffany nodded. The blurred feeling was going. The moment of wide-awakeness had faded like a dream. *But I must remember that it wasn't a dream.*

'How did you get away from the huge wave?' she asked.

'Ach, we're fast movers,' said Rob Anybody. 'An' it was a strong lighthoose. O' course, the water came up pretty high.'

'A few sharks were involved, that kind of thing,' said Not-as-big-as-Medium-Sized-Jock-but-bigger-than-Wee-Jock-Jock.

'Oh, aye, a few sharkies,' said Rob Anybody, shrugging. 'And one o' them octopussies—'

'It was a giant squid,' said William the gonnagle.

'Aye, well, it was a kebab pretty quickly,' said Daft Wullie.

'Ha' a heidful o' heid, you wee weewee!' shouted Wentworth, overcome with wit.

William coughed politely. 'And the big wave threw up a lot of sunken vessels full o' trrrreasure,' he said. 'We stopped off for a wee pillage . . .'

The Nac Mac Feegles held up wonderful jewels and big gold coins.

'But that's just dream treasure, surely?' said Tiffany. 'Fairy gold! It'll turn into rubbish in the morning!'

'Aye?' said Rob Anybody. He glanced at the horizon. 'OK, ye heard the kelda, lads! We got mebbe half an hour to sell it to someone! Permission to go offski?' he added to Tiffany.

'Er . . . oh, yes. Fine. Thank you—'

They were gone, in a split-second blur of blue and red.

But William the gonnagle remained for a moment. He bowed to Tiffany.

'Ye didnae do at all badly,' he said. 'We're proud o' ye. So would yer grrranny be. Remember that. Ye are not unloved.'

Then he vanished too.

There was a groan from Roland, lying on the turf. He began to move.

'Weewee men all gone,' said Wentworth sadly, in the silence that followed. 'Crivens all gone.'

'What *were* they?' muttered Roland, sitting up and holding his head.

'It's all a bit complicated,' said Tiffany. 'Er . . . do you remember much?'

'It all seems like . . . a dream . . .' said Roland. 'I remember . . . the sea, and we were running, and I cracked a nut which was full of those little men, and I was hunting in this huge forest with shadows—'

'Dreams can be very funny things,' said Tiffany carefully. She went to stand up and thought: I must wait here a while. I don't know why I know, I just know. Perhaps I knew and have forgotten. But I must wait for something . . .

'Can you walk down to the village?' she said.

'Oh, yes. I think so. But what did—?'

'Then will you take Wentworth with you, please? I'd like to . . . rest for a while.'

'Are you sure?' said Roland, looking concerned.

'Yes. I won't be long. Please? You can drop him off at the farm. Tell my parents I'll be down soon. Tell them I'm fine.'

'Weewee men,' said Wentworth. 'Crivens! Want bed.'

Roland was still looking uncertain.

'Off you go!' Tiffany commanded, and waved him away.

When the two of them had disappeared below the brow of the hill, with several backward glances, she sat down between the four iron wheels and hugged her knees.

Far off, she could see the mound of the Nac Mac Feegle. Already, they were a slightly puzzling memory, and she'd seen them only a few minutes ago. But when they'd gone, they left the impression of never having been there.

She could go to the mound and see if she could find the big hole. But supposing it wasn't there? Or supposing it was, but all there was down there were rabbits?

No, it's all true, she said to herself. *I must remember that too.*

A buzzard screamed in the dawn greyness. She looked up as it circled into sunlight, and a tiny dot detached itself from the bird.

That was far too high up even for a pictsie to stand the fall.

Tiffany scrambled to her feet as Hamish tumbled through the sky. And then – something ballooned above him and the fall became just a gentle floating, like thistledown.

The bulging shape above Hamish was Y-shaped. As it got bigger, the shape become more precise, more . . . familiar.

He landed, and a pair of Tiffany's pants, the

long-legged ones with the rosebud pattern, settled down on top of him.

'That was *great*!' he said, pushing his way through the folds of fabric. 'Nae more landin' on my heid for me!'

'They're my best pants,' said Tiffany wearily. 'You stole them off our clothes line, didn't you . . . ?'

'Oh aye. Nice and clean,' said Hamish. 'I had to cut the lace off 'cuz it got in the way, but I put it by and ye could easily sew it on again.' He gave Tiffany the big grin of someone who, for once, has not dived heavily into the ground.

She sighed. She'd liked the lace. She didn't have many things that weren't necessary. 'I think you'd better keep them,' she said.

'Aye, I will, then,' said Hamish. 'Noo, what wuz it . . . ? Oh, yes. Ye have visitors comin'. I spotted them out over the valley. Look up there.'

There were two other things up there, bigger than a buzzard, so high that they were already in full sunlight. Tiffany watched as they circled lower.

They were broomsticks.

I *knew* I had to wait! Tiffany thought.

Her ears bubbled. She turned and saw Hamish running across the grass. As she looked, the buzzard picked him up and sped onwards. She wondered if he was frightened or, at least, didn't want to meet . . . whoever was coming

The broomsticks descended.

The lowest one had two figures on it. As it landed, Tiffany saw that one of them was Miss Tick, clinging anxiously onto a smaller figure who'd been doing the steering. She half climbed off, half fell off, and tottered over to Tiffany.

'You wouldn't believe the time I've had,' she said. 'It was just a nightmare! We flew through the storm! Are you all right?'

'Er . . . yes . . .'

'What happened?'

Tiffany looked at her. How did you begin to answer something like that?

'The Queen's gone,' she said. That seemed to cover it.

'What? The Queen has *gone*? Oh . . . er . . . these ladies are Mrs Ogg—'

'Mornin',' said the broomstick's other occupant, who was pulling at her long black dress, from under the folds of which came the sounds of twanging elastic. 'The wind up there blows where it likes, I don't mind telling you!' She was a short fat lady with a cheerful face like an apple that has been stored too long; all the wrinkles moved into different positions when she smiled.

'And this,' said Miss Tick, 'is Miss—'

'Mistress,' snapped the other witch, dismounting.

'I'm so sorry, *Mistress* Weatherwax,' said Miss Tick. 'Very, *very* good witches,' she whispered to Tiffany. 'I was very lucky to find them. They *respect* witches up in the mountains.'

Tiffany was impressed that anyone could make Miss Tick flustered, but the other witch seemed to do it just by standing there. She was tall – except, Tiffany realized, she wasn't *that* tall, but she *stood* tall, which could easily fool you if you weren't paying attention – and like the other witch wore a rather shabby black dress. She had an elderly, thin face that gave nothing away. Piercing blue eyes looked Tiffany up and down, from head to toe.

'You've got good boots,' said the witch.

'Tell Mistress Weatherwax what happened—' Miss Tick began. But the witch held up a hand and Miss Tick stopped talking immediately. Tiffany was even more impressed now.

Mistress Weatherwax gave Tiffany a look that went right through her head and about five miles out the other side. Then she walked over to the stones, and waved one hand. It was an odd movement, a kind of wriggle in the air, but for a moment it left a glowing line. There was a noise, a chord, as though all sorts of sounds were happening at the same time. It snapped into silence.

'Jolly Sailor tobacco?' said the witch.

'Yes,' said Tiffany.

The witch waved a hand again. There was another sharp, complicated noise. Mistress Weatherwax turned suddenly and stared at the distant pimple that was the pictsie mound.

'Nac Mac Feegle? *Kelda?*' she demanded.

'Er, yes. Only temporary,' said Tiffany.

'Hmmph,' said Mistress Weatherwax.

Wave. Sound.

'*Frying pan?*'

'Yes. It's got lost, though.'

'Hmm.'

Wave. Sound. It was as if the woman was extracting her history from the air.

'*Filled buckets?*'

'And they filled up the log box too,' said Tiffany.

Wave. Sound.

'I see. Special Sheep Liniment?'

'Yes, my father says it puts—'

Wave. Sound.

'Ah. Land of snow.' Wave. Sound. 'A queen.' Wave. Sound. 'Fighting.' Wave, sound. 'On the sea?' Wave, sound, wave, sound . . .

Mistress Weatherwax stared at the flashing air, looking at pictures only she could see. Mrs Ogg sat down beside Tiffany, her little legs going up in the air as she made herself comfortable.

'I've tried Jolly Sailor,' she said. 'Smells like toenails, don't it?'

'Yes, it does!' said Tiffany gratefully.

'To be a kelda of the Nac Mac Feegle, you have to marry one of 'em, don't you?' said Mrs Ogg, innocently.

'Ah, yes, but I found a way round that,' said Tiffany. She told her. Mrs Ogg laughed. It was a sociable kind of laugh, the sort of laugh that makes you comfortable.

The noise and flashing stopped. Mistress Weatherwax stood staring at nothing for a moment, and then said: 'You beat the Queen, at the end. But you had help, I think.'

'Yes, I did,' said Tiffany.

'And that was—?'

'I don't ask you *your* business,' said Tiffany, before she even realized she was going to say it. Miss Tick gasped. Mrs Ogg's eyes twinkled, and she looked from Tiffany to Mistress Weatherwax like someone watching a tennis match.

'Tiffany, Mistress Weatherwax is the most famous witch in all—' Miss Tick began severely, but the witch waved a hand at her again. I really must learn how to do that, Tiffany thought.

Then Mistress Weatherwax took off her pointed hat and bowed to Tiffany.

'Well said,' she said, straightening up and staring directly at Tiffany 'I didn't have no right to ask you. This is your country, we're here by your leave. I show you respect *as you in turn will respect me.*' The air seemed to freeze for a moment and the skies to darken. Then Mistress Weatherwax went on, as if the moment of thunder hadn't happened: 'But if one day you care to tell me more, I should be grateful to hear about it,' she said, in a conversational voice. 'And them creatures that look like they're made of dough, I should like to know more about them too. Never run across them before. And your grandmother sounds the kind of person I would have liked to meet.' She straightened up. 'In the meantime, we'd better see if there's anything left you can still be taught.'

'Is this where I learn about the witches' school?' said Tiffany.

There was a moment of silence.

'Witches' school?' said Mistress Weatherwax.

'Um,' said Miss Tick.

'You were being metapahorrical, weren't you?' said Tiffany.

'Metapahorrical?' said Mrs Ogg, wrinkling her forehead.

'She means metaphorical,' mumbled Miss Tick.

'It's like stories,' said Tiffany. 'It's all right. I worked it out. *This* is the school, isn't it? The magic place? The world. Here. And you don't realize it until you look. Do you know the pictsies think this world is heaven? We just don't look. You can't give lessons on witchcraft. Not properly. It's all about how you are . . . you, I suppose.'

'Nicely said,' said Mistress Weatherwax. 'You're sharp. But there's magic too. You'll pick that up. It don't take much intelligence, otherwise wizards wouldn't be able to do it.'

'You'll need a job too,' said Mrs Ogg. 'There's no money in witchcraft. Can't do magic for yourself, see? Cast-iron rule.'

'I make good cheese,' said Tiffany.

'Cheese, eh?' said Mistress Weatherwax. 'Hmm. Yes. Cheese is good. But do you know anything about medicines? Midwifery? That's a good portable skill.'

'Well, I've helped deliver difficult lambs,' said Tiffany. 'And I saw my brother being born. They didn't bother to turn me out. It didn't look too difficult. But I think cheese is probably easier, and less noisy.'

'Cheese is good,' Mistress Weatherwax repeated, nodding. 'Cheese is alive.'

'And what do you *really* do?' said Tiffany.

The thin witch hesitated for a moment, and then:

'We look to . . . the edges,' said Mistress Weatherwax. 'There're a lot of edges, more than people know. Between life and death, this world and the next, night and day, right and wrong . . . an' they need watchin'. We watch 'em, we guard the sum of things. And we never ask for any reward. That's important.'

'People give us stuff, mind you. People can be very gen'rous to witches,' said Mrs Ogg happily. 'On bakin' days in our village, sometimes I can't move for cake. There's ways and ways of not askin', if you get my meaning. People like to see a happy witch.'

'But down here people think witches are bad!' said Tiffany, and her Second Thoughts added: *Remember how rarely Granny Aching ever had to buy her own tobacco?*

'It's amazin' what people can get used to,' said Mrs Ogg. 'You just have to start slow.'

'And we have to hurry,' said Mistress Weatherwax. 'There's a man riding up here on a farm horse. Fair hair, red face—'

'It sounds like my father!'

'Well, he's making the poor thing gallop,' said Mistress Weatherwax. 'Quick, now. You want to learn the skills? When can you leave home?'

'Pardon?' said Tiffany.

'Don't the girls here go off to work as maids and things?' said Mrs Ogg.

'Oh, yes. When they're a bit older than me.'

'Well, when you're a bit older than you, Miss Tick here will come and find you,' said Mistress

Weatherwax. Miss Tick nodded. 'There're elderly witches up in the mountains who'll pass on what they know in exchange for a bit of help around the cottage. This place will be watched over while you're gone, you may depend on it. In the meantime you'll get three meals a day, your own bed, use of broomstick... that's the way we do it. All right?'

'Yes,' said Tiffany, grinning happily. The wonderful moment was passing too quickly for all the questions she wanted to ask. 'Yes! But, er...'

'Yes?' said Mrs Ogg.

'I don't have to dance around with no clothes on or anything like that, do I? Only I heard rumours—'

Mistress Weatherwax rolled her eyes.

Mrs Ogg grinned cheerfully. 'Well, that procedure does have something to recommend it—' she began.

'No, you don't have to!' snapped Mistress Weatherwax. 'No cottage made of sweets, no cackling and no dancing!'

'Unless you want to,' said Mrs Ogg, standing up. 'There's no harm in an occasional cackle, if the mood takes you that way. I'd teach you a good one right now, but we really ought to be going.'

'But... but how did you manage it?' said Miss Tick to Tiffany. 'This is all chalk! You've become a witch on chalk? How?'

'That's all *you* know, Perspicacia Tick,' said Mistress Weatherwax. 'The *bones* of the hills is flint. It's hard and sharp and useful. King of stones.' She picked up her broomstick, and turned back to Tiffany. 'Will you get into trouble, do you think?' she said.

'I might do,' said Tiffany.

'Do you want any help?'

'If it's my trouble, I'll get out of it,' said Tiffany. She wanted to say: Yes, yes! I'm going to need help! I don't know what's going to happen when my father gets here! The Baron's probably got really angry! But I don't want them to think I can't deal with my own problems! I ought to be able to cope!

'That's right,' said Mistress Weatherwax.

Tiffany wondered if the witch could read minds.

'Minds? No,' said Mistress Weatherwax, climbing onto her broomstick. 'Faces, yes. Come here, young lady.'

Tiffany obeyed.

'The thing about witchcraft,' said Mistress Weatherwax, 'is that it's not like school at all. *First* you get the test, and then afterwards you spend years findin' out how you passed it. It's a bit like life in that respect.' She reached out and gently raised Tiffany's chin so that she could look into her face. 'I see you opened your eyes,' she said.

'Yes.'

'Good. Many people never do. Times ahead might be a little tricky, even so. You'll need this.'

She stretched out a hand and made a circle in the air around Tiffany's hair, then brought her hand up over the head while making little movements with her forefinger.

Tiffany raised her hands to her head. For a moment she thought there was nothing there, and then they touched . . . something. It was more like a sensation in the air; if you weren't expecting it to be there, your fingers passed straight through.

'Is it *really* there?' she said.

'Who knows?' said the witch. 'It's *virtually* a pointy hat. No one else will know it's there. It might be a comfort.'

'You mean it just exists in my head?' said Tiffany.

'You've got lots of things in your head. That doesn't mean they aren't real. Best not to ask me too many questions.'

'What happened to the toad?' said Miss Tick, who *did* ask questions.

'It's gone to live with the Wee Free Men,' said Tiffany. 'It turned out it used to be a lawyer.'

'You've given a clan of the Nac Mac Feegle their own lawyer?' said Mrs Ogg. 'That'll make the world tremble. Still, I always say the occasional tremble does you good.'

'Come, sisters, we must away,' said Miss Tick, who had climbed on the other broomstick behind Mrs Ogg.

'There's no need for that sort of talk,' said Mrs Ogg. 'That's theatre talk, that is. Cheerio, Tiff. We'll see you again.'

Her stick rose gently in the air. From the stick of Mistress Weatherwax, though, there was merely a sad little noise, like the *thwop* of Miss Tick's hat point. The broomstick went *kshugagugah*.

Mistress Weatherwax sighed. 'It's them dwarfs,' she said. 'They *say* they've repaired it, oh yes, and it starts first time in their workshop—'

They heard the sound of distant hooves. With surprising speed, Mistress Weatherwax swung herself off the stick, grabbed it firmly in both hands, and ran away across the turf, skirts billowing behind her.

She was a speck in the distance when Tiffany's father came over the brow of the hill on one of the farm horses. He hadn't even stopped to put the leather shoes on it; great slices of earth flew up as hooves the size of large soup plates,* each one shod with iron, bit into the turf.

Tiffany heard a faint *kshugagugahvvvvvoooom* behind her as he leaped off the horse.

She was surprised to see him laughing and crying at the same time.

It was all a bit of a dream.

Tiffany found that a very useful thing to say. It's hard to remember, it was all a bit of a dream. It was all a bit of a dream, I can't be certain.

The overjoyed Baron, however, was very certain. Obviously this – this Queen woman, whoever she was, had been stealing children but Roland had beaten her, oh yes, and helped these two young children to get back as well.

Her mother had insisted on Tiffany going to bed, even though it was broad daylight. Actually, she *didn't* mind. She was tired, and lay under the covers in that nice pink world halfway between asleep and awake.

She heard the Baron and her father talking

---

* Probably about eleven inches across. Tiffany didn't measure them this time.

downstairs. She heard the story being woven between them as they tried to make sense of it all. Obviously the girl had been very brave (this was the Baron speaking) but, well, she was nine, wasn't she? And didn't even know how to use a sword! Whereas Roland had fencing lessons at his school . . .

And so it went on. There were other things she heard her parents discussing later, when the Baron had gone. There was the way Ratbag now lived on the roof, for example.

Tiffany lay in bed and smelled the ointment her mother had rubbed into her temples. Tiffany must have got hit on the head, she'd said, because of the way she kept on touching it.

So . . . Roland with the beefy face was the hero, was he? And she was just like the stupid princess who broke her ankle and fainted all the time? That was *completely* unfair!

She reached out to the little table beside her bed where she'd put the invisible hat. Her mother had put down a cup of broth right through it, but it was still there. Tiffany's fingers felt, very faintly, the roughness of the brim.

We never ask for any reward, she thought. Besides, it was her secret, all of it. No one else knew about the Wee Free Men. Admittedly Wentworth had taken to running through the house with a tablecloth round his waist shouting, 'Weewee mens! I'll scone you in the boot!' but Mrs Aching was still so glad to see him back, and so happy that he was talking about things other than sweets, that she wasn't paying too much attention to what he *was* talking about.

No, she couldn't tell anyone. They'd never believe her, and suppose that they did, and went up and poked around in the pictsies' mound? She couldn't let that happen.

What would Granny Aching have done?

Granny Aching would have said nothing. Granny Aching often said nothing. She just smiled to herself, and puffed on her pipe, and waited until the right time . . .

Tiffany smiled to herself.

She slept, and didn't dream.

And a day went past.

And another day.

On the third day, it rained. Tiffany went into the kitchen when no one was about and took down the china shepherdess from the shelf. She put it in a sack, then slipped out of the house and ran up onto the downs.

The worst of the weather was going either side of the Chalk, which cut through the clouds like the prow of a ship. But when Tiffany reached the spot where an old stove and four iron wheels stood out of the grass, and cut a square of turf, and carefully chipped out a hole for the china shepherdess, and then put the turf back . . . it was raining hard enough to soak it in and give it a chance of surviving. It seemed the right thing to do. And she was sure she caught a whiff of tobacco.

Then she went to the pictsies' mound. She'd worried about that. She knew they were there, didn't she? So, somehow, going to check that they were there would be . . . sort of . . . showing that she doubted if they would be, wouldn't it? They were busy people. They had lots to do. They had the old kelda to mourn. They were probably very busy. That's what she told herself. It wasn't because she kept wondering if there *really* might be nothing down the hole but rabbits. It wasn't that at all.

She was the kelda. She had a duty.

She heard music. She heard voices. And then sudden silence as she peered into the gloom.

She carefully took a bottle of Special Sheep Liniment out of her sack and let it slide into darkness.

Tiffany walked away, and heard the faint music start up again.

She did wave at a buzzard, circling lazily under the clouds, and she was sure a tiny dot waved back.

On the fourth day, Tiffany made butter, and did her chores. She did have help.

'And now I want you to go and feed the chickens,' she said to Wentworth. 'What is it I want you to do?'

'Fee' the cluck-clucks,' said Wentworth.

'Chickens,' said Tiffany severely.

'Chickens,' said Wentworth obediently.

'And wipe your nose *not on your sleeve*! I gave you a handkerchief. And on the way back see if you can carry a whole log, will you?'

'Ach, crivens,' muttered Wentworth.

'And what is it we don't say?' said Tiffany. 'We don't say the—'

'– the crivens word,' Wentworth muttered.

'And we don't say it in front of—'

'– in fron' of Mummy,' said Wentworth.

'Good. And then when I've finished we'll have time to go down to the river.'

Wentworth brightened up.

'Weewee mens?' he said.

Tiffany didn't reply immediately.

Tiffany hadn't seen a single Feegle since she'd been home.

'There might be,' she said. 'But they're probably very busy. They've got to find another kelda, and . . . well, they're very busy. I expect.'

'Weewee men say hit you in the head, fishface!' said Wentworth happily.

'We'll see,' said Tiffany, feeling like a parent. 'Now please go and feed the chickens and get the eggs.'

When he'd wandered away, carrying the egg basket in both hands, Tiffany turned out some butter onto the marble slab and picked up the paddles to pat it into, well, a pat of butter. Then she'd stamp it with one of the wooden stamps. People appreciated a little picture on their butter.

As she began to shape the butter she was aware of a shadow in the doorway, and turned.

It was Roland.

He looked at her, his face even redder than usual. He was twiddling his very expensive hat nervously, just like Rob Anybody did.

'Yes?' she said.

'Look, about . . . well, about all that . . . about . . .' Roland began.

'Yes?'

'Look, I didn't— I mean, I didn't lie to anyone or anything,' he blurted out. 'But my father just sort of assumed I'd been a hero and he just wouldn't listen to anything I said even after I told him how . . . how . . .'

'– helpful I'd been?' said Tiffany.

'Yes . . . I mean, no! He said, he said, he said it was lucky for you I was there, he said—'

'It doesn't matter,' said Tiffany, picking up the butter paddles again.

'And he just kept telling everyone how brave I'd been and—'

'I said it doesn't matter,' said Tiffany. The little paddles went *patpatpat* on the fresh butter.

Roland's mouth opened and shut for a moment.

'You mean you don't mind?' he said at last.

'No. I don't mind,' said Tiffany.

'But it's not fair!'

'We're the only ones who know the truth,' said Tiffany.

Patapatpat. Roland stared at the fat, rich butter as she calmly patted it into shape.

'Oh,' he said. 'Er . . . you won't tell anyone, will you? I mean, you've got every right to, but—'

Patapatapat . . .

'No one would believe me,' said Tiffany.

'I did try,' said Roland. 'Honestly. I really did.'

I expect you did, Tiffany thought. But you're not very clever and the Baron certainly is a man without

First Sight. He sees the world the way he wants to see it.

'One day you'll be Baron, won't you?' she said.

'Well, yes. One day. But look, are you really a witch?'

'*When you're Baron* you'll be good at it, I expect?' said Tiffany, turning the butter around. 'Fair and generous and decent? You'll pay good wages and look after the old people? You wouldn't let people turn an old lady out of her house?'

'Well, I hope I—'

Tiffany turned to face him, a butter paddle in each hand.

'Because *I'll* be there, you see. You'll look up and see my eye on you. I'll be there on the edge of the crowd. All the time. I'll be watching everything, because I come from a long line of Aching people and this is my land. But you can be the Baron for us and I hope you're a good one. If you are not . . . there will be a reckoning.'

'Look, I know you were . . . were . . .' Roland began, going red in the face.

'Very helpful?' said Tiffany.

'. . . but you can't talk to me like that, you know!'

Tiffany was *sure* she heard, up in the roof and on the very edge of hearing, someone say: 'Ach, crivens, what a wee snotter . . .'

She shut her eyes for a moment, and then, heart pounding, pointed a butter paddle at one of the empty buckets.

'Bucket, fill yourself!' she commanded.

It blurred, and then sloshed. Water dripped down the side.

Roland stared at it. Tiffany gave him one of her sweetest smiles, which could be quite scary.

'You won't tell anyone, will you?' she said.

He turned to her, face pale. 'No one would believe me . . .' he stammered.

'Aye,' said Tiffany. 'So we understand one another. Isn't that nice? And now, if you don't mind, I've got to finish this and make a start on some cheese.'

'Cheese? But you . . . you could do anything you wanted!' Roland burst out.

'And right now I want to make cheese,' said Tiffany calmly. 'Go away.'

'My father owns this farm!' said Roland, and then realized he'd said that out loud.

There were two little but strangely *loud* clicks as Tiffany put down the butter paddles and turned round.

'That was a very brave thing you just said,' she said, 'but I expect you're sorry you said it, now that you've had a really good think?'

Roland, who had shut his eyes, nodded his head.

'Good,' said Tiffany. 'Today I'm making cheese. Tomorrow I may do something else. And in a while, maybe, I won't be here and you'll wonder: Where is she? But part of me will always be here, always. I'll always be thinking about this place. I'll have it in my eye. And I *will* be back. Now, *go away*!'

He turned and ran.

After his footsteps had died away Tiffany said: 'All right, who's there?'

'It's me, mistress. No'-as-big-as-Medium-Sized-Jock-but-bigger-than-Wee-Jock-Jock, mistress.' The pictsie appeared from behind the bucket, and added: 'Rob Anybody said we should come tae keep an eye on ye for a wee while, and tae thank ye for the offerin'.'

It's still magic even if you know how it's done, Tiffany thought.

'Only watch me in the dairy, then,' she said. 'No spying!'

'Ach, no, mistress,' said Not-as-big-as-Medium-Sized-Jock-but-bigger-than-Wee-Jock-Jock nervously. Then he grinned. 'Fion's goin' off to be the kelda for a clan over near Copperhead Mountain,' he said, 'an' she's asked me to go along as the gonnagle!'

'Congratulations!'

'Aye, and William says I should be fine if I just work on the mousepipes,' said the pictsie. 'And . . . er . . .'

'Yes?' said Tiffany.

'Er . . . Hamish says there's a girl in the Long Lake clan who's looking to become a kelda . . . er . . . it's a fine clan she's from . . . er . . .' The pictsie was going violet with embarrassment.

'Good,' said Tiffany. 'If I was Rob Anybody, I'd invite her over right away.'

'You dinnae mind?' said Not-as-big-as-Medium-Sized-Jock-but-bigger-than-Wee-Jock-Jock hopefully.

'Not at all,' said Tiffany. She did a little bit, she had to admit to herself, but it was a bit she could put away on a shelf in her head somewhere.

'That's grand!' said the pictsie. 'The lads were a bit worried, ye ken. I'll run up an' tell them.' He lowered his voice. 'An' would ye like me to run after that big heap o' jobbies that just left and see that he falls off his horse again?'

'No!' said Tiffany hurriedly. 'No. Don't. No.' She picked up the butter paddles. 'You leave him to me,' she added, smiling. 'You can leave everything to me.'

When she was alone again she finished the butter . . . *patapatapat* . . .

She paused, put the paddles down, and with the tip of a very clean finger, drew a curved line in the surface, with another curved line just touching it, so that together they looked like a wave. She traced a third, flat curve under it, which was the Chalk.

Land Under Wave.

She quickly smoothed the butter again and picked up the stamp she'd made yesterday; she'd carved it carefully out of a piece of apple wood that Mr Block the carpenter had given her.

She stamped it onto the butter, and took it off carefully.

There, glistening on the oily, rich yellow surface, was a gibbous moon and, sailing in front of the moon, a witch on a broomstick.

She smiled again, and it was Granny Aching's smile. Things would be different one day.

But you had to start small, like oak trees.

Then she made cheese . . .

. . . in the dairy, on the farm, and the fields unrolling, and becoming the downlands sleeping under the hot midsummer sun, where the flocks of sheep, moving slowly, drift over the short turf like clouds on a green sky, and here and there sheepdogs speed over the grass like shooting stars. For ever and ever, wold without end.

Author's Note

The painting that Tiffany 'enters' in this book really exists. It's called *The Fairy Fellers' Master-Stroke*, by Richard Dadd, and is in the Tate Gallery in London. It is only about 21 inches by 15 inches. It took the artist nine years to complete, in the middle of the nineteenth century. I cannot think of a more famous 'fairy' painting. It is, indeed, very strange. Summer heat leaks out of it.

What people 'know' about Richard Dadd is that 'he went mad, killed his father, was locked up in a lunatic asylum for the rest of his life and painted a weird picture'. Crudely, that's all true, but it's a dreadful summary of the life of a skilled and talented artist who developed a serious mental illness.

A Nac Mac Feegle does not appear anywhere in the painting, but I suppose it's always possible that one was removed for making an obscene gesture. It's the sort of thing they'd do.

Oh, and the tradition of burying a shepherd with a piece of raw wool in the coffin was true too. Even gods understand that a shepherd can't neglect the sheep. A god who didn't understand would not be worth believing in.

There is no such word as 'noonlight', but it would be nice if there was.

Tiffany Aching's story
continues in:

Turn the page for an extract
from her next adventure!

CHAPTER 1

Leaving

It came crackling over the hills, like an invisible fog. Movement without a body tired it, and it drifted very slowly. It wasn't thinking now. It had been months since it had last thought, because the brain that was doing the thinking for it had died. They always died. So now it was naked again, and frightened.

It could hide in one of the blobby white creatures that baa'd nervously as it crawled over the turf. But they had useless brains, capable of thinking only about grass and making other things that went baa. No. They would not do. It needed, needed something better, a strong mind, a mind with power, a mind that could keep it safe.

It searched . . .

The new boots were all wrong. They were stiff and shiny. Shiny boots! That was disgraceful. Clean boots, that was different. There was nothing wrong with putting a bit of a polish on boots to keep the wet out. But boots had to work for a living. They shouldn't *shine*.

Tiffany Aching, standing on the rug in her bedroom, shook her head. She'd have to scuff the things as soon as possible.

Then there was the new straw hat, with a ribbon on it. She had some doubts about that too.

She tried to look at herself in the mirror, which wasn't easy because the mirror was not much bigger than her hand, and cracked and blotchy. She had to move it around to try and see as much of herself as possible and remember how the bits fitted together.

But today . . . well, she didn't usually do this sort of thing in the house, but it was important to look smart today, and since no one was around . . .

She put the mirror down on the rickety table by the bed, stood in the middle of the threadbare rug, shut her eyes and said:

'See me.'

And away on the hills something, a thing with no body and no mind but a terrible hunger and a bottomless fear, felt the power.

It would have sniffed the air, if it had a nose.

It searched.

It found.

Such a strange mind, like a lot of minds inside one another, getting smaller and smaller! So strong! So close!

*It changed direction slightly, and went a little faster.
As it moved, it made a noise like a swarm of flies.*

*The sheep, nervous for a moment about something
they couldn't see, hear or smell, baa'd . . .*

. . . and went back to chewing grass.

Tiffany opened her eyes. There she was, a few feet
away from herself. She could see the back of her own
head.

Carefully, she moved around the room, not looking
down at the 'her' that was moving, because she found
that if she did that then the trick was over.

It was quite difficult, moving like that, but at last
she was in front of herself and looking herself up and
down.

Brown hair to match brown eyes . . . there was
nothing she could do about that. At least her hair was
clean and she'd washed her face.

She had a new dress on, which improved things a
bit. It was so unusual to buy new clothes in the Aching
family that, of course, it was bought big so that she'd
'grow into it'. But at least it was pale green, and it
didn't actually touch the floor. With the shiny new
boots and the straw hat she looked . . . like a farmer's
daughter, quite respectable, going off to her first job.
It'd have to do.

From here she could see the pointy hat on her head,
but she had to look hard for it. It was like a glint in the
air, gone as soon as you saw it. That's why she'd been
worried about the new straw hat, but it had simply
gone through it as if the new hat wasn't there.

This was because, in a way, it wasn't. It was in-visible, except in the rain. Sun and wind went straight through, but rain and snow somehow saw it, and treated it as if it were real.

She'd been given it by the greatest witch in the world, a real witch with a black dress and a black hat and eyes that could go through you like turpentine goes through a sick sheep. It had been a kind of reward. Tiffany had done magic, serious magic. Before she had done it she hadn't known that she could; when she had been doing it she hadn't known that she was; and after she had done it she hadn't known how she had. Now she had to *learn* how.

'See me not,' she said. The vision of her ... or whatever it was, because she was not exactly sure about this trick ... vanished.

It had been a shock, the first time she'd done this. But she'd *always* found it easy to see herself, at least in her head. All her memories were like little pictures of herself doing things or watching things, rather than the view from the two holes in the front of her head. There was a part of her that was always watching her.

Miss Tick – another witch, but one who was easier to talk to than the witch who'd given Tiffany the hat – had said that a witch had to know how to 'stand apart', and that she'd find out more when her talent grew, so Tiffany supposed the 'see me' was part of this.

Sometimes Tiffany thought she ought to talk to Miss Tick about 'see me'. It felt as if she was stepping out of her body, but still had a sort of ghost body that could walk around. It all worked as long as her ghost eyes didn't look down and see that she *was* just a ghost body. If that happened, some part of her panicked and she found herself back in her solid body immediately. Tiffany had, in the end, decided to keep this to herself. You didn't have to tell a teacher *everything*. Anyway, it was a good trick for when you didn't have a mirror.

Miss Tick was a sort of witch-finder. That seemed to be how witchcraft worked. Some witches kept a magical lookout for girls who showed promise, and found them an older witch to help them along. They didn't teach you how to do it. They taught you how to know what you were doing.

Witches were a bit like cats. They didn't much like one another's company, but they *did* like to know where all the other witches *were*, just in case they needed them. And what you might need them for was to tell you, as a friend, that you were beginning to cackle.

Witches didn't fear much, Miss Tick had said, but what the powerful ones were afraid of, even if they didn't talk about it, was what they called '*going to the bad*'. It was too easy to slip into careless little cruelties because you had power and other people hadn't, too easy to think other people didn't matter much, too easy to think that ideas like right and wrong didn't apply to *you*. At the end of *that* road was you dribbling and cackling to yourself all alone in a gingerbread house, growing warts on your nose.

Witches needed to know other witches were watching them.

And that, Tiffany thought, was why the hat was there. She could touch it any time, provided she shut her eyes. It was a kind of reminder . . .

'Tiffany!' her mother shouted up the stairs. 'Miss Tick's here!'

Yesterday, Tiffany had said goodbye to Granny Aching . . .

The iron wheels of the old shepherding hut were half buried in the turf, high up on the hills. The pot-bellied stove, which still stood lopsided in the grass, was red with rust. The chalk hills were taking them, just like they'd taken the bones of Granny Aching.

The rest of the hut had been burned on the day she'd been buried. No shepherd would have dared to use it, let alone spend the night there. Granny Aching had been too big in people's minds, too hard to replace. Night and day, in all seasons, she *was* the Chalk country: its best shepherd, its wisest woman, and its memory. It was as if the green downland had a soul that walked about in old boots and a sacking apron and smoked a foul old pipe and dosed sheep with turpentine.

The shepherds said that Granny Aching had cussed the sky blue. They called the fluffy little white clouds of summer 'Granny Aching's little lambs'. And although they laughed when they said these things, part of them was not joking.

No shepherd would have dared presume to live in that hut, no shepherd at all.

So they had cut the turf and buried Granny Aching in the Chalk, watered the turf afterwards to leave no mark, then they burned her hut.

Sheep's wool, Jolly Sailor tobacco and turpentine . . .

. . . had been the smells of the shepherding hut, and the smell of Granny Aching. Such things have a hold on people that goes right to the heart. Tiffany only had to smell them now to be back there, in the warmth and silence and safety of the hut. It was the place she had gone to when she was upset, and the place she had gone to when she was happy. And Granny Aching would always smile and make tea and say nothing. And nothing bad could happen in the shepherding hut. It was a fort against the world. Even now, after Granny had gone, Tiffany still liked to go up there.

Tiffany stood there, while the wind blew over the turf and sheep bells *clonked* in the distance.

'I've got . . .' She cleared her throat. 'I've got to go away. I . . . I've got to learn proper witching, and there's no one here now to teach me, you see. I've got to . . . to look after the hills like you did. I can . . . *do* things but I don't *know* things, and Miss Tick says what you don't know can kill you. I want to be as good as you were. I will come back! I will come back soon! I promise I will come back, better than I went!'

A blue butterfly, blown off course by a gust, settled on Tiffany's shoulder, opened and shut its wings once or twice, then fluttered away.

Granny Aching had never been at home with words. She collected silence like other people collected string. But she had a way of saying nothing that said it all.

Tiffany stayed for a while, until her tears had dried, and then went off back down the hill, leaving the everlasting wind to curl around the wheels and whistle down the chimney of the pot-bellied stove. Life went on.

Turn the page to
discover the rest of the
Tiffany Aching sequence.

Wintersmith

The third book in
the Tiffany Aching sequence

Disaster has struck.

Tiffany has accidentally danced with the Wintersmith.
And now the Wintersmith has a bit of a crush on Tiffany.

If she doesn't shake off her admirer soon,
the Chalk will never see another springtime . . .

'Characteristically entertaining'
Sunday Times

I Shall Wear Midnight

The fourth book in
the Tiffany Aching sequence

When the Baron dies, and Tiffany is blamed for his death,
it's clearer than ever that she is alone.

Now Tiffany must journey to Ankh-Morpork, to inform
the Baron's heir, Roland, of his father's death.
But on the way she meets something – an evil ball
of spite and malice that has only now woken up.

And it is out to get witches everywhere . . .

'High peaks of imagination'
Sunday Times

The Shepherd's Crown

The fifth and final book in the Tiffany Aching sequence

Tiffany Aching is finally a witch (and a respected
one at that). Overworked and underpaid,
that's for certain, but a witch nonetheless.

However, as new friends are made and old ones return,
enemies are stirring. With her beloved Chalk in jeopardy,
Tiffany will face the toughest challenge of her life.

There will be a reckoning . . .

'Brilliant . . . This is a book worth reading twice
in quick succession'
Daily Mail

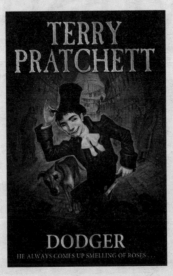